THE FLAME AND THE SWORD

When Perdita was rescued from the forest by the Earl of Athelstan, she was at first afraid of the dark secrets of the castle, but then she discovered that her lover was a man who stood head and shoulders above others of his time, and she was proud to love him. Even though it meant that she must risk the threat of excommunication – or even her own life – to follow her heart.

THE FLAME AND THE SWORD

The Flame And The Sword

by

Anne Herries

Magna Large Print Books
Long Preston, North Yorkshire,
BD23 4ND, England.

British Library Cataloguing in Publication Data.

Herries, Anne
     The flame and the sword.

     A catalogue record of this book is
     available from the British Library

     ISBN   978-0-7505-2723-1

First published in Great Britain in 1987 by
Mills & Boon Limited

Copyright © Anne Herries 1987

Cover illustration © Richard Clifton-Day by arrangement with
Alison Eldred

The moral right of the author has been asserted

Published in Large Print 2007 by arrangement with
Linda Sole

Magna Large Print is an imprint of Library Magna Books Ltd.

Printed and bound in Great Britain by
T.J. (International) Ltd., Cornwall, PL28 8RW

CHAPTER ONE

Where could she hide? Hearing the sound of horses' hooves, the girl was seized by terror. They sounded so close! They were coming after her, hunting her down like an animal. The forest was dark and dense, and she had hoped to escape her pursuers by entering it. For a while she had thought she had succeeded, but now she could hear the blood-curdling cry of a hound and knew the huntsmen would catch her in the end. Before nightfall Sir Edmund Mortimer would have her fast in his net, and then she would pay dearly for her defiance! He would make her suffer for the humiliating wounds she had inflicted on him as she struggled in his hateful embrace. She would suffer as that sweet lady she had loved so dearly had done before her; but Mathilda was dead, and she herself was at the mercy of a man she hated.

For a moment fear held her rooted to the ground, her limbs leaden and heavy. She was so tired, but she had to go on – there was no turning back now! Pain tore at her breast as she gulped for air, fighting to recover her breath. It was some hours since she had fled in panic from the manor house that had been home to her for the past sixteen years, when she had been taken there as a nameless orphan to live as the beloved child of Lady Mathilda. It had been home to her then, but of late it had become a prison. She had borne it for many months, but today her fear had made her desperate.

Dusk was falling swiftly around her and the forest had become a place of shadows, bringing an added menace to that she already dreaded. It was said to be haunted by a monster, who snatched those unwary travellers who dared to venture too deeply into its heart. She had seen the dark, forbidding expanse of trees often enough from the window of her solar, but never before had she dared to venture further than the tiny village clustered at its edge. Sir Edmund laughed at the peasants' tales – but then, what monster would dare to attack him? The girl shuddered at the memory of his fury as she struck at him with her nails, gouging deep scratches in his cheek. He would never forgive her for that – or for what she had said to him. Her distress had led her into foolishness, and she had blurted out things which would have been better left unsaid. No, he would never forgive her. There was nowhere she could hide, nowhere she could live in peace. Wherever she went, his hand would reach out to claim her.

Yet she would rather die than become what he would have her be!

She had to escape. That was the one thought beating in her brain as she renewed her headlong flight deeper into the forest, heedless of the cruel branches that whipped into her face or the brambles ripping her kirtle. If she could but evade the merciless hounds that Sir Edmund used to hunt both man and beast, she cared not what became of her. Perhaps she could live in the woods, scavenging for her food – or perhaps she could find sanctuary with the nuns? Anything, even death, was preferable to what awaited her if she was dragged back to the manor by Sir Edmund's men. In her distress she almost wished that her blow had killed him, but she knew he had merely been stunned, recovering soon after she had fled from the chamber.

The baying of that hound chilled her blood as it came ever closer. It was a fearful sound, and one she had heard often enough in the years she had spent at the manor, but never quite like this. The peasants called their lord's dogs 'the Hounds of Hell', and now she knew they were right. The cry that struck ice into her veins was like the moaning of a tortured soul echoing in the stillness of the forest.

Now she had reached a clearing, and she hesitated, looking frantically from right to left as she tried to decide which path to follow. Which way lay the Abbey and her only chance of sanctuary? If she could but plead with the Abbess, that devout lady might take her in for the sake of... A scream of horror burst from the girl's lips as a huge black dog came hurtling towards her from the trees. In an instant she realised that it came from in front of her and not behind, and despair swept over her as she realised she was trapped. Somehow the huntsmen must have encircled her. Unable to move, she flung up her arms to protect her throat as the beast sprang, its teeth sinking into her flesh as she screamed yet again.

'Down, Beelzebub, you damned cur!'

She heard the command as she went down beneath the huge creature, the weight of its warm body smothering her and blocking her view so that she could not see the horseman or the servant who ran towards her. Pain seared her, combining with the terror to rob her mind of rational thought. She was aware that, miraculously, the dog had ceased to savage her, but it still stood over her, guarding her with a growling vigilance. She was swooning with fear, her senses swimming as a hand reached out to haul the beast from her, and she stared up in bewilderment into the face of the man who bent over her – a face so ugly and fearful that she thought it was the demon who haunted these woods, and she screamed wildly again and again until the blackness took possession of her mind and she lay limply at his feet.

In the brief instant before the darkness enfolded her, she heard another voice issuing commands to the dog. Her eyelids fluttered as she struggled to see who was speaking, but even as he brought his horse closer she slipped into unconsciousness, unheeding of the startled oath he uttered as he gazed down at her crumpled form.

'It's a child, Balsadare! Has the dog killed her?'

Balsadare bent his head, pressing his ear against the girl's bosom and frowning in concentration; then a smile flickered across his deeply scarred features as his sharp hearing caught the faint beat of her heart.

'No, my lord, she lives still.'

The master dismounted and stood beside his servant. Tall and lean in his hunting garb of black velvet, there was an almost feline grace about him that belied his steely strength. Soft, straight hair swept the collar of his severe tunic, framing the pale features. His grey, thoughtful eyes were glittering with anger as they surveyed the girl, absorbing the scratches on her face and legs – and the blood trickling from her arm where the dog had mauled her.

He frowned, realising that she was not

quite the child he had at first believed her to be. Though slight and thin, she had the features of a girl who had been gently bred – that complexion had never been exposed to work in the fields! Yet her gown was of a rough woollen material and her feet were bare.

'If she breathes yet, it is no thanks to you or that cur,' he said. 'You lost control of him, Balsadare.'

'Beelzebub would not have attacked if she had not shown fear.'

'Fear of us – or of another?' Fine brows rose in lazy enquiry. 'Did it not seem strange to you that we passed riders and hounds an hour since? What quarry did they hunt, think you, Balsadare?'

'I saw no sign of any beast, my lord. Yet the dogs were excited...'

'They did not hunt boar or stag.' The grey eyes narrowed to menacing slits. 'For that reason, I crossed their path and scattered the powder that destroyed the scent Sir Edmund's hounds followed. He shall not feed on this flesh tonight. We shall take her to the castle.'

'To the castle, my lord?' Pity for the un-conscious girl at his feet made the servant bold. 'Would it not be better to deliver her up to the Abbess? She is but a child. You do not mean...?'

A slender, black-gloved hand touched his

14

arm; the fingers applied no pressure and yet he was silenced. 'You question my orders, sirrah?'

'Forgive me, my lord.' Balsadare met his burning gaze unflinchingly. 'My life is yours – take it if I have offended you.'

'You tempt me, Balsadare.' A smile lurked at the corners of his master's lips but did not reach the eyes. 'Yet I shall spare you for … the sake of your beauty…'

Choking on a smothered oath, Balsadare bent to lift the unconscious girl in his arms. Though squat and misshapen, he had immensely strong shoulders and the girl was light. He carried her as easily as if she were but a sack of goose-feathers, following obediently behind his master's horse. The huge black dog loped at their heels as they disappeared into the trees, leaving no trace of their presence for the huntsmen to find…

'You dare to tell me you have failed? How could a mere girl escape you when men have been caught within the hour?' Sir Edmund glared at the unfortunate wretch cowering before him. Fury made him lash out, and he struck the man's cheek with the full force of his strength, causing him to stagger and fall to his knees in fear.

'The hounds lost her scent, Sir Edmund. It was as if they were bewitched, one moment in full cry, and then…' He faltered at the rage in his master's eyes. 'They are still acting strangely.'

'What do you mean?' Thick brows met in a frown. 'These tales of witchery will not save you, Fulk.'

'Have you not noticed the hounds are strangely silent, my lord? Two of them were so afflicted that we had to carry them home.'

'This is foolish talk, sirrah! If the dogs are ill, you must have fed them poisoned meat.' Sir Edmund's fleshy face tightened with anger. 'Fools! Must I always be served by idiots and laggards? You lost the girl and so you blame the hounds. I'll have you flayed for this!'

His fingers strayed to the deep lacerations on his cheek and he almost choked on the bile that rose in his throat. The sting from these petty wounds was as nothing to the thundering ache in his skull where *she* had struck him with a heavy iron taper-stick, yet neither wound was as sharp as the blow her words had dealt to his pride. That *she* should dare to defy him! That slut! His tawny eyes were flecked with tiny gold spots as the anger flamed inside him. To be overset by a mere wench – it was not to be borne! It made him look a fool and pricked his vanity. Grown men were wont to turn pale when he looked at them, but *she* had dared to mock him. He had thought her spirit crushed after so many months of virtual imprisonment, believing that she would accept his plans for her meekly – even gratefully. It seemed she had deceived him, the cunning witch! When she was his once more, she would learn how he punished those who dared to disobey him. He had been too easy with her, but now she would suffer for her impudence.

The fleshy face twisted with spite as he looked at his henchman. 'Tomorrow you will search again, and this time you will find her, Fulk. If you fail me…' He left the threat unspoken, a cruel sneer on his thick lips. 'The wench must be brought back alive. Do you understand me?'

Fulk's face drained of colour as he read his fate in the other's eyes. His master was not given to idle threats. If the girl was not found, he would die before sunset on the morrow…

She was conscious of the pain long before her eyes opened. It hurt so terribly that she could scarcely bear it. Her head turned from side to side on the pillow as she cried out, staring up as the nameless terror gripped her and she was suddenly wide awake. She began to whimper with fright, thrashing wildly as her lips opened to scream. A shadowy figure moved towards the bed, bending over her in concern, and she found herself looking into the face of an

17

angel. At least it was so fair and sweet that, in the circle of light afforded by a rush taper, she thought it must be Gabriel himself until he spoke.

'Do not be frightened,' he said gently. 'No one shall harm you while I am here to protect you.'

She swallowed, the tip of her tongue moving over dry lips. 'Water...' Her voice was a harsh croak, and sounded strange to her ears. 'Who... Where am I?'

The youth poured water into a pewter cup and bent to place an arm beneath her shoulders, lifting her so that she could drink a few drops of the blessedly cool liquid. She gulped greedily until he removed the cup, then she sighed, sinking back against the softness of feather pillows and staring at him in bewilderment. She felt so strange ... as if she were floating...

'My name is Gervase,' the beautiful youth said with a smile, his blue eyes reminding her of a summer sky. 'Beelzebub attacked you, and they brought you here.' He laughed gaily as he saw the startled look on her face. 'No, you were not brought here by the prince of evil spirits! Beelzebub is a dog, though some would say both he and his master were forged in the fires of Hell!' A shadow passed across his face and was dismissed swiftly. 'Now, lady, tell me who you are and whence you came?'

For a moment the girl stared at him blankly, then a look of fear began to cloud her dark eyes, turning them almost black. She felt a surge of panic and clutched desperately at his arm, a faint moan issuing from her lips.

Seeing her distress, Gervase frowned. 'What ails you, sweet mistress? Is the pain so bad?'

Tears slipped beneath her thick lashes as she moved her head negatively on the pillow. 'I – I do not know...' she whispered, catching her breath on a sob. 'I cannot remember.'

Gervase stared at her in surprise. 'You cannot remember your name? Surely it cannot be so! Think carefully now, lady. You were in the forest and the dog attacked you. You fainted when Balsadare came to your aid. Now it must come back to you, I think?'

'No,' she whispered, the tears sliding silently down her cheeks. 'There is nothing in my mind but vague shadows... Ah!' She sat up in bed, tearing at her hair as a feeling of terror swept over her. 'Help me... They will kill me!'

The youth caught her hands, holding them tightly as she fought him wildly. Capturing her at last, he held her pressed against him, soothing her with gentle words until she quietened. At last she drew away from him, staring at his face anxiously.

'Who am I, sir? Pray tell me my name at least.'

He shook his head sadly. 'I fear I know only as much as I have told you. My brother may know more, but he has not confided in me as yet.'

'Your brother?' she asked wonderingly, looking about the chamber as if seeking a clue to light the darkness in her mind. 'Who is he, and what is this place?'

The warmth left his eyes, and he became so cold and withdrawn that she shivered. 'My brother has many names, mistress, but I am wont to call him Athelstan. If you should have cause to speak with him...' Gervase drew a sharp breath as if the thought distressed him. 'It would be proper for you to address him as Lord Athelstan.'

'Lord Athelstan...' A little chill ran down her spine as she repeated the name. 'Is this your brother's house, sir?'

The youth looked at her, shaking his head slightly as if in amusement. 'I shall not have you call me "sir". We are to be friends, little mistress. I have need of a companion in this … place. No, it is not a house but a castle; the Earl of Athelstan's stronghold and the source of his power.'

'His power?' She glanced at him in puzzlement, sensing that he was fighting some inner struggle. Meeting her curious gaze, he got to his feet and walked away from the bed. She noticed for the first time that he had a deformity which caused him to drag one leg behind the other. 'Oh...'

He turned, and his mouth twisted wryly. 'Do not pity me, girl. I have no pain, and it does not distress me.'

Instantly she sensed the deep bitterness his words were meant to hide, and she knew that his deformity was indeed a source of pain to him, even if that pain were not physical.

'It was not pity, sir, only surprise,' she said. 'Forgive me if I have offended you.'

'You will offend me only if you persist in calling me "sir".' He returned to the bed and smiled down at her. 'It is late, and I must leave you. I believe you will sleep when I have gone, but if you should be frightened or ill you must pull the rope beside the bed and Griselda will come.'

'Griselda?' She raised her brows at him as he paused at the door.

'Griselda was my nurse, and my brother's before me. It was she who tended your hurts when they brought you here, but she is old and I sent her to rest while I watched over you.'

The girl lay back against the pillows as he went out and pulled the door to behind him, her fingers tangling in the coverlet of heavy silk. Gervase had left the taper-stick for her and she was grateful for the kindness of this thought; if she had been plunged into darkness, the panic she was barely keeping in check might have overcome her. Her eyes moved round the large chamber, resting briefly on the two heavy oak coffers that stood at either end of the room. There was little else to catch her interest except a table covered with a tapestry by the narrow window. In this light she could catch the gleam of silken threads, but the subject of the fine work eluded her. It was the only ornament, save for the thick bed-hangings, and seemed out of place in the austere chamber, almost as if it had been placed there to bring some comfort for her sake – but that was mere foolishness. Why should anyone go to so much trouble for a stranger – a girl who did not know her own identity?

Now the panic was filling her again, making her want to call the youth back to her side. While he had stayed with her she had managed to keep the fear at bay, but now it plucked at her nerves like a minstrel at the strings of his harp, stretching so tautly that she was in agony. Who was she, and what was the fearful thing lurking in the shadows of her mind? Was it because of that fear that she had forgotten her own name?

She believed it must be so. Because she did not want to recall whatever had caused her fear, she had somehow brought down a curtain to shut out the things that were painful to her. The feeling of sheer panic began to fade as she explored the thought. She was conscious of an inner strength she had not been aware of until this moment. She was alive, and it seemed that she had much to be grateful for. What did it matter that she had no name? If she could not remember her true title, she would invent one for herself.

Names drifted through her mind as her eyelids grew heavier, and the images blurred, making the room appear full of strange shapes and shadows. Anne, Bronwen, Elena... She dismissed them all, and then her lips curved in a little smile of triumph. Perdita... She would call herself Perdita. In Latin it meant 'lost', and she was certainly that! How did she know that? How could she recall the meaning of a word and not know her own name? It puzzled her, but then she dismissed it, determined not to give way to the panic again. It did not matter how she knew these things. One day she would remember everything, and until then she would call herself Perdita. With the decision came peace, and her eyes closed as she drifted into a dreamless sleep.

It was morning when she awoke and the sun was filtering through the tiny window, warming a patch of the stone floor to dancing colour. She saw that the colour was reflected from the tapestry, and recognised that the silken threads were woven to represent the passion of Christ. Once, she herself had worked on such a tapestry... She remembered the cloth quite clearly and knew that it had been a source of great pleasure to her, where and when this work had been done remained hidden in the mists that still held her mind. Oh, why could she not remember her own name?

For a moment the panic returned, then she recalled the decision she had made before she slept. Her name was to be Perdita. The memory gave her something to cling to. When she drew back the bed-hangings, she saw that an old woman was bending over one of the chests, laying something down carefully.

Hearing the swish of the curtains, the woman turned to look at her, and Perdita saw that she was indeed very old. Her face was so wrinkled that her chin turned upwards and her eyes were mere slits in the loose folds of skin. She walked towards the bed, her back bent and her steps slow.

'So you're awake then, mistress?' The voice was surprisingly young and clear, and when Perdita met her eyes she felt a little tingle as she saw how bright they were. 'You are to dress and come down, girl. The master wishes to see you before he leaves.'

'Is Lord Athelstan going away?' Perdita asked as she threw back the covers and stepped out on to the chill of the floor, wearing only a thin shift. She saw the sharp look the old woman gave her, and hid her smile,. 'I was told I was a guest in Lord Athelstan's home last night. Forgive me, I have no right to pry into your master's affairs. It was but an idle question.'

''Tis not my forgiveness you'll be needing if you meddle in what does not concern you, wench.' The woman brought her bright gaze up to study the girl intently. 'I know not who you are or how you came here, but I advise you to leave as soon as you may. This is no place for the likes of you.'

'Why do you say that, Griselda?' Perdita frowned as she saw the woman's chin shake with annoyance. 'Your master's brother told me that it was your name... He told me you would help me if I needed you.' The wistful note in her voice made the old crone bite back the scolding words she had been about to deliver.

'Does your arm pain you?' she asked, her words reflecting a grudging concern. 'Come, let me apply fresh salves, then I'll help you to dress – and we must do something about that hair!' She muttered crossly beneath her breath as she began to unwind the stained linen from the girl's arm, but Perdita felt that she was not really angry.

Griselda's remark about her hair made her curious, and she glanced at the tresses falling loosely on her shoulders. Her hair was thick and luxuriant, its dark brown shade tinged with a hint of burgundy. She realised suddenly that she did not know what she looked like or even the colour of her own eyes.

'Tell me, Griselda,' she said hesitantly, 'am I pretty or – or plain featured?'

'What vanity is this?' Griselda scowled as she applied a strong-smelling ointment to the girl's wound, tutting as she flinched and gasped. 'That dog is a dangerous brute. If I had my way it would be destroyed – and also that imp of Satan who cares for it!'

'Why did the dog attack me?' Perdita wrinkled her brow as she struggled to remember the incident and failed. 'Was I trespassing on your master's land?'

'Questions! Always questions!' Griselda grumbled as she finished binding the wound with clean linen. 'I have learned not to ask questions in this household. Wash your face and slip on that gown, then I shall dress your hair.' She pointed to a tunic of blue silk edged with silver lying on the nearest coffer.

Meekly, Perdita obeyed her, realising that the woman knew no more than she did. She looked at the fine garment, touching its material and feeling sure that it was not her own. Judging by the amount of blood on the stained bandage, her own gown must have been ruined when the dog savaged her. She wondered who the tunic really belonged to, but decided not to ask; Griselda would not tell her. She sat on a stool in silence, patiently staring before her as the nurse brushed and braided her hair into a wide coronet round her head, fastening it with a silver net caught with seed-pearls. It was soothing to sit thus, and it felt strangely familiar, as if it had often happened in the past.

When Griselda had done, she gave a grunt of satisfaction and stood back to study her work. Looking into the wide, innocent eyes of the girl she had transformed into a beauty, she felt a flicker of fear and frowned, wishing there was some way to dim the brilliance of those velvety brown eyes.

'You look well enough, mistress,' she muttered, answering the girl's unspoken question. 'I have obeyed my master's orders. You must not blame me for what happens now. I have given you warning. Heed me or not as you please.'

Perdita gazed at her apprehensively. Griselda's hints were beginning to make her feel anxious.

'What warnings has this hag been whispering, sweet lady?' Gervase appeared on the threshold, and her unease fled as she saw his eyes light with admiration. 'My faith, Athelstan was right – you are beautiful!'

Perdita rose to her feet, smiling shyly as he

came limping towards her. This morning he was dressed in a tunic of silver and blue, seeming even more handsome than he had the previous night. 'You flatter me, Gervase. I do not think your nurse approves!'

Mischief glowed in the blue eyes. 'Griselda is old, and we shall not heed her. If she ever approves of you, you will know you are on your deathbed!'

'That is unkind,' she reproved him with a frown.

'Take no notice, girl,' Griselda grunted. 'His tongue is not always as fair as his face – but it cannot hurt me. It was this hag he spurns who fed and bathed him when he was still a spewling infant, these hands that set him on his feet and wiped his tears when he fell. He is a child yet, when he needs me and the sickness is on him...'

'Still your clattering tongue, woman!' Gervase's voice was oddly harsh, and the old woman nodded, a glint of spite in her eyes as though she nursed some secret triumph.

'Ay, still your tongue, Griselda. Ask no questions. See nothing and hear less... It's a wise head that keeps its own counsel in this accursed place!' She was muttering angrily as she hobbled from the room, leaving the young people eyeing each other awkwardly.

'She is old,' Perdita said quietly. 'I think she means no harm.'

A wry smile lit his eyes. 'She would die for me, but her last breath would be spent in scolding me. Come, we must keep Athelstan waiting no longer.'

A spasm of fear passed across her face. Why was it that the very mention of that name was enough to set her trembling? Could it be that he was connected with the terror that lurked at the back of her mind? She considered the idea and then dismissed it. Although her fears were shadowy, she felt that she had been in grave danger. If Lord Athelstan meant her harm, she would not have been so gently used in his home. Taking her escort's arm, she allowed him to lead her through the echoing passages and down a spiral staircase to the gallery, dismissing her vague feelings of apprehension as the direct consequence of her uncertain situation. It was natural that she should feel a little nervous of meeting her host for the first time. She was beholden to him for the bed she had slept in last night and the clothes she wore. Since he could turn her from his house at a moment's notice, she would be a fool not to feel some trepidation. She was a stranger in this place, and though she had been treated with kindness, she could not expect Lord Athelstan to give her a home. Somehow she had to remember who she was and why she had been in the forest.

Feeling her hand jerk on his arm, Gervase

glanced at her white face. 'Do not be frightened, lady. My brother has sworn to me that he means you no harm. There are those who have cause to fear – even to hate – him. Sometimes I am one of them, but I know him for a man of his word.'

Far from reassuring her, his words sent little chills down her spine. It was not the first time he had hinted at some mystery surrounding his brother, and Griselda's warnings hovered in her mind. Why did everyone seem to fear Lord Athelstan? Was he some kind of a monster?

They had travelled the length of the gallery and now stood at the head of a wide stone stairway, leading down to what was obviously the great hall. Massive stone pillars carved with intricate designs supported ornate wooden arches embellished with gilding, and the domed ceiling was painted with fantastic figures in gaudy blues, reds and gold. Here and there narrow windows allowed a glimmer of light, but the chamber was dark, and try as she might, Perdita could not make out the features of the men standing at the far end. Feeling oddly breathless, she kept her eyes downcast as Gervase led her slowly down the stairs and across the tiled floor, stopping when they reached the huge open hearth, where a fire was burning despite the wintry sunshine she had glimpsed through the solar window.

'You are welcome, lady.'

The soft, husky voice brought her head up swiftly in surprise, and then she drew a sharp breath. Two men were standing side by side in front of the roaring flames. One was squat and ugly, his face scarred by purple welts that looked as if he had at some time been badly burned. His wide shoulders gave him a top-heavy look that was almost a deformity. Studying him intently for a moment, she felt that she had seen him before but could not remember when or where; probably in the forest before she fainted. This, she believed, was Balsadare, the master of the dog who had attacked her. She could see a gleam of curiosity in his eyes, and gave him a shy smile. Then she turned her gaze to the second man, and her heart jerked strangely. He was tall and serious-looking, with intelligent eyes that seemed to see into her very soul. There was a quietness and a watchfulness about him that made her slightly apprehensive. Why was he staring at her so intently? Unsure of what to do, she sank into a graceful curtsy, knowing immediately that he was Lord Athelstan.

'I thank you for your welcome, my lord – and for graciously allowing your servant to tend my hurts.'

'I need no thanks, lady. It was the least I could do, since it was my dog that caused your pain. Balsadare is anxious to beg your pardon for his slowness in controlling the beast.'

The servant muttered something that might have been an apology, and Perdita shook her head. 'I am sure it was not intended, sir.'

Athelstan's lips curved. 'There, you are forgiven, Balsadare. I shall not have you beaten after all.' The idle jest brought a gasp from Perdita and the colour drained from her cheeks. Seeing her look, Athelstan's fine brows rose. 'They told me you had recovered from your fright, but I see that all is not well with you. Forgive me for bringing you from your bed. I wished only to speak with you for a moment before I set out.'

'I am well enough, my lord, although if I am to leave here, I know not where I shall go.'

'Have I said that you must leave?'

The hint of reproach in his soft voice brought a flame to her cheeks. 'No, my lord. I meant not to offend you.'

'Did you not?' A slight smile played about his mouth as he looked at her, enjoying the clear evidence of her discomfort. As he had suspected from the first, she was beautiful and she had spirit. His curiosity was aroused, and he was sure that he would be well rewarded for bringing the wench to the castle. It was obvious that Gervase had already fallen beneath her spell. 'Well, then, you shall not go until you wish it. Tell me, lady, have you recalled your name?'

She shook her head, staring at him uneasily as she tried to decide whether he was mocking her. He seemed to have a rather black sense of humour – at least she thought he had been jesting when he threatened his servant with a beating! Now he was studying her with a cool calculation that made her nervous. Did he imagine she was pretending a loss of memory in order to force him into offering extended hospitality? A surge of pride brought a sparkle to her eyes.

'I know not who or what I am, but I have decided I shall be called Perdita...' She broke off indignantly as she heard his husky chuckle. 'It is as good a name as any, since I have none of my own.'

'Indeed it is, lady.' Athelstan's eyes registered silent appreciation of her choice.

'Why Perdita?' asked Gervase, frowning. 'You might as well be Margaret or Isabelle.'

'I think not.' Athelstan's tone was chiding. 'Have you forgot all your Latin?'

A grin lit the youth's face as he realised the significance of the name she had chosen. 'By my faith, even you could not have named her better, brother.'

'Perhaps not so well, Gervase. At least we know something of our guest at last.' He smiled as she looked at him enquiringly. 'You are plainly of gentle birth and have received some tuition – that in itself is something unusual. Another day we shall endeavour to discover the extent of your learning, Perdita, but first we must try to establish who you really are. You may have an anxious family...' His words trailed into silent suspicion as he saw her sudden look of fear. Was it possible that she was trying to deceive them? 'Why do you tremble so, Perdita? Can it be that you know what I shall discover? Come, tell me the truth, and I shall protect you from whatever it is you fear!' His face had become stern, and it frightened her.

Tears stung her eyes, but she blinked them back as pride came to her rescue. Clearly, he thought that she was lying to preserve some shameful secret. The knowledge that she could not be sure of her own innocence made his doubt of her even more bitter. There was a chiding look in his eyes that made her feel like a naughty child, and because of it she found herself reacting childishly.

'You are cruel to taunt me, sir. Send me away if you think so ill of me, but do not accuse me of lying to you!' She brushed away her tears, and as she did so, a smear of blood from her wound transferred itself to her cheek. 'I do not know who I am or how I came to be where you found me. I – I did not mean to trespass on your land...' A sob escaped her despite all her efforts to control it, and she saw him frown.

Athelstan felt a prick of disappointment. She was but a child after all, although he had briefly seen something in her that stirred an unwonted interest. Mere beauty could never captivate him for more than a few days; he needed the stimulation of a challenge and for a moment he had believed that she might supply the lack he had felt for so long. But no matter. She was in need of help, and a guest in his house.

'You are ill, child, and should not have been brought from your bed.' He turned to his brother with a sigh that seemed to condemn her as an irritant that must be swiftly dealt with. 'Take her to Griselda, brother. She is to stay in her chamber and rest until she is well enough for company.'

'But, Athelstan,' Gervase protested, 'she was perfectly well until you tormented her.'

A tiny nerve flicked in Athelstan's cheek and the grey eyes were suddenly flinty. From no one else would he take such presumption. Sometimes he wondered if he had indulged his young brother too much for his own good, but it was hard to be other than gentle with him in the circumstances. And yet... He dismissed the thought as swiftly as it had entered his mind. Gervase enjoyed his little games. He found it amusing to see just how far he could provoke the brother he resented. Theirs was a strange relationship, but the ties that bound them were strong, though neither could be quite sure whether love or hatred was supreme.

'Do as I ask you, Gervase,' he said quietly, his gaze meeting the youth's in silent conflict. He saw mutiny flare, and then the blue eyes dropped. 'I shall be gone some hours, perhaps for a day or two. I shall hope to see you much recovered when I return, lady.' With a curt nod of his head he turned and strode from the chamber, the tread of his leather buskins making little sound on the flagstones. At his heels, Balsadare followed as silently as his shadow.

Fighting her tears, Perdita had missed the small confrontation between Athelstan and his brother. She thought that his coldness had been meant for her, and she felt hurt by the unfairness of it. She watched until the two figures disappeared from sight; then, as Gervase turned to her, she gave a little cry and ran from him, rushing up the stairs. She knew she must seek sanctuary in her chamber before the tears could flow and shame her.

CHAPTER TWO

Tears blurred Perdita's eyes as she ran, smarting with indignation at Athelstan's dismissive treatment. It was obvious from his attitude that he thought her a troublesome child whom he was forced to succour by the laws of hospitality until he could discover her true identity – and since he meant to lose no time in doing what he could to trace her family, it was clear that he could not wait to be rid of his unwelcome charge.

Tortured by her thoughts, it was several minutes before she realised that she had somehow missed her way. The passage she had entered ended in a stout door, iron-studded and set at the top of a tiny flight of steps; it was similar to the chamber she had left earlier, but was not the same. She stopped running, catching her breath as she looked about her. That door was the entrance to one of the castle's towers, so she must retrace her steps and try to find her own chamber, for she had seen no sign of any servants.

As she was about to turn away, the door opened and she paused, thinking it might be sensible to ask for help rather than spend hours wandering about the bewildering maze of rooms and possibly trespassing where she was not permitted to go. As she stood hesitating, a man came out and paused at the top of the stairs, a look of surprise on his face as he saw her. He had a large frame with powerful shoulders, and a hard face; in a gown of dark blue velvet over a short silver tunic and hose, his demeanour was full of pride and arrogance.

'Who are you?' he demanded, his eyes narrowing menacingly. 'What are you doing here? Have you been spying on me?'

Perdita took a step backwards, feeling threatened by his belligerent manner. 'Why should I spy on you, sir? I do not know you. I lost my way and was about to return to the great hall. When you came out, I thought to ask for help...'

'If you are lying, wench...' He made a move towards her, and she gave a squeal of fright.

'Perdita! Why did you run from me?'

Hearing Gervase's voice, she looked behind her and felt a surge of relief. He would tell this angry nobleman – for by his dress and manner he could be no less – that she had not meant to invade his privacy. She bit her lip as she saw the flush of annoyance on her rescuer's face, and noticed that his limp was more pronounced as he hobbled towards her.

'I am sorry to put you to so much trouble,' she said contritely, going to meet him. 'It was foolish of me to flee like that, and I am well served for my pains. I – I seem to have intruded into this ... gentleman's private domain.' She glanced nervously over her shoulder at the stranger, seeing that he still looked angry.

Gervase followed the direction of her gaze. He bowed his head in stiff acknowledgment. 'Your pardon, sir. We meant not to disturb you. Perdita is my brother's guest. She does not yet know her way about the castle.'

'Since you vouch for her, I accept that it was an accident.' The stranger's eyes glittered oddly. 'You will not speak of this, wench. If gossip should reach Athelstan's ears, he would know what must be done. Never say that you have seen me here. Do you understand?'

'I do not know you, sir. Why should I speak of you?' Her voice and face were defiant as she felt an instinctive dislike of him.

'Do not, if you value your tongue.' The stranger turned his hard gaze on Gervase. 'I must speak with Athelstan before I leave. Have him attend me immediately.'

'My brother rode out a short time ago, sir. He said that he might be gone for a day or two. I am sure he would not have left if he had thought you might need him.'

'Gone?' The heavy brows met in a frown.

'Where? He said naught of this when we spoke last night.'

'Athelstan goes where he pleases,' Gervase said, an odd touch of malice in his tone. 'He does not confide in me. I know no more of his business today than of his talks with you. Yet, if I can be of service, I am at your command, my lord.'

'No...' The stranger seemed to dismiss him with a curt nod. 'Stay, perhaps you can be of service. Tell Athelstan only that I shall go to France as we agreed. He is to wait until he hears from me, as he knows, but he will need a sign. My messenger will bring him this ring. Here, take it and examine it well so that you may know it again.' He gave Gervase a heavy gold ring.

Unable to contain her curiosity, Perdita glanced at it as it lay on the palm of his hand. The stone was flat and of a curious blackish colour flecked with red; it had the head of a leopard carved deeply into it, and as she looked at the emblem she had a peculiar sensation of falling and had to clutch at a stone pillar to steady herself. She had seen that ring, or one very similar, somewhere before – but where? Her head was whirling, and she saw Gervase give her an odd glance as he returned the ornament to its owner, who slipped it back on the middle finger of his left hand.

'What ails the wench?' he asked, frowning.

'She has been ill,' Gervase said swiftly. 'I shall deliver your message to my brother as soon as he returns.'

'Good! Remember, only if you see this ring will the courier have come from me.' He scowled, giving Perdita one more penetrating look. 'Go now, both of you. And remember my warning, wench.'

Perdita nodded, taking Gervase's arm as they walked away. She was conscious of the stranger's eyes watching them until, at last, they turned the corner.

'Why did you almost faint just now?' Gervase asked, looking down at her.

'That ring...' She frowned, trying desperately to recall some tiny clue. 'I have seen it – somewhere before. Who was that man, Gervase?'

'You must not ask me that. He is a person of some importance. I can tell you only that. Athelstan warned me not to be curious.' He frowned at her. 'We live in uneasy times. Since the Duke of Gloucester was foully murdered, no man can sleep soundly in his bed. There is no law or justice in England when the King orders and parliament obeys...'

'But was it not said that the Duke died of an apoplectic fit?' Perdita wrinkled her brow. 'I remember...' She seemed to see the gentle face of a woman. There was a fire flickering in the hearth, and a bible spread on the table before them... The image faded, and she gave a cry of distress. 'Oh, why do I recall such foolish things and not my own name?'

'There were many rumours at the time of Gloucester's death, but few believed them. It is common knowledge that King Richard was determined to be revenged on his uncle for forcing him to sign the commission that almost stripped him of his royal power. Gloucester was certainly murdered, and it is only a matter of...' Suddenly Gervase realised he had said too much, and he gave her a calculating look that reminded her of his brother. 'Were you sent here to spy on us, Perdita? Have you really forgotten your name, or is it part of some plot to trap Athelstan?'

'No!' she cried, her face clouding with distress. 'Oh, please do not look at me like that. I swear to you that I know nothing of these things. My mind is full of hazy pictures and sometimes I recall a word or an object, but all the rest is merely shadows.'

'I believe you.' Gervase relaxed as he saw that she was genuinely upset. 'For a moment I thought that one of my brother's enemies might have set a trap for him, but I see that I was mistaken. You must never repeat any of this, Perdita. That man was never here, and I said things that would have been better left unspoken. Give me your promise that you will not betray us.'

'I have seen and heard nothing, Gervase.' She lifted her clear eyes to his. 'In truth, I wish I had not. That man frightened me. There was something about him that reminded me...' She shivered and shook her head. 'No, I cannot remember anything except that I was very frightened. Do you think I ever shall?'

'Athelstan said he believed it was the shock of being attacked by the dog. When you have had time to recover, you may be able to remember everything.'

'And if I do not?' Her bottom lip trembled. 'Will—Will Lord Athelstan let me stay here?'

'Perhaps, if I ask him.' Gervase laughed hollowly. 'You may not wish to stay here. Indeed, most of my brother's guests are only too anxious to leave!'

'What do you mean?'

He shook his head, a distant expression stealing into his eyes. 'It was merely a jest. You have nothing to fear. You are not like the others.'

'The others?'

Seeing her anxiety, he smiled. 'Do not concern yourself. I have been babbling like a fool! It is so pleasant for me to have your company, and yet I seem intent on trying to frighten you away. Griselda says I have a cruel streak in my nature and perhaps she is right, but I do not wish to hurt you.

Athelstan can be ruthless, but he would not harm you. He is not a monster, despite what some may say of him. Sometimes I blame him, but he is not responsible...'

The bleak look in his eyes told her that he was thinking of his deformity. She was saddened by the knowledge of his suffering, and she laid her hand gently on his arm, wanting to reach out to him.

'I am not afraid when you are with me, Gervase.'

His face lit up as he looked down at her. 'I am glad Athelstan found you! I hope he fails to discover your true identity, Perdita. I want you to stay here with us for ever.'

There was something a little disturbing in the brilliance of his eyes at that moment. His hand clutched her wrist, the fingers tightening until she cried out. In that instant he seemed to realise what he was doing, and he released her.

'You should rest now,' he said with a harsh laugh. 'My brother commanded it – and we must all obey him.'

With that, he turned from her, his twisted foot dragging awkwardly as he walked slowly away.

The congealing remains of a meal were scattered on the oak board before Sir Edmund as he sat brooding into his tankard of ale. His servants had been scouring the woods since first light, but so far the troublesome wench had avoided them. Their task was made more difficult because only a handful of the dogs were able to join them. He had inspected the pack himself the previous night and found that Fulk was telling the truth; the dogs were acting strangely, yet they were in no pain. He knew his servants were convinced it was witchcraft, but he was a practical man and he did not believe in such nonsense – though he doubted not that some mischief had been done to his hounds. But who would dare to risk his wrath? Certainly it could be none of his own people... He looked up, frowning, as a servant approached.

'Well,' he barked. 'What is it, man?'

'There – is a visitor, Sir Edmund.'

'A visitor?' The Baron's thick brows met in a frown. There had been few enough visitors to the manor since the death of his wife; he was not popular with his nearest neighbours, and he disliked being forced to provide food and lodging for a gaggle of greedy relatives. Besides, he had his own reasons for keeping the curious at bay. He wanted no prying eyes until that slut had been brought back and dealt with as she deserved! He waved a dismissive hand. 'I'll see no one today.'

The servant gave him a startled glance, but he was afraid of his master and dared not argue. He turned away, but even as he did so a figure appeared at the doorway, advancing in to the room uninvited.

'My master can see no one...' His protest died as he caught the flash of anger in the grey eyes and he looked nervously over his shoulder.

'I believe Sir Edmund will see *me*.' The visitor's calm voice carried a hint of authority.

Sir Edmund's startled gaze flew to the face of the man who had spoken, and he rose to his feet with a smothered oath. 'Athelstan! I did not know it was you.' He glared at the hapless servant. 'Fool! Why did you not say it was Lord Athelstan? Go, bring wine for my guest!' As the servant hastened to obey, he gestured to an oak settle by the fire. 'Will you not sit and take wine with me, my lord? I am honoured by your visit.'

A wry smile flickered over Athelstan's lips. Although their estates were separated only by the forest – which was the property of the crown and leased to Athelstan – they scarcely met, and this was the first time he had entered his neighbour's house for more than ten years. Mortimer was a bully and a coarse-tongued braggart; his company did not appeal to his overlord, though they met occasionally in Nottingham or at council when called upon by the King. For the lands he held, Sir Edmund owed fealty to the Earl of Athelstan and was required to keep ten fighting men, who could be called upon by

46

the Earl at any time.

'I hope I do not find you indisposed, Mortimer?' Athelstan glanced at the empty ale-jugs and the remains of food strewn on the table, then back to his host's face.

Sir Edmund flushed as he saw the glimmer of scorn, feeling suddenly conscious of the stains on his tunic. The Earl was well known for his fastidiousness at table and in the manner of his dress. 'The servants grow idle with no mistress to scold them,' he muttered. 'I'll have all this cleared at once.'

'Do not trouble yourself on my account. I came only to inspect your men-at-arms, for I may have need of them quite soon.'

The Baron blinked stupidly. 'Do you mean to go on a journey, my lord? A pilgrimage, perhaps?'

'Of a kind, perhaps.' A tiny smile flickered in the grey eyes. 'Well, why do you delay? I have said I would inspect your retainers.'

'Had you sent word of your coming, my lord, I should have been delighted to arrange a fine show for you – hand-to-hand fighting by my very best men, but…' He made an expressive gesture with his hands. 'All my people are out searching the forest…' He was halted by the forbidding arch of Athelstan's fine brows.

'I believe I gave permission for you to hunt on twenty-five days of the year – this is not one of them, I think?'

The Baron squirmed uneasily beneath the probe of his overlord's gaze. He was well aware that he had often flouted the licence granted to him by Athelstan, but had believed it went unnoticed. 'The huntsmen do not seek boar or stag.' He scowled, avoiding the other's pointed stare. 'They hunt a runaway, my lord. A wench who has been treated with nothing but kindness in this house suddenly became hysterical, attacking me for no reason.' He touched the scratch-marks on his cheek ruefully.

'She attacked you for no reason?' Athelstan's frown relaxed, and he seemed to invite the Baron's confidence. 'Come, sir, we are both men of the world! The wench resisted your advances with some spirit, and you threatened her with retribution. She fought you and fled in fear of her life... Is that not the truth?'

'She has run mad, I tell you.' Sir Edmund's voice rose in anger. 'If you have found her, you must not listen to a word she says. She is an evil wench, and I was questioning her about ... something, when she started to yell and scream abuse at me.'

'This wench...' Athelstan's look made him flinch. 'I seem to remember hearing that your good wife had an adopted daughter of whom she was very fond?'

An unbecoming mottling stained the Baron's cheeks. 'My wife was a fool to take the slut! Mathilda doted on her – and yet, when she lay close to death, the girl stole from her. She took a ring from her finger and left my wife alone to die in some distress.'

'Indeed? Then you had good cause to punish her for her wickedness. Yet I believed Lady Mathilda died some three months ago?'

'I have been too overset by grief to punish the girl before this, my lord. For my wife's sake I wished to spare her...' He sighed deeply. 'But had she stayed at the bedside, Mathilda might yet live. She had taken a sleeping-potion to ease the pain, and was smothered in her pillows.'

'And so you think the wench is in part to blame?' Athelstan nodded, hiding his disgust with difficulty. He believed nothing this man said, but knew he must tread carefully. The girl was Sir Edmund's ward, and if he demanded her return the law would oblige him to comply. 'Then you are well rid of her! If any of my servants discovers her hiding on my land, I shall see she is dealt with in a suitable manner.'

The Baron looked at him suspiciously. 'I would not have her punished too harshly, my lord. If she is returned to me, I shall make sure that she does penance for her neglect of a woman who was all but a mother to her.'

'She deserves a beating at the very least,'

Athelstan agreed. 'Such ingratitude towards a woman who had taken her in and cared for her from a babe is base indeed. Where did your wife find the child, sir?'

'She was born in the Abbey, of a woman the good nuns found wandering in the woods. They took the mother in and cared for her, but she died after the child was born.'

'And did no one come to claim the child?'

'The mother was unwed. She died in shame, and would tell no one her name or whence she came. The Abbess begged my wife to give the babe a home, knowing that Mathilda was unable to bear her own babes...' He crossed himself piously. 'God rest her soul. She loved the girl as much as and more than if she were indeed her own.'

'Lady Mathilda was a good woman,' said Athelstan. 'I shall intrude upon your grief no more, Sir Edmund. Yet I charge you to have your men practise daily with their arms in case I have need of them.'

Sir Edmund bowed his head respectfully. 'Send word of your coming, my lord, and I shall prepare some fine combat for your entertainment.'

Athelstan nodded, moving towards the door. There he paused to look back as if in afterthought. 'Tell me, what was the wench called?'

'Rosamund.' The Baron scowled, unable

to hide his anger at the mere mention of her name. 'We named her after my wife's sister, who died when still a child.'

'A pretty enough name for an ungrateful wench.'

For a moment the two men measured each other, and then the Baron's eyes dropped. Athelstan smiled inwardly as he left the chamber, not deceived by the other's meek manner. He knew that Sir Edmund's thoughts were already seeking for a way of discovering whether the girl was at the castle. He would not find it easy, however, for the Earl's servants had been carefully chosen for their loyalty.

In the courtyard, Balsadare was waiting patiently with the horses. He came to help his master to mount and was waved away as Athelstan swung himself into the saddle, his eyes gleaming with an inner triumph.

'You were right, my lord!' Balsadare saw the look he knew so well. 'Do we return to the castle now?'

'No, I think not. I would speak first with the Abbess, my friend. There is some mystery here, and I think she may hold the key.'

'And when you have discovered the truth?' Balsadare looked at him hard. 'Will you deliver the girl to the Abbess for safe keeping?'

'Perhaps.' His eyes mocked the servant's serious manner. 'Are you afraid I shall corrupt her innocence, Balsadare? Believe me,

I intend the girl no harm. She interests me…'

As he urged his horse forward, Balsadare crossed himself swiftly before mounting his own horse and following at his master's back.

'Athelstan asks that you sup with us, Perdita, and I am sent to fetch you,' Gervase said from the doorway.

Perdita got to her feet eagerly. She was bored with the enforced confinement in her chamber – which had lasted for two whole days – and she had been hoping that Griselda's work would not go unremarked. Tonight the woman had brought her a softly-flowing gown of emerald green, the waist accentuated by a wide girdle of golden threads. On the girl's feet were leather slippers embroidered with gold thread, and a thin gold circlet rested on her brow. Griselda had washed her hair with sweet-smelling soap and left it flowing loosely on her shoulders.

'When did your brother return?' she asked, as Gervase led her from the room. 'Do you know if he has news for me?'

He gave a hollow laugh. 'Think you he would tell me his news? I know only that he seemed mightily pleased about something. Whether it concerns you, I know not.'

If Lord Athelstan was pleased, it probably meant that he had discovered who she was and where she came from, Perdita thought. Her nerves jangled as she wondered whether she was about to be sent back to ... wherever she belonged...

As they paused at the head of the main stairway, she gave a little gasp of surprise. The great hall was lit by a multitude of flaring torches and was ablaze with light. The tables were laden with food, and at least a hundred men were seated on benches at either side – but the most amazing thing was that every one of them was dressed in green and black. Except for Athelstan. He came to meet her as she walked down the stairs, his gown was of black velvet over a tunic of cloth of gold.

He stood watching her in silence, and she caught her breath at the look in his eyes. It was the look of a hunter – and she was very much afraid that she was his prey. Then he smiled and held out his hand imperiously. She left Gervase and went to him uncertainly.

'So, you are feeling rested, Perdita?'

'Yes, my lord.' She flicked her lashes down, unable to bear his piercing look. 'I – I wish to apologise...'

'Nonsense!' He would not let her continue. 'Away with your sighs, lady. You will smile for me this evening, will you not?'

'I shall try – if it pleases you.'

'And do you wish to please me, Perdita?'

He seemed to dwell on her name for a moment, and she gazed up at him. 'Pray do not tease me, my lord. Have you news for me? Do you know who I am?'

'Such impatience!' he chided with a mock sigh. 'Are you so eager to leave us? Have we given you a dislike of our company?'

Colour flooded her cheeks. 'I am not so ungrateful, my lord. Yet– Yet I know I may not trespass on your hospitality too long…'

'When I am weary of your company, I shall say so.' His smile was enigmatic. 'For this evening, I would have you sit beside me. It is too long since I had such a charming guest.'

As he drew her towards the table at the head of the hall, Perdita realised that the men's eyes had turned to her as if of one accord. She was uncomfortably aware of the amused glances towards her, and of the jests in harsh whispers that were yet loud enough to reach her ears.

Athelstan saw her blushes and chuckled softly. 'You must not mind their jests. It is strange for them to see their lord with a lady – and such a fair one! They will learn better manners in time.'

It pleased him and his men to mock her, but she was determined not to behave childishly. She had been reduced to tears by his scorn once, but it would not happen again. Instinctively, she knew that this man would respect her only if she stood her ground with him.

'Men learn from their master, sir. If you treat me with respect, they can do no less.'

His eyes gleamed, and she saw that her answer had pleased him. 'Your argument is sound, Perdita, but might prove awkward if taken to excess.' As she looked at him in confusion, his brows went up. 'If I should adore you and worship at your feet – must they follow suit?'

If he had hoped to bring a blush to her cheek once more, he was disappointed. Perdita frowned, lifting her head with a touch of hauteur. 'Now indeed you mock me, Lord Athelstan. You do not deserve an answer – nor shall I give you one.'

'I stand rebuked and must hang my head in shame.'

He did not look shamed. In fact, it was obvious to her that he was enjoying himself at her expense. She suspected that this verbal combat was meat and drink to him; the intelligence in those grey eyes scared her, for she wondered if she was capable of parrying his sharp thrusts.

They had almost reached the high table now, and as if he had guessed her thoughts, Athelstan pointed out the one man in the room who was not wearing his colours. 'Father Jonathan was my brother's tutor. Tomorrow you will begin your lessons with him, Perdita. I wish to discover how much you have been taught.'

He paused at the edge of the dais, drawing her forward to face the brown-robed priest. 'This is the lady of whom I told you, Father. I believe you will find her an apt pupil, though she will need all the patience I know you possess to help her to find her way.'

'Lady, I welcome you,' said the priest, his plump face wreathed in smiles. 'It will be good to have a pupil again – for I fear Gervase neglects his studies.' His words held no malice, but he glanced chidingly at the youth who had followed close behind them.

Perdita looked over her shoulder and saw Gervase's resentful expression. She felt a surge of sympathy for his tutor, realising that it could not be easy to manage such a difficult pupil. Already she was aware that Gervase used his deformity as a weapon to bend others to his will. He could be moody and bitter on occasion, but there was such sweetness in his smile that she thought few could resist when he chose to charm them.

Seeing her look at him, Gervase laughed ruefully. 'If I had had Perdita to share my lessons, I might not have found them so dull!'

'I should be glad if you would join us,' said Perdita, giving him a warm smile. 'I fear I may disappoint Father Jonathan, and you can help me if you will.'

The storm-clouds vanished, and his voice was warm. 'For the first time in my life I shall look forward to conjugating verbs!'

'You are a fool to yourself, Gervase,' his brother said, frowning. 'You have a good brain, and you choose to waste it in pursuit of idle pleasure.'

'Should I employ my time as you do, brother?' There was an ugly harshness in Gervase's voice. 'Nay, I think one Athelstan is enough in any household... I prefer my music. It brings pleasure, not pain.'

Perdita felt the man at her side stiffen. She sensed the anger in him and waited for the outburst that must surely come, but to her surprise Athelstan made no reply. Instead, he proceeded to the high-backed chair at the centre of the table. As he reached it, every man in the hall rose to his feet, remaining at attention until he took his seat, motioning Perdita to the place of honour at his right hand. Gervase came to sit beside her, leaving empty his accustomed position at his brother's left hand. Athelstan's face was expressionless as he glanced at the priest, who hastened to obey the unspoken command. He obviously considered it an honour, and at once attempted to engage the Earl in conversation.

'I have received the copies of John Wycliffe's bible that you ordered transcribed, my lord.'

'This is good news.' Athelstan's interest was caught. 'You will keep one for your own use, as we agreed, the other shall be placed in the village church so that all may have access to the scriptures.'

'It is a most generous gift, my lord. Father Thomas has long wished to own a copy of Wycliffe's translation, but he could not afford to have it transcribed.'

A wave of Athelstan's hand dismissed the subject. 'What news of the lad you spoke of some days ago? Will his parents consent to the proposal you made them?'

'They are still reluctant to part with him.' The priest frowned. 'They are ignorant folk, and they have heard tales that frightened them. Perhaps they would listen to you, my lord?'

'Perhaps. We shall speak of this again in private.'

Athelstan turned to glance at the girl beside him. She was laughing at something Gervase had whispered to her, and her dark eyes had a brilliance that made the Earl regret the passing of his youth. He knew himself to be almost twice her age, and felt the gap to be a yawning chasm between them. She was beautiful, spirited, and she aroused emotions in him that he had thought himself beyond experiencing. For a long time now he had denied the physical side of his nature, devoting himself to the work that took so much of his time and his thoughts. To allow himself to be distracted by this girl, even for a moment, was folly. Yet a man needed more than the sterile existence his life had become ... he needed the warmth of a woman's body in his bed... Even so, he knew he would find the mere physical satisfaction of his lust an empty act, unless... A wry smile flickered briefly in his eyes. Was he really thinking of love? He had long ago reached the conclusion that romantic love was a myth of minstrels' songs for the pleasure of those who paid for them. Some were so enamoured of the minstrels' art that they beggared themselves to pay for flowery sonnets, particularly if the poet was wise enough to praise the beauty of his mistress. Athelstan did not subscribe to the pursuit of pleasure for its own sake, though he could appreciate a skilled musician at the appropriate time and welcomed wandering players to his board at Christmastide...

'Why do you frown so, my lord?' Perdita asked when she could bear his silent scrutiny no longer. 'Have I offended you?'

'Nay, my thoughts were elsewhere,' he lied, and wondered at himself. A youth might be forgiven for mistaking passion for love, but he was no longer a green boy. 'Think you will be happy to make your home with us, Perdita? At least until you remember who you are?'

'Then you have discovered nothing?' Perdita felt a surge of relief. She was safe for the time being.

'I cannot tell you who you really are.' That much was true, for the Abbess had added little to Sir Edmund's tale. The child's mother had died without revealing her secret, the only clue to her identity being a ring she had worn on a ribbon about her neck. 'But I do not believe you leave a grief-stricken family behind you, lady. When we found you in the forest, it seemed that you were running from something – or someone – you feared.'

Perdita gazed at him, sensing that his judgment was a fair one in the circumstances. She must have been there for some reason. 'I wish I could remember my name, if nothing more,' she said wistfully.

'A name means little. You are Perdita – and the castle is your home. It is my wish that it should be so. You are not to think of leaving us.'

His words were a command, she thought, but was too grateful to question the nature of the meaning behind them. Despite having felt the sharpness of his tongue, she saw no need to fear the man who had given her shelter. Griselda's warnings had been but the mumblings of an old woman, she decided, and Gervase's resentment of his brother was quite clearly rooted in the bitterness he felt because of his lameness. Or that was how it seemed to her. The only danger she saw was that she might come to like Lord Athelstan a little too much.

She smiled up at him, her shyness bringing a pale rose colour to her cheeks. 'Why are you so kind to me, my lord? How can you be sure that I am not a thief, or – or something worse?'

'What? Will you have me believe you a desperate character now?' His eyes mocked her. 'Are you a murderess or, more like, a witch? Yes, I think you are an enchantress sent here by the Devil to ensnare me in your web. You will pluck my heart from my breast and carry it back with you to your underworld palace.'

'You mock me, my lord!' She stared at him indignantly.

His husky laughter sent little shivers right down to her toes. 'But you tempt me to it, Perdita. When you look at me with such innocence in those lovely eyes, you raise a tiny demon in me.'

'I think the demon was there long before you met me, my lord!'

'Ah, now you speak the truth, my fair one. I confess that it was so.' He took the hand that lay on the table near him, turning it to examine the soft palm. 'This hand has never been used to rough work, Perdita. Witch or woman, you are of gentle birth. I know not who you truly are, but I like what I see. I would keep you with me.'

Her hand trembled, and he held it tighter as she would have torn it from his grasp. Her eyes were wide and scared as she looked at him. What lay behind that intense gaze?

'You do not know me, my lord. Why should you wish to keep me with you?'

His finger rested on the pulse at her wrist, as if he could feel the fire leaping through her veins. 'Why indeed, Perdita? It may be that I feel the need of a companion. Is it so strange that I should find you attractive? Your skin is soft, and there is temptation in your eyes. A man can find the long nights lonely...'

She gasped and drew back. 'Please, I beg you, do not ask me to be your – your mistress.' Her cheeks were burning with embarrassment. 'I do not wish to offend you. I know how much I owe you, but I cannot consent to such an arrangement.'

'Why?' The grey eyes searched her face. 'Do you find me repulsive?'

'No, of course not!'

'Are you afraid of me?'

'No...' Her answer was less certain, this time. 'At least, only a little, when you look at me as you are doing at this moment.'

'And how do I look at you?' he asked, clearly amused once more.

'You– You have the anticipation of a hunter in your face. Like a wolf before it makes its kill.'

'And you feel as if you are my prey?' His soft chuckle made her gaze up at him. 'Well, if it is so, I have snared you my little bird. I have you fast in my lair, and you may not go unless I will it.'

She stared at him doubtfully. Was he merely mocking her again or was that gleam in his eyes a sign of something more sinister? 'You–You are really frightening me now, my lord,' she whispered. 'Am I to be your prisoner?'

The gleam faded from his eyes, leaving them serious. 'I would not have you go in fear of me, Perdita. I was merely teasing you. It is my way. A fault in my nature, perhaps? I cannot help the way I look at you – any man with red blood in his veins would feel as I do. Be at ease; I shall not force you to share my bed if you do not wish it. Yet it would have been pleasant enough, I think...'

Now his expression was cold and distant again, and she sensed his disapproval. His words had been merely dalliance, after all, and she had reacted like an immature girl. She felt that she had somehow disappointed him. Her own emotions were confused, and just as she sought desperately for something to say that would lessen the strain between them, there was a disturbance in the hall and a newcomer appeared at the far end. He was not wearing Athelstan's colours, and was still heavily cloaked against the cold, as if he had journeyed far to reach the castle. Attempting to advance towards the high table, he was detained by the Earl's men, one of whom questioned him sharply before coming forward himself and bowing to his lord.

'This messenger comes from the King and would approach you, my lord.'

Watching Athelstan's face from the corner of her eye, Perdita saw a tiny nerve pulse in his cheek. She sensed the tension in all those present as the Earl gave permission for the royal courier to approach.

He advanced towards them through the ranks of Athelstan's men and bent the knee before him; then he unrolled an important-looking parchment that bore an impressive seal, clearing his throat as he began to read in a loud voice.

'His most royal Majesty Richard II of England doth hereby notify and inform the Earl of Athelstan and all those Barons, esquires and freemen residing within the bounds of his lands, that they are together and separately charged with having cons-pired with certain enemies of the King's person. In his mercy, His Majesty has granted pardon for these various crimes, and will on payment of one thousand silver marks for each man above the rank of esquire and one hundred silver pennies for each freeman, sign a charter for the said pardon of these crimes. His Majesty charges the Earl of Athelstan to collect these monies and deliver them within the space of eight and twenty days...'

Athelstan leapt to his feet, his face white with anger. 'Does Richard mean to bleed us dry? By God! This new fine he lays upon us is iniquitous and shall not be paid.'

There was a rousing cheer from the hall, and every one of the men was suddenly on his feet. 'Athelstan ... Athelstan ... Athelstan...'

The royal courier glanced about him with scared eyes, his breath catching in his throat as he sensed the mounting anger all round him. Seeing the clenched fists that had been raised on all sides, he knew that his own life was in danger. The mood of these men was much as he had encountered across the breadth of the country, but more openly expressed. Since the scandal of the Duke of Gloucester's death and the banishment of the Dukes of Hereford and Norfolk, any Baron who had ever shown favour to these men had felt the sting of the King's vengeance. Richard now believed his power to be absolute, and he assumed that none of his Barons would dare to defy him. Gone were the days when his uncles had attempted to restrain his excesses, and now he indulged in any amount of extravagance, extorting from his unwilling nobles the money to pay for his pleasures. Until this moment the courier had met with frowns and black stares when he read out the King's demands, but this stubborn refusal to comply with the royal command stunned him. As he stood rooted to the ground in fear, the Earl held up his hand for silence, and an expectant hush fell over the gathering.

'You may carry this message to the King, sir: The Earl of Athelstan and his adherents have never shown disloyalty to the Crown. We shall neither sue for pardon nor pay this fine that is unwarranted and therefore not forfeit. However, I am myself prepared to stand trial before my peers, and will prove my innocence by wager of battle against any who accuse me.'

His words were greeted by another burst of cheering and the stamping of feet as the men showed their approval of his words. The noise rebounded from the vaulted roof, almost deafening the courier, who shook visibly. His cheeks were ashen, for he dared not return to Court with such a message – it was virtually a challenge to the King himself! He trembled as the cheers faded, and his voice was thin with fear.

'I – I dare not carry your message, Lord Athelstan,' he croaked. 'The King's anger would fall on any who dared to speak such treason.'

Athelstan nodded, still angry but in perfect control. 'You shall carry a sealed letter so that Richard's wrath will not fall on your head. Come, we shall retire to my chambers and prepare the letter at once. Then you may rest and eat before continuing your journey at first light.' He turned to the priest beside him. 'I shall require your services, Father.'

'Are you sure this is wise, my lord? Would it not be wiser to plead for time to collect these heavy fines?' The priest swallowed nervously, seeming as if he wished to protest further but was prevented by the Earl's frown. He got to his feet, following hurriedly behind his patron as he walked round the table.

The men began to talk excitedly one to the other as Athelstan left the hall, with the courier and his personal confessor at his heels. Perdita had sat in stunned silence while the little scene was enacted; now she turned to Gervase with a puzzled look.

'What is happening?' she asked anxiously. 'Why is your brother so angry? Does he really mean to defy the King?'

'It would appear so. Like many others in this land, he grows tired of Richard's tyranny.'

'What do you mean?'

'When Richard was first crowned it was thought that he would be a just ruler. He acquitted himself with honour when he rode out to speak to the people at the time of the peasants' revolt, but Wat Tyler was stabbed to death within his sight and he did nothing to prevent it. He made the people all manner of promises, that were broken shortly afterwards. Some years ago his uncles formed a council that sought to control his power, and for almost a year he was virtually deposed. Gloucester was at the council's head, and though Richard appeared to forgive him for the part he played in this humiliation, he harboured a deep resentment. Finally, he had Gloucester arrested under guise of extending the hand of friendship. Gloucester died before he could be brought to trial – and his friends cried murder. Since then, the King has sought to punish anyone who spoke against that foul murder by the imposition of heavy fines. Athelstan has already paid several large sums to the King – but this latest demand is outrageous!'

'If he defies the King, will he not be punished?'

Gervase shrugged carelessly. 'Athelstan will never bow his head to a tyrant. Besides, even if he paid, we should none of us be truly safe. The Duke of Norfolk was forced to go on a pilgrimage to the Holy Land because he dared to voice his fears of Richard's retribution, and Hereford has been banished to France. If his father – the great John of Gaunt – should die while he is banished, and it is likely that he will for he is sick almost unto death, his son could lose his inheritance. Richard has promised that Hereford shall inherit no matter what – but he has broken so many promises, who can believe him?'

Perdita's head whirled. She seemed vaguely to remember having heard snatches of talk about these things at some time, but they were very muddled in her mind.

'Was–Was there not some quarrel between the Dukes of Norfolk and Hereford?'

'Yes, that is so. It was agreed by the High Court of Chivalry that the dispute between them should be settled by a trial of arms in accordance with custom, but...' Gervase broke off, frowning. 'Is your memory returning, Perdita?'

'A little, I think. I – I am beginning to see more and more pictures in my mind,' she admitted. 'Often now I can see a room and a woman's face – a woman who was dear to me, for I feel happy when the vision of her comes to me. I believe it was she who taught me all I know of life, but I cannot remember her name. I – I think she must be connected with whatever it is that I do not want to remember...' She touched his arm, her face anxious. 'Go on with your story. My memory is not important for the moment.'

'Well, the contest was to take place at Coventry, but before it could begin Richard threw down his warder and the Earl Marshal stopped the combat. Norfolk was exiled for life, and Hereford for ten years – but that sentence was reduced by a half after submission by Hereford.'

'And when did this happen?'

'Three months ago – in September.'

'And, since then, the King has imposed these fines on Athelstan?'

'My brother was unwise enough to object to Hereford's banishment at council, and his words were construed as treason. No one else was involved, but the King has chosen to punish all our people.'

Her cheeks paled. 'If he defies the King now…'

'He risks imprisonment – or banishment.' Gervase gave her an odd look. 'It is not like Athelstan to act so rashly. What was he saying to you just before the courier arrived?'

'N-Nothing of importance. He was teasing me a little, that's all.'

'I thought he spoke of… But no matter…' Gervase sipped his wine thoughtfully. 'If the King summons Athelstan to Court, he will be in grave danger. My brother has many enemies who would enjoy watching him humbled.'

'Why has he so many enemies?'

'They are jealous of his wealth – and of the power that wealth brings him.' Gervase stared moodily in front of him. 'Many have tried to learn his secrets – women as well as men. They whisper behind his back that he is in league with … the Devil, but they dare not say it to his face, for they are afraid of him. Yet, if he makes an enemy of the King…'

'You think they would choose that moment to move against him?'

'Who knows?' He shrugged. 'Athelstan is not a fool. He can muster over three hundred fighting men if need be – and he has his friends. Powerful friends…'

'But that would indeed be treason, if…' Her eyes dilated and she caught her breath. The stranger she had accidentally seen when she lost her way had spoken of a trip to France. Could it be that Athelstan had already been contemplating some dreadful act against his sovereign? She shivered at the thought, shocked by the enormity of the crime. Even if Richard were the tyrant Gervase claimed, treason against an anointed king was a fearful thing.

Gervase noticed the way her eyes had darkened, and he frowned at her. 'You must not let this incident tonight upset you, Perdita. My brother has faced danger many times before and survived it. Forget what has happened; it need not concern you.'

'Do you not fear for your brother's safety?' she asked, looking at him oddly.

'Why should I?' He gave a careless flick of his hand. 'Athelstan can take care of himself. Forget him, Perdita. Shall I send for my harp? Would you like me to sing for you?'

She blinked stupidly, trying to collect her wandering thoughts. Suddenly, she realised how foolish it was to concern herself over Athelstan's affairs. She could do nothing to influence his decision one way or the other. Even if she begged him to take more care, he would laugh at her and think her a silly child. Besides, it was not her affair – yet the thought of his being in danger was vaguely distressing. She fought to clear her mind, smiling at Gervase.

'Will you really sing for me?' she asked, a surge of pleasure running through her. 'I should be honoured, sir.'

The clouds vanished from the youth's blue eyes. He summoned a servant, who disappeared into the ante-chamber, reappearing in a moment with his master's instrument. Gervase took it from him, running his fingers lightly over the strings. As he did so a hush fell over the hall, and all eyes turned in their direction as the youth started to sing. He began with a love song, looking directly into Perdita's eyes.

It was the story of a young man who had

fallen in love with a beautiful girl. For a time, the girl responded to his advances and they spent the summer wandering in scented meadows, talking of their love and stealing innocent kisses. Then a rich lord spied the girl and carried her off to his castle. She fought his embraces; but then she gave in to his insistent passion and fell in love with the lord, who showered her with gifts. One day, while she was walking in the village market-place the young man managed to reach her side, and he begged her to run away with him, but she spurned him and he went sadly away. The winter was now upon the land and he lay in the fields, weeping until he died of cold.

'Oh…' Perdita cried as the last strains of the poignant music died away. 'That is such a sad song – and the girl was so cruel to treat her former lover so unkindly…' She broke off abruptly as she heard a soft chuckle behind her. Absorbed by Gervase's song, she had not seen Athelstan return.

'Such is the way of women,' he said, with a wry twist of his lips. 'It was cruel, perhaps, but very practical. The young lover was obviously a poor man, and the rich lord had more to offer her.'

'You are unkind to mock me, my lord,' Perdita protested, seeing Gervase's flush of annoyance. 'I do not believe all women are so cruel! Anyway, it was a beautiful story, and I loved it.'

Gervase glanced at her. 'Then I am well rewarded for my pains. I composed it for you, Perdita.'

'For me?' She looked at him in surprise, her cheeks flushing as she realised he was angry. Did he imagine that she was like the girl in his song? 'Your heroine was a shallow person, Gervase,' she said with a touch of hauteur. 'If she had truly loved her first lover she would not have fallen so easily into the rich lord's arms.'

'Would she not?' Athelstan's eyes sparkled with amusement. 'Would you give up the love of a rich man to run away with a penniless lover, Perdita? Think carefully! It would mean that you might have to sleep beneath the hedges and dine on nothing more than a crust of bread.'

Perdita looked at him provocatively. 'Perhaps, if I loved the poor man enough. But I admit I would prefer to have both love and a comfortable bed to sleep in, my lord!'

He shouted with laughter, thumping his hand on the table in triumph at her answer. 'I knew you were a sensible young woman,' he said. 'Love is but a momentary thing – the sparkle of a dewdrop before it vanishes forever with the sun. A pretty thing, but not to be compared with the comfort of a warm bed.'

She smiled, pleased that she had made

him laugh so freely. When genuine laughter took the seriousness from his lean face, it seemed to her that he became another man. At that moment she knew that his life had contained little true happiness, and it was almost as if she caught a glimpse of the man's soul. As a sharp pain twisted inside her, she caught her breath, turning her gaze because she could not bear the expression in his eyes. She was afraid of the challenge they flung at her, afraid of the new, disturbing emotions he had aroused in her.

'You know I did not mean it in that way,' she said quietly. 'Besides, how can I know what I would do? I believe love must always be unpredictable. No one knows how she will behave until faced with a choice.'

'You speak with a wisdom beyond your years.' Athelstan's smile faded as he looked at her. 'We all have choices to make – some much harder than others. It is time for me to bid you good-night, lady. The hour grows late, and you must be fresh when you begin your lessons in the morning.'

He was dismissing her. Had she offended him again? Something had brought a bleak look to his eyes, but it could not be anything she had said. There was a distance in him now, as if his mind had turned to more important things. Of course, she was merely a source of amusement to him when he had time for leisure, to be sent away when more serious matters awaited his attention. He had business to discuss with the men he trusted, and she was only a woman...

She got to her feet, nodding her head at him with carefully controlled dignity. He should not again be given cause to scorn her as a child.

'Good-night, my lord,' she said in a clear, calm tone. 'I wish you pleasant dreams. Good-night, Gervase – Father Jonathan.'

'May God keep watch over you, daughter,' the priest said with a warm smile.

'I shall escort you to your chamber, Perdita.'

She was surprised when the youth got to his feet. Surely he must wish to stay and hear his brother's views on this new fine imposed on them by the King? If Athelstan truly meant to defy the order, it must also affect Gervase. Knowing it was not her affair, however, she did not protest at his accompanying her as they left the hall together.

Gervase seemed to be sunk in some mood of his own, and it was not until they stopped outside her chamber that he looked at her. She sensed the anger that she had glimpsed earlier, and laid her hand on his arm.

'What is it, Gervase? Why are you angry with me?'

'I am not angry,' he replied, but there was bitterness in his tone. 'Very well, if you must have the truth, I disliked the way you behaved this evening.'

'The way I behaved?' She stared at him in astonishment. 'What did I do that was so terrible?'

'I saw the look in your eyes when he spoke to you – you were simpering like a fool!'

'When who spoke to me?'

'My brother, of course! I have seen the way he looks at you. He wants you – and when he is ready, he will take you. You will fall into his arms as easily as *she* did!'

'I don't know what you are talking about, Gervase, but I find your remarks very insulting. I have no intention of falling into anyone's arms. Besides, he thinks of me as a foolish child...' She blushed, knowing that her statement was not quite true. There had been that moment when Athelstan seemed to suggest... But he had only been mocking her!

Gervase saw her blush, and scowled. It was as he had suspected, she was already beginning to succumb to his brother's charm. There was something about Athelstan that drew women to him. His jealousy made the bitter words spill out of him in a torrent.

'He likes to tease you as he did Jania at the start. It is a part of his nature that he must always enslave those around him. You must have seen how his men worship the very ground he walks on. He bewitches them as he will you – as he did Jania! He taunted her and led her on until she was mad for him, and then he lay with her – but when she gave him her love, he cast her aside. As he will you, if you are foolish enough to let him capture your heart.'

Perdita stared at him, her pulses racing wildly. What was he trying to tell her? Who was the girl Athelstan had cast aside, and why was Gervase looking at her in that way?

'Who is Jania? Please do not speak in riddles, Gervase. If you are warning me against your brother, please speak plainly.'

His face twisted with pain, and she glimpsed his torment. 'Jania was my betrothed. I saw them together, and she laughed when I accused her. She laughed and said she would wed only him; but he spurned her and called her a whore, and when she realised he would not marry her, she killed herself.'

Perdita's blood seemed to run cold. She was frozen with horror, staring at him in disbelief. 'No! It cannot be true – I cannot believe that anyone could be so cruel.'

'Can you not?' His face was stony. 'I was glad when she died. I would not have had her to wife once she had lain with him – though she knelt at my feet and begged me to forgive her with tears in her eyes...' He had begun to shake as though he had a fever.

It was a shameful story, and one that made

Perdita feel sick and dizzy. She could not wonder that Gervase should be bitter, and she experienced a rush of sympathy for him.

'Oh, Gervase,' she whispered, her throat stinging with emotion, 'how hurt you must have been. I am so sorry she betrayed you.'

He gave her a twisted smile, unable to hide the pain that still mingled with the bitterness. 'I was but a boy of fourteen then, Perdita. It was three years ago and I have forgotten her. She was nothing. A whore – no more.'

It was obvious to Perdita that Jania had meant much more to him than he would admit. He would never forget or forgive the way his brother had taken his betrothed from him, she realised. Now she understood why he had sung his tale of tragedy for her: it was a warning. A warning against giving her trust to the man who had taken control of her life. He was afraid that she, too, would fall beneath his brother's spell and act the part of a strumpet.

'Thank you for telling me,' she said, her throat tightening. 'I shall be on my guard from now on.'

His eyes held a strange brightness as he looked at her. 'I should not want you to die, Perdita.'

She watched as he limped away from her, feeling chilled by something she had glimpsed in his eyes. There were two sides to

Gervase, she thought: it was almost as if two people lived within him, each struggling for supremacy – and one of them was distinctly unpleasant. She could not help feeling sorry for him and saw that he had good reason for his moods, yet she sensed that there was a malicious streak in him. Gervase would make a bad enemy, she thought.

Even so, who could blame him for his bitterness? His deformity was enough to sour his life without all the rest – and when he was in a good mood he could be charming. Indeed, there was a strong likeness between the two brothers. It seemed that neither was as he appeared on the surface, and she suspected that each was equally dangerous in his own way. If she were not to fall prey to one or the other, she must tread carefully.

Shivering, she went into her chamber and began to undress. The castle was a strange place, full of mysteries and shadows...

CHAPTER THREE

The room was in darkness when Perdita woke. For a moment she lay shivering, wondering what had disturbed her sleep. If she had been dreaming she could not recall her dream, though it would be hardly surprising if her rest had been uneasy after all that had happened the previous evening! What with Athelstan's outburst of defiance against the King, and Gervase's terrible revelations, it was a wonder she had slept at all.

It was just as she was drifting into a semi-conscious state again that she heard the scream. She sat bolt upright, her nerves alive and jangling. Another scream, even more terrifying than the first, made her cross herself superstitiously. The sound seemed to be all around her, echoing from the walls of her chamber, yet curiously muffled as though it originated deep within the castle. How could she have heard it through the stone walls that must be several feet thick? she wondered. Were all the walls as thick as they seemed? Was it not possible that there were secret, hollow ways leading down to the very bowels of the castle, and that the echo had travelled a long way because of that? It was beyond her comprehension and she might have thought she had imagined it if it had not happened twice.

Rising, Perdita slipped on soft leather shoes and covered herself with a loose, thick gown over her night-attire. She knew she could never rest without at least trying to discover who had screamed like that. Whoever it was had been in agony, of that much she was certain. Before leaving her chamber, she paused to light a taper from the smouldering embers in the hearth, for at this hour the smoky torches that were used to light the passages would have burnt out.

In the narrow corridor it was dark and bitterly cold. The chill struck into her bones as she moved instinctively in the direction the scream seemed to have come from. From somewhere in the region of the great hall, she thought, but it sounded as though it had issued from beneath the ground, spiralling up to reach her room. Were there dungeons at the castle, she wondered, a little shiver curling up her spine. Was Athelstan the kind of man who would imprison and torture his enemies? All she had so far seen of him told her that it was unlikely. He did not appear to be a brutish savage who would enjoy hurting people, but would he do so if he considered it a necessary evil? The answer was chilling. The Earl was a man who would always carry out what he saw to be his duty, no matter how painful.

Reaching the head of the main stairway, Perdita paused, listening as she strained her eyes towards the shadowed darkness of the vast hall. She had heard nothing more since leaving her own chamber. Everywhere was as still and silent as the grave, making her feel that she alone was wakeful in this house. It must want an hour to cock-crow and no one was stirring, not even the kitchen boy.

She felt uneasy, her pulses pounding madly as she considered returning to her own room. It had been foolish of her to leave it. How could she hope to discover the source of that scream? There must be hundreds of rooms and passages, and she could wander about the castle for hours, eventually becoming lost. She was still unsure of her way, and most of the rooms were unexplored territory for her. Besides, it was really not her affair. She had almost convinced herself and was about to turn away, when she heard a noise below in the hall. Her nerves prickled, raising little hairs on the nape of her neck. It sounded as if someone had closed a door – a heavy door that swung on creaking hinges.

She drew a deep breath, knowing that she had to go on, and began to creep softly down the stairs, hardly daring to breathe. She knew that what she was doing was foolish. She had no right to pry into things that did not concern her, but her curiosity had been aroused. Something very strange was happening, and she wanted to know more about it. Gervase had shocked her with his bitter tale of betrayal and tragedy. It seemed that the master of the castle was a more sinister man than she had at first thought – was it possible that he was playing with her as a cat with a mouse, teasing her until he was ready for the kill?

She had reached the bottom of the stairs. Her taper threw out a pale yellow glow, illuminating a small area around her; but beyond the haven of light, the hall stretched echoingly into a menacing blackness. She hesitated, her breath coming in harsh gasps as she took a firmer grip on her nerves. She had come so far, was she to retreat like a coward now? She walked very slowly, holding her chamber-stick at arm's length and moving it from side to side in an effort to see into dark corners. What dangers might be lurking there? How different the huge room seemed now that it was deserted, the voices of Athelstan's men a forgotten echo…

A slight sound behind her made her jump. She half turned, gave a cry of alarm as a shadow moved swiftly towards her, and dropped her taper. The sound of metal striking stone reverberated loudly as she was plunged into a blackness so complete that it was as if the sight had been taken from her eyes, and it terrified her. She screamed, starting forward with her hands outstretched in blind panic. Her fingers pressed against something soft – soft, but with an underlying hardness. As she moved them frantically over the object blocking her path, her wrists were suddenly encircled in an imprisoning grip.

'Be still, you foolish girl,' Athelstan's voice commanded. 'You will wake the household with your noise. Stand quite still while I light a candle.'

Her tongue flicked nervously over dry lips as she obeyed. She could not have moved one step even if he had not commanded her to stay where she was. Fear held her rooted to the spot as she heard him strike a tinder somewhere close by. She blinked in the sudden blaze of light as he applied the flame to a branch of fat wax candles. His face looked pale and threatening in the candle-light, his eyes dark with anger as he turned to her.

'What are you doing here, Perdita? Could you not sleep – or did you come here to spy on me?' He frowned as he saw her pupils dilate, making her eyes look almost black. 'Are you ill?'

'No...' She swallowed hard, the saliva forming a lump in her throat. 'I – I heard something.'

'You heard?' Athelstan frowned, obviously suspicious. 'What did you hear, Perdita?'

She hesitated, afraid of his anger, and yet defiant. He seemed to be accusing her of some crime, when all she had done was to investigate the cry of someone in pain. Surely that was not so very wrong! Common sense came to her aid, and her panic subsided.

'Screaming...' she said slowly. 'I heard someone screaming as if they were in terrible pain – and I came to discover if that person needed help. Was that such a terrible thing to do?'

Athelstan was silent as he studied her face. His first flush of anger subsided as he saw the look in her eyes, and he drew a sharp breath. God! but she was lovely, and that fire in her eyes... Her beauty stirred him strangely, making him aware of long-forgotten emotions. Once he had been as young as she, full of hopes and youthful ideals that heated his blood and made him love life. He had wanted to ride out, sword in hand, to set right the wrongs of an evil world; now he knew too much of that world, and of all the heaving rottenness that crawled like maggots in the minds of men. His pilgrimages and journeys had brought him knowledge, but with that knowledge came the realisation of suffering beyond all human aid. Only his firm belief in an omnipotent being gave him the strength to carry on his work – though in his secret thoughts he was not always sure whether that being was God or the Devil.

'Why do you frown so, my lord?' Perdita asked, feeling uncomfortable beneath his stare. 'Are you angry with me for prying into something that is not my affair?'

'No, I am not angry,' he said at last, but his voice throbbed with passion and there was an odd glitter in his eyes. 'You would have done better to stay in your chamber, but I am willing to believe your motives were unselfish.'

His words were forgiving, but his manner was not. She sensed the swirling whirlpool of emotion beneath the calm exterior, and her knees felt weak. She had brought his anger on herself by her own behaviour, but it was still mortifying. Gazing into his eyes, she was drawn into that seething emotion like a straw into a floodtide.

'Who was it that screamed so – so piti-fully?' she whispered, her breath dying as a silver flame illuminated those grey orbs and they seemed to penetrate her very soul.

'A boy from the village,' said Athelstan. 'His leg had been crushed beneath the wheel of a farm cart, and his parents brought him to me. He was in great pain, and I am known to have some skill in these matters. Unfortunately, the sleeping potion I gave him was not strong enough; he woke while I was still … tending his wounds.'

'Oh…' His explanation was simple, so why did she feel that he was not telling her the whole truth? There was something more – something he was hiding from her. 'I – I see.'

'No, you do not see, do you?' His penetrating gaze sent a little tremor through her. 'You think I am lying, but why should I lie, Perdita? What tales have you been listening to, that you should think me some kind of a monster? Has that old hag Griselda been gossiping?'

There was a rasp in his voice that made her flinch from him, but she was determined not to let him vanquish her so easily. She would stand her ground with him, no matter how he frowned at her! Lifting her head, she smiled coolly, her face touched with pride.

'No. Griselda tells me nothing – she would not dare! If you think that I do not believe you, my lord, it is your own conscience dictating to you. Only you know whether what you say is the whole truth.'

She had come too close to reality for comfort. He had told a small lie to ease her mind, for it was unlikely that she could accept the whole. He felt a surge of fury as he looked down into that beautiful face. Who was she to question what he did? She was but a child, after all – and yet those were a woman's eyes… His anger at that moment was not for her alone, but for all those bigoted fools who refused to accept his work for what it was – a tiny flame in the darkness of man's ignorance. They looked at him with suspicion and fear, whispering of things that were beyond their comprehension, dismissing endless hours of painstaking experimentation as witchcraft. Superstitious fools! Would that it were possible to conjure up some demon out of Hell to work a spell! He would sell his soul gladly if he could but find the answers he sought. So perhaps they were in part right when they condemned him as a servant of the Devil – those high and mighty churchmen who should know better than the blind, ignorant peasants they led by the nose, deliberately keeping knowledge to themselves in order that the common folk should be more easily subjugated. They had tried to ban Wycliffe's translation of the bible because it spoke of the freedom that should belong to all; they would stifle all learning and progress, if they could. They mouthed their inane objections to each new discovery, hiding behind the word of God and condemning what they did not understand as the work of Satan...

Suddenly the barriers holding back the torrent of seething passion within him gave way before his surging anger. He reached out for her, his fingers grasping her shoulders with painful intensity. Seeing her eyes darken with fear, he felt an urge to punish her for being one of the doubters. He had foolishly expected more from her, believing her to be a kindred spirit, a spirit that needed only a little nurturing to blossom into glowing life. Now he realised that she was the same as all the rest, and the realisation of his loneliness turned to him like the point of a blade. She was not the woman he had searched for all his life – even so, there was still one way she could serve him! He was a man, and he had a man's basic needs.

His mouth came down to subjugate hers. As Perdita felt the burn of his kiss, her whole body tensed with a kind of fear. Her lips felt as if they were on fire, and her will was dissolving in the heat of his desire. It was a terrifying experience for an innocent girl. This was no gentle lover's kiss, but the demanding embrace of a starving man. She was afraid of the fierce emotion raging within him, yet she could not find the strength to resist him. The flame was spreading along her veins like molten lead, making her feel as if she were being consumed by hell-fire. This must surely be what it was like to die, she thought dazedly. She was being drawn down into the eternal cauldron – into the Devil's arms!

She had been yielding to him, her body unconsciously curving itself into the hardness of his frame. Her hands had somehow stolen over the arch of his shoulders, seeking to entwine themselves in his hair. She was on the verge of surrendering to him! The realisation was like a douche of cold water, putting out the flames that engulfed her.

She pushed against his chest, shaking her head in bemused denial as he relaxed his hold to look questioningly into her face. 'Ah... No, my lord,' she whispered, trembling as she saw the smouldering desire in his eyes. 'I am no whore, nor shall I be used as one. I – I am not Jania.'

His face contracted with a pain so sharp that she gasped, wondering at his agony of mind. 'What do you know of her?' he demanded harshly. 'Who told you of ... Jania?'

Perdita blinked, wishing she could retract her careless words. There was such suffering in his face that she felt it strike her to the heart.

'I – I did not mean...' she croaked, her throat closing with emotion. 'Gervase told me she – she...' It was impossible to continue when confronted by the raw agony he was unable to hide. She stared at him in confusion, knowing she was seeing him exposed and naked without the mask he habitually wore. Surely this was not the reaction of a man who had dismissed his brother's betrothed as a whore after carelessly seducing her!

Slowly Athelstan's features settled into the habitual expressionless mask. 'You have heard that she took her own life after I rejected her?' His eyes narrowed as Perdita nodded. He hesitated as if wishing to say more, then she saw his mouth harden. 'So – you believe the worst of me, Perdita? You too think I serve the Devil? Perhaps you believe I deliberately drove her to her death? Or mayhap I killed her myself. Is that why you stare at me so accusingly?'

Outwardly, he was calm, but she sensed the bitter rage in him and drew back in alarm as if she was afraid he would seek to take her life, too. Her mind was whirling into darkness, and the fear was closing in on her. She was alone in the forest and she could hear the blood-curling cries of the hounds. They were gaining on her, and when they caught her... She screamed wildly as the horror of the unknown pressed down on her, and the grey web seemed to wind itself about her mouth so that she could not breathe.

'Oh! They will catch me – they will take me back,' she cried, her head moving from side to side in frantic denial. 'The dog comes ... oh...' Her mouth opened as if to scream again as the panic gripped her.

Realising instantly that she had somehow slipped into a nightmarish revival of her ordeal in the woods, Athelstan administered a sharp, stinging slap that cut off the scream before it left her throat. She stared at him in stunned dismay; then her face crumpled and tears began to flow silently down her cheeks.

'Foolish child,' he said gruffly. 'The dog won't harm you again. Forgive me for frightening you. You are safe enough now. I give you my word.'

She could not speak or move, merely staring at him with the eyes of a trapped doe. He gave a sigh of exasperation, bending down to sweep her up in his arms and hold her gently pressed to his chest. He frowned as he felt her tremble, knowing that he had been to blame for what had happened. She had suffered a terrible shock, and in his impatience he had almost pushed her too far.

'No, I am not going to seduce you, Perdita,' he said as she looked up at him beseechingly. 'I am merely taking you to your own bedchamber.'

She saw the flicker of a smile about his mouth and knew that the anger had drained out of him. Sighing, she hid her face against his velvet jerkin, clinging to him as she tried to block out the terrible pictures in her mind. They frightened her much more than his anger; and held comfortingly against his breast, she felt only a sapping weakness that made her want to hold on to him. He was her rock in the midst of a turbulent sea. Without him she would surely be swept into those black waters that threatened to drag her down! She let her mind empty completely as he carried her up the stairs and through the shadowed passages to her chamber. It was still hardly light, but his footsteps were sure and firm, almost as though he could see in the dark like a cat. Perhaps he really was a servant of the Devil! Perhaps that explained the strange power he seemed to have over her? The weakness in her that had so nearly caused her downfall – that might do, even yet! For she knew that if he was intent on making her his mistress, he would succeed. She had fought against his domination because he was so fierce that he frightened her, but this new gentleness in him had broken her will.

Lulled to a false security by the warmth of his body, Perdita was hardly aware that they had reached her room. When he laid her down on the bed, she was conscious of a sense of loss and nearly cried out in protest, needing the comfort he had supplied. He bent over her, tucking the covers about her with a chiding look as though she were indeed the child he sometimes seemed to think her.

'Are you still frightened?' he asked, his hand stroking the dark strands from her forehead with a tenderness that set her pulses racing. 'Shall I stay here beside you until you sleep?'

'No...' If he stayed, she would betray herself! She swallowed hard, suppressing the great tide of choking emotion his touch aroused in her. Suddenly she knew how easy it would be to act as foolishly as Jania had before her. She was surely bewitched! What else could cause her limbs to tremble like this? 'I am better now, my lord. It was only the dream of the forest.'

'Have you experienced it before?'

'Yes. It comes to me both waking and sleeping. I am pursued by something so horrible that I know I shall die if I let it catch me,' she whispered, looking at him fearfully. 'Yet I know that if I am ever to remember who I am, I must first remember who – or what – it is I am running from.'

'Poor little Perdita,' he said softly, brushing his lips over hers. 'Do not try to remember. If you are patient you may find that nothing is as terrible as the unknown. Sleep now, child. Believe me, you are safe from the terror that haunts you within these walls. I shall not let harm come to you.' With that promise, he got to his feet and left her.

Sighing, Perdita closed her eyes. A strange weariness was sweeping over her, making her limbs heavy. She wanted to lie awake and think about the man who had so completely dominated both her body and her thoughts tonight; but she could not fight this creeping lassitude and soon she slept.

Outside the door, Athelstan kept a silent vigil until he heard the sound of steady, regular breathing and knew that she was at peace.

'Griselda, whose gown was this?' Perdita touched the pale gold tunic she was wearing, and looked up. 'Did it once belong to Jania?'

'Who told you of her?' The old woman's hands shook as she smoothed a dark tress. 'Who has been gossiping? If it was one of the servants, Athelstan will have him whipped. I'll see to that – I'll not have them spreading tales behind my lamb's back...'

She was so obviously angry that Perdita's curiosity was aroused. 'What tales, Griselda? Gervase told me she took her own life. Is that not true?'

The nurse's eyes glittered beneath her hooded lids. 'Why should Gervase lie? The servants whisper – but it is all lies! Ask Athelstan, if you do not believe me...' Her lips curved with scorn. 'Ask him, if you dare!'

'What do the servants say, Griselda?' Perdita felt a prick of unease. 'Not that – Athelstan killed her?'

'It is all lies, I tell you!' Griselda muttered, dragging the comb cruelly through the girl's hair so that it pulled in the tangles. 'Have I not warned you to keep from prying, girl?'

'Yes, I am sorry, Griselda.' Perdita winced as the woman tugged at her hair. 'I only wanted to know if I am wearing Jania's clothes.'

'They were made for her, but she never wore them. They were to have been her bride clothes. Now, ask me no more, for I shall not answer.'

'I see.' She shivered slightly. It was strange to be wearing garments made for Gervase's tragic bride.

'There's no need to pull such a face,' Griselda said grumpily. 'The master has already sent to town for new garments, though I cannot see why. These are perfectly good, and better than you're used to, judging by the rags you were wearing when he brought you here. I'll have you know, mistress, that I've had the trouble of shortening the hem of all these gowns– Jania was taller than you by half a head.'

'I am sorry you were put to so much work on my behalf,' Perdita said meekly. 'Do you still have the gown I was wearing when I came here? Could I see it, please?'

'I burnt everything. It was done on the master's orders.' Griselda clamped her lips shut, and the girl realised the discussion was finished.

Perdita sighed deeply. She did not really

care about the clothes, but it was just possible that the sight of them might have triggered her memory. She felt she was so close to recalling everything now. Last night the door in her mind had opened slightly, revealing a glimpse of what lay behind it. She knew now that she had been running from a man. She had seen herself struggling in his arms, but his face had been veiled from her as if by a grey mist. Then the door had slammed shut, leaving her with such a feeling of terror that she had clung to Athelstan out of sheer self-preservation...

'Are you ready, Perdita?'

Jumping as her thoughts were interrupted, she turned to look at Gervase standing on the threshold. He moved so silently that she had not heard him come. This morning he was wearing his favourite shade of blue, his eyes as clear as a summer sky with no sign of the shadows that had clouded them the previous evening.

'She is ready now,' said Griselda, fastening a veil of filmy gauze to the coronet of gold. 'Did you sleep well, my lamb?'

Gervase scowled at her. 'You know well enough, old hag. You made sure that I should not wake, didn't you?'

She smiled maliciously, nodding her secret triumph. 'You drank my posset, master, knowing well it would give you ease – but blame me if it pleases you. I am old, and my time is coming. One day soon you will have no one to curse.'

'Come, Perdita,' Gervase said with a touch of his brother's imperiousness. 'Father Jonathan is waiting for us.' He was angry, but she saw him flinch as if the nurse's words had pricked him.

Perdita took his arm, wondering at the relationship between the old woman and her former charge. Gervase obviously resented the hold she still had over him, but his need of her was plain. He provoked her, using harsh words to wound, and yet it was clear that she retained her unique position in his life. He had said his leg did not pain him, but he seemed to suffer from sleepless nights unless he drank the possets specially prepared for him by his devoted nurse.

'Did you sleep well, Perdita?' Gervase gazed at her intently. 'You look tired.'

'I – I had a bad dream.'

'Do you have them, too?' A look of eagerness came into his face. 'Sometimes I am afraid to sleep – the Black Watcher is always at my shoulder, waiting for me to close my eyes.' He shuddered as if a chill hand clutched at him. 'Are you afraid of dying, Perdita? I am – though I know I shall die quite soon.'

'Gervase, you should not say such things!' she exclaimed, stopping to stare at him in dismay. 'You cannot know how long your life will be. It is in God's hands, and we can none of us know His will!' She felt shocked as she saw the odd, wistful expression on his face.

'So many die before they are thirty – shall I live when others die? A cripple who…' His eyes slid away from hers. 'Do you know how many were claimed by the Reaper in the year of 1349 by the Black Death? Thousands were taken, Perdita, both here and across Europe. They fell in the streets, rotting in the heat, while their bodies blackened and the stench of death befouled the air…'

'Stop it!' Perdita cried, her face white. 'I refuse to listen to your morbid tales, Gervase. If you cannot talk of pleasanter things, I shall go to my lessons alone.'

His eyes had a glazed look. She shook his arm, and he blinked at her as though he found it difficult to bring himself back from wherever he had been; then he seemed to wake up and gave her a rueful smile.

'It was the old hag's fault. Forgive me! I know I have a preoccupation with death, but – I am afraid of the Black Watcher, Perdita.'

She squeezed his arm, moved to pity by his vulnerability and wanting to comfort him. He was a strange person, but she sensed the loneliness in him and wanted to show him that she was his friend. Perhaps it was not surprising in the circumstances that his thoughts should be so morbid. With only Griselda for company, it could hardly be otherwise.

'I forgive you,' she said. 'Now, tell me more about your music. Have you composed other songs beside the one you sang for me last night?'

'I spend most of my day composing songs. Athelstan thinks it is a waste of time, but I could not live without my music. It – it brings me release and so much pleasure.'

'He cannot really think it a waste of time,' Perdita said indignantly. 'You have a beautiful voice – and I liked your song, even if it was sad.'

'I have almost finished another,' Gervase confided with a smile. 'This time I wrote a happy story to please you. I shall sing it for you later, if you wish?'

'Oh yes, I should like to hear it! But first we must attend to our lessons. You will help me, Gervase? I am so nervous. What will Athelstan think of me if I have no learning?'

He frowned, looking down at her with raised brows. 'Does it matter so much? You are beautiful – and that is enough for any woman.'

'Indeed?' Her eyes sparkled. 'Then you believe a woman can be an empty-headed ninny so long as she has beauty? Should my days be spent in spinning and weaving – or staring aimlessly from my solar window?'

'I did not mean to offend you!' Gervase looked surprised. 'I had not thought of you as a scholar, Perdita.'

She bit her lip in troubled concentration; until this moment she had not known that it was so important to her. 'I think that everyone should reach out towards that ... certain something that is within them. For you, it is music – for me, it is the right to be myself...' She laughed self-consciously. 'I suppose that sounds very foolish?'

'It sounds admirable, Perdita.' Athelstan's voice behind them made them both start as he came up with them. He smiled at the girl, nodding coolly to his brother. 'Father Jonathan is waiting for you and you should not keep him waiting.'

'Are– Are you coming with us?' she squeaked nervously. The thought of those cool grey eyes watching her at her lessons made her knees quake. If he were present, she would be sure to make a fool of herself!

Athelstan's lips curved as if he had read her mind and found her thoughts amusing. 'No, I came only to make sure you were well enough to begin your lessons. I shall not stay to spy on you.' He nodded to them both, and walked on.

'Father Jonathan will tell him everything he wants to know anyway,' Gervase said sulkily. 'Athelstan has him in the palm of his hand – as he has us all.'

'It is natural that a tutor should make a report on his pupils,' said Perdita, wishing that he would not seize on every opportunity to attack his brother, even if he did have good cause to feel bitter.

'Perhaps.' Gervase shrugged his shoulders. 'Well, here we are, Mistress Perdita. I wish you well with your studies.'

'Are you not coming in?'

'No, I think not.' His mouth twisted scornfully. 'I have not your love of learning. I shall see you later. Perhaps you will have time to walk with me in the castle gardens after your lessons?' He did not wait for her answer to a question that was clearly meant to sting her with sarcasm, limping away as she stood outside the priest's chamber.

Perdita watched him for a moment or two, frowning. He had meant to stay and take his lessons with her, she was sure, but something had changed his mind. Was it because he thought she had defended Athelstan's right to hear the priest's report on their progress? She shook her head and sighed. Gervase was almost as difficult to understand as his brother!

Pushing her doubts to one side, Perdita knocked at the door Gervase had indicated. The priest called out that she might enter, and she went in, looking about her with interest. It was a small, comfortable chamber similar to her own, with a fire burning welcomingly in the grate. A plain oak table stood before the hearth with three stools, and several scrolls and parchments were set out neatly in readiness; there was also a large leather-bound bible fastened with a silver clasp. The priest himself had been busily writing something, but now he stood up to greet her with a smile.

'Come, sit here and warm yourself, lady. The Earl has generously permitted us this good fire. He does not believe that physical suffering is necessary for the acquisition of learning, as some others do.' His bright eyes went past her in expectation, dimming slightly in disappointment as he saw she was alone. 'You are by yourself?'

'Yes – Gervase changed his mind. I am sorry, Father. I think perhaps I may have upset him.'

'You must not blame yourself, daughter.' He smiled at her kindly, beckoning her to a stool near the hearth. 'The Earl has told me of your unfortunate situation. You need not fear that I shall push you too swiftly. For today we shall try to discover if you can read.' He waited while she warmed her hands and sat at the table. 'Here is a bible, see if you can make out any of the words.'

Perdita reached for the heavy book, her fingers moving lovingly over the beautiful binding and the intricate silver clasp. The Earl had obviously gone to great expense to have it transcribed and bound. She opened it with shaking hands, almost afraid to touch something so exquisite and valuable. Her eyes moved slowly over the delicate script with its illuminated capitals in gold leaf and bright colours, and she gave a cry of delighted surprise.

'Why, it is in English, Father!' she said, looking up at him. 'I have been used to reading passages from it in Latin.' It was strange, but she could recall the scene so clearly – it was a room very similar to this, but her companion had been a woman.

The priest looked at her excitedly as the words died on her lips. 'You can read Latin, my child? You are certain of this?'

'Yes ... I believe so. I can certainly read this.' She ran her finger beneath the passage in front of her. 'And God so loved the world that he...'

'Yes, yes, you can read English,' said the priest, obviously convinced and impatient to get on. 'Now, what can you read from this?' He unrolled a yellowed parchment and laid it before her on the board. 'Read this for me, Perdita.'

'*Beati monoculi in regione caecorum,*' she read obediently. 'It is a proverb, Father. It means: In the kingdom of the blind, the one-eyed are kings.' The priest stared at her oddly, and she blushed. 'Have I made a mistake?'

'No, Mistress Perdita.' He smiled benevolently. 'Will you read some more for me, please?'

She obeyed, realising very quickly that the scroll was one he must have prepared himself for her or Gervase's benefit. It contained a series of phrases and sayings that a pupil might learn by heart, but nothing of consequence. After a moment, she looked up at him. 'Is there nothing else we could read?'

His eyes gleamed with real pleasure. 'Lord Athelstan has many books in his possession. His collection rivals that of Gerard of Abbeville – and in 1338, over sixty years ago, that was said to number some 1,722 volumes. The Earl is a man of great learning and equal generosity. He will, I know, be pleased to allow us access to anything we might desire. I can think of several texts that might interest you – though much of it is theology or about chemistry. Perhaps you would like to begin with the histories of Alexander the Great? Did you know it was recorded that he made a glass barrel and descended to the bottom of the sea to study the fishes?'

She looked at him curiously, hardly able to believe such a story. If it had been anyone but the priest, she would have thought they were teasing her. 'No... Do you believe he could really do that, Father? How would he breathe?'

'Perhaps it is not true, my daughter.' He chuckled. 'But it was recorded – and I shall show you a drawing of how it might have been done. The Earl himself was very interested in the theory, and we have spent many happy hours exploring its feasibility. There are so many wonderful things to study and discuss if one has an open mind. Too many are closed to learning; so many people waste their lives these days in the pursuit of idle pleasures. We are fortunate to live beneath Lord Athelstan's roof in such dark times.'

'You – like him, don't you?' He was the first person she had spoken to since her arrival who seemed not to be afraid of the Earl.

'I respect Lord Athelstan. He gave me a place of honour in his household when I was dismissed from my parish by the Bishop of Nantes for preaching Wycliffe's treatise. He is a generous patron, and I have much to thank him for. Not least is the opportunity he has given me of working with such a bright pupil!'

Perdita blushed at his praise. 'I fear I may know very little. Although I have been taught to read, I have never heard of men descending to the bottom of the ocean in glass barrels. I believe the bible may have been my only opening to this vast store of learning you speak of, Father.'

'It would surprise me if it were not so! Few people have access to a wealth of reading matter such as the Earl possesses. You were fortunate that someone taught you to read and understand Latin so well; not many have such opportunities.' He looked at her curiously. 'Can you not remember who it was that took such pains with your education?'

'I – I believe it must have been *her*,' Perdita said slowly. 'I remember a woman's face, and I know she was dear to me.' Tears welled up in her eyes and she blinked them away. 'Oh, Father, shall I ever recall my own name and whence I came?'

He placed a gentle hand on her head, his face full of sympathy. 'You must trust in God, daughter. Would you like to pray with me? It might ease you.'

'Yes. Yes, I should like it,' she said, realising that it was what she needed. 'I am so afraid of what I might have done. You do not think that this affliction was put upon me by God to punish me for some terrible sin?' She raised her eyes to his in a misty appeal.

'There are those in the Church who might say that it was indeed a punishment from God – but I am not one of them, my child. I believe in a gentle God who loves all his children. I think that this is more likely the work of the Devil.'

Perdita shivered, crossing herself swiftly. 'Am I possessed by Satan, Father?'

He looked into her innocent face, and smiled. 'No, I do not think so – but the Devil is always waiting to snatch the souls of the unwary, daughter. We should all be on our guard against him. Yet God will protect those who truly love him. Come, kneel and pray with me.'

Obediently she slipped to her knees and closed her eyes, repeating the words of a prayer after him. It came to her lips easily and had a familiarity that eased her. She knew instinctively that this was something she had done often before. Rising at the priest's behest, she opened her eyes in time to see him take a heavy silver cross and chain from about his neck. Smiling, he lowered it over her head.

'Wear this, and remember that God is always with you, daughter,' he said.

She touched the beautiful silver cross with reverent fingers. 'But it is yours, Father!'

'I have another. Take it with my blessing.'

He held out his hand, and she kissed it. 'Thank you. You have been kind to me.'

'It is a pleasure to instruct one so eager to learn. Now, child, we have done enough for one day, I think. When you come tomorrow, I shall be better prepared.'

'And will Lord Athelstan be pleased by your report, Father?'

Perdita could not keep the eagerness from her face, and seeing it, the priest frowned.

He realised that in his admiration for the Earl he might have praised him too highly. The girl was young and, despite the Earl's good qualities, he was a man like any other. It was clearly his duty to protect such innocence.

'I am sure that Lord Athelstan must be pleased by what I have to tell him, but you should not study only to please your patron, Mistress Perdita. He is a busy man and cannot always be bothering his head about a girl he found in the forest. Besides, it is not seemly that you should spend too much time with him.'

Perdita stared at the floor, feeling herself rebuked. The priest's manner was stern, unlike the gentleness he had shown her earlier. She knew he was right. She must not expect too much of the man who had given her a home. She was merely a nameless wench he had taken pity on, and the priest was right to remind her of her station, though it made her face flame as though she had been slapped.

'I – I wished only to please him, since he…'

The door opened behind her and she turned to look, half fearful that it would be Earl come to enquire after her progress; but it was only Gervase, and in her relief she gave him a radiant smile.

'Are you ready, Perdita?' he asked. 'Athelstan wants you to come and watch his men in the courtyard – they are training a hawk, and he bade me fetch you.'

Forgetting the priest's warning, Perdita clapped her hands in delight at the prospect of such a treat. It was the first time she had left the main building since her arrival, and she had seen only as much of the castle grounds as were visible from her own window. She murmured a hasty farewell to Father Jonathan, and took Gervase's arm in a surge of excitement.

'Is it a wild bird?' she asked. 'Or was it bred in captivity?'

'Balsadare took it from the nest when it was almost ready to fly,' said Gervase, his eyes mirroring her own excitement. 'He has a way with wild creatures. He once had an eagle trained to the lure.'

'An eagle?' She looked at him disbelievingly. 'The eagles are too fierce to train! You are teasing me, I think?'

'No. I tell you it is true. That's why Athelstan always takes him when he goes to the forest. Balsadare can track anything: humans, animals or birds. Nothing escapes his keen eyes.'

'He found me, didn't he?' Perdita frowned. 'Who is he, Gervase? He is not like the Earl's other men – and he has such terrible scars...' She shivered as a chill ran through her. 'Where did he come from? I do not think he is English…'

'I am not sure. I know Athelstan found him in Italy on one of his journeys, but I do not know if it was the country of his birth. He had been tortured by a rich nobleman for daring to stare too hard at his lady. They tortured him with hot irons and then threw him out to die by the roadside. My brother saved his life and brought him back to England. Now, Balsadare is so grateful that he trots behind him like a little dog.'

Gervase's scornful tone made Perdita frown. She had witnessed Balsadare's devotion to his lord, and heard the way Athelstan mocked him unmercifully, wondering at such loyalty. Now she thought she understood why Balsadare did not resent his master's barbs.

Gervase was hurrying her through a part of the castle she had not seen before. As they left the living quarters and stepped outside, she shivered in the sudden chill of the wind, wishing she had stopped to fetch a cloak, but in her excitement she had not thought of it – and Gervase was certainly in too much hurry. The inner courtyard was a scene of bustle, with men engaged in many varied tasks. Two servants were rolling great casks of ale from the winery to the kitchen door, while others were busy making similar casks. Blacksmiths, weavers and bakers were all in their own allotted spaces. Carpenters and stonemasons were working on repairs to one of the tower gates, and she could hear the ring of metal against metal as an armourer sweated at his bench. She had not previously been aware of so much going on, and realised that her room must face the other way. Why, it was like a small town, she thought, where almost everything the inmates needed could be supplied by their own labour. Glancing at the high, protective walls and the slanting steps leading to the battlements and watch towers, Perdita understood that it was an impregnable fortress. A siege might last for months and still fail unless proper provision had been made, she guessed. And as she saw the bulging granaries, stew-ponds and dovecots, it occurred to her that that provision had been made. It was as though Athelstan expected to be attacked!

As they left the first courtyard, her impression of preparation for war grew stronger. Several of the Earl's men were practising with a quarter-staff, their shouts and laughter attracting the attention of a noisy audience. Others fought fiercely with halberd, mace or the two-handed broadsword, while yet another tilted at the quintain. She saw men with cross-bows, and several strange engines of war that she could not name. Puzzled, she looked enquiringly at her companion.

'Is the Earl preparing for an attack?'

'No more than usual.' Gervase laughed harshly. 'My brother believes in being prepared! I told you he had enemies. Besides, it keeps the men fit and alert.'

'Yes, but…'

She forgot what she had meant to say as Gervase grabbed her arm and pointed to the sky. 'Look, Perdita!'

The hawk was soaring, and she held her breath in wonder at its magnificence as it hovered just above their heads and then swept down, disappearing from their view.

'Hurry,' Gervase urged, catching her hand and pulling her beneath an arch to the walled gardens beyond. There she saw a pleasant area of shrubberies, a herb garden and a lily pool. Beyond the pool was an open space where Athelstan stood with Balsadare and another man. As she watched, the young hawk dived at the lure and was drawn back to the gloved hand of the falconer. 'Did you see that, Perdita? We are too late. It will not fly again today.'

He sounded disgruntled, and she realised he was annoyed at having been sent to fetch her. 'Perhaps they will let it fly once more, if you wish it, Gervase?'

Scowling, he shook his head. 'No. They are putting the hood on. We delayed too long.'

'I'm sorry… It was my fault.'

He did not contradict her, though she had

apologised only to soothe him. His face was sulky at being denied the chance to watch the young bird. 'Athelstan sent me to bring you,' he muttered. 'Why could he not have waited for us? I wanted to stay, but he ordered, and I am forced to obey him.'

'Don't be cross with me, Gervase,' Perdita pleaded. 'May we not find something else to do? Could we not walk in the garden – or watch the men practising?'

His eyes were moody as he looked at her, then they began to snap with mischief. 'I know what we'll do,' he said, a note of excitement in his voice. 'Come on, I'll show you something!'

Relieved, Perdita laughed up at him, letting him take her by the hand and tug her towards a small building at the far end of the garden. 'Where are we going?' she asked, thinking he was playing a game with her, but he only laughed.

The building seemed to be set apart from the rest of the castle, almost hidden behind a mass of trailing ivy and with an air of disuse about it. As they reached it, Perdita saw that the iron-studded door had fine cobwebs over it, as if it had not been opened for some time. A feeling of sadness and oppression seemed to emanate from the neglected area and she felt reluctant to enter, hesitating and staring at it uneasily. The arch above the door was carved with grotesque figures, and some words in a strange script had been cut deeply into the stone. She tugged at Gervase's hand, trying to free herself as he lifted the latch.

'What is this place?' she whispered, her heart jerking. 'I – I do not want to go in there.'

'Are you afraid of the dead, Perdita?' Gervase laughed mockingly. 'Most of my ancestors lie here – I shall join them one day.'

'It is your family tomb?' she gasped, trying harder to free herself now. 'I won't go in there. Let me go, Gervase! This is morbid, and I refuse to be a part of it.'

The door swung inward on creaking hinges, revealing a flight of three crumbling stone steps. Perdita hung back reluctantly, but Gervase had a surprisingly strong grip and she could not break free. He dragged her behind him, grinning as she struggled.

'You shouldn't be afraid of the dead,' he chided. 'They won't hurt you. It's the living you should be wary of, Perdita. Come, look at their faces, see how peaceful they are. If I were sure it would be so peaceful, I would not be afraid to die.'

He had dragged her towards the tomb of a knight. The stone effigy was beautifully carved; and unable to resist Gervase's urging, Perdita's gaze was drawn unwillingly to the image of the dead man's face. She drew a sharp breath, feeling dizzy as she saw

Athelstan lying there. The floor seemed to be coming up to meet her and she swayed, hearing the sound of her tormentor's laughter as if from a distance.

'He was our grandfather, Perdita. Is he not very like my own dear brother? I thought you would like to see how Athelstan will look when he lies here. For he is mortal, like the rest of us. He, too, will die one day.'

'You– You are sick!' she cried, feeling the vomit rise in her throat. 'Let me go! I refuse to listen to you.'

'But I have more to show you,' he said persuasively. 'You must see just one more of – my family. Then I shall release you.'

His fingers were biting into her flesh, and she knew he would not let her go until he had taken sufficient revenge. She had caused him to miss the hawk's flight, and this was his way of punishing her. She had foolishly allowed him to see her dislike of his morbid preoccupation with death and he was deliberately using it to hurt her. Griselda was right, she thought; he did have a cruel streak in his nature. Suddenly she understood that her resistance would only prolong her agony.

'Oh, very well,' she said, ceasing to struggle. 'If it amuses you to taunt me, Gervase, I shall look. But I am angry with you, and I shall not easily forgive this childish prank.'

He scowled, pulling her further into the darkness of the vault. 'Look now,' he insisted, his voice oddly quiet. 'Was she not beautiful?'

This time the tomb belonged to a woman – no, to a very young girl, Perdita realised. The mason had carved the face of an innocent child, her eyes closed and her lips curved in a sweet smile. Her slender hands were crossed over small, pointed breasts, and she looked as though she were sleeping.

'Oh, how young she was,' Perdita said sadly. 'Who was she?'

His free hand moved lingeringly over the carved features, seeming to stroke them. Then he suddenly let go of her wrist, clenching both fists to smash them against the stone image.

'She was a whore!' he cried wildly. 'I'm glad she's dead – I hate her!'

'Jania…' she gasped, her knees shaking as she realised why he had forced her to come here. 'Gervase, don't be so bitter! She is dead, so why can't you forget and forgive her?'

He whirled to face her, his eyes glittering strangely. 'Why should I forgive her, Perdita? I loved her, and she laughed in my face – she laughed at me! She vowed she would never marry a cripple.' He was shaking from head to foot, his gaze becoming glazed as the shudders intensified.

All at once, Perdita realised he was ill. This was not merely anger, something was terribly wrong with him. His body was jerking with uncontrollable shudders – and he was beginning to froth at the mouth. As she watched, unable to think clearly, he fell to the ground, kicking and twitching grotesquely.

'Gervase!' she whispered, horrified. 'What is the matter? What can I do?'

'Nothing. Get out of here!' Athelstan's harsh command made her turn to stare at him with frightened eyes. 'You cannot help him, and he will never forgive you if he knows you have seen him like this.'

He moved past her and knelt on the ground beside his brother. She hesitated, watching in helpless fascination as he slipped a silver disk between Gervase's teeth. Holding him as still as possible, Athelstan glanced over his shoulder.

'I told you to go! Gervase will remember nothing – but if he sees you when he comes to himself, he will know you witnessed his shame and he will hate you for it.' She stared at him, still frozen into immobility by shock, and his eyes flamed with anger. 'Go, you foolish girl. Leave us!'

Finally, he had reached her. She gave a little cry of fright, and ran from the vault. Once outside, the shock of what she had seen lent wings to her feet. She fled beneath the arch, through the courtyards, past the astonished eyes of the Earl's men and into the safety of the keep, not stopping until she reached the seclusion of her own chamber.

CHAPTER FOUR

Sobbing, Perdita threw herself on the bed, letting the tears flow freely. She was weeping not merely because of what she had just seen, but for herself and for the uncertainty of life itself. Despite his sometimes cruel nature, Gervase was her friend. She believed he liked her even though he delighted in teasing her, and her feelings for him were a mixture of sympathy, friendship and a certain unease. At this moment she was conscious of a deep sadness. Now she could fully understand the bitterness inside him and why he resented the hold his old nurse still had over him. Life had been cruel to the youth, and if he sometimes felt the need to strike back at those around him who were strong and healthy, it was surely only a sign of his humanity? It was better that he should show his temper from time to time than sink into a mindless apathy, becoming a creature to be despised and pitied.

As her thoughts clarified, Perdita ceased to weep. She had been shocked and distressed by Gervase's illness, but now that her first feelings of horror had subsided, she felt ashamed of her own weakness. She should have done something to help him rather than running away like a frightened child. Getting up, she poured cold water from a silver ewer into a basin and washed the tear-stains from her face. She was just wondering what she ought to do next when someone knocked at her door.

'Come in,' she called, thinking it must be Griselda or one of the servants. The colour drained from her cheeks as the door was opened and Athelstan entered, closing it firmly behind him. 'Oh… It is you, my lord.'

Athelstan stared at her without speaking, and she flushed, feeling uncomfortable beneath those coldly assessing eyes. 'You have been crying,' he said at last. 'I am sorry that you had to witness such an unpleasant scene. It has not happened for some months, and I had hoped that Gervase's sickness was under control. For it is an illness, Perdita. Some call it the "falling sickness" – others talk of madness or possession by devils. My brother is not mad, neither is he possessed.'

'Oh, I did not think…' She bit her lip, sensing his anger. 'I – I behaved foolishly. Please forgive me? But you were so angry, and I was frightened.'

His smile sent little tremors through her. 'I was not angry, Perdita, only anxious that Gervase should not come to his senses and see you standing there. He feels that his illness is shameful, and it would hurt him to know that you had seen him like that. I want you to promise me that you will never speak of it – to anyone.'

'Oh, I shall not,' she said quickly. 'As God is my witness, I shall never mention the incident. But what must I say if Gervase should ask me what happened?'

'He will remember nothing; but if he should mention taking you to the vault, say that you ran away because you were frightened of the tombs and that he laughed at you for it.'

'Yes, he will believe that, for it was true. He– He only took me there to punish me because we had missed the hawk's flight.'

'So you have already discovered that Gervase's claws are sharp! I hope you will not turn against him, Perdita? My brother needs a friend. Since his illness began he has refused to visit our neighbours or the Court in case he should have an attack.'

'Then he was not always thus?'

'No...' Athelstan tensed, and she sensed some intense emotion within him. 'It began some three years ago.'

'Oh!' It must have been at the time of Jania's death, she realised, finding it difficult to meet his eyes. Her sympathy for Gervase made her mouth firm into an uncompromising line. 'No, I shall not turn against Gervase, my lord. He is my friend.'

'Good.' He was silent for a moment and

she was puzzled by the expression on his face. He seemed to be waiting for something – but what? What did he want of her?

'Where is Gervase now? May I see him?'

'He is sleeping. You will see him this evening. I shall leave you now, Perdita.' He turned away as if she had somehow disappointed him.

'My lord...' He paused at the door to glance back, his brows raised. 'What am I to do? What is my place in your household?'

'You are my guest, Perdita. I thought I had made that plain.' He frowned as she hung her head awkwardly. 'Are you unhappy here?'

'Oh no!' Her head jerked up. 'It is just – just that I do not care to be idle. Is there not something I could do to earn my keep – some sewing or accounts?'

Laughter swept the sternness from his features and his eyes were suddenly free of shadows. 'Forgive me, lady. I am not used to requests for work. Most find me a hard taskmaster! I had thought your lessons with Father Jonathan would be more than enough employment, but I see that I was wrong.' His amused gaze moved round the bare bedchamber. 'I have been remiss in my hospitality – my mind was, I fear, otherwise occupied – but your needs shall be filled today.'

'It was only that I wished to be of service

to you, my lord.'

'I have servants enough, Perdita. Your company is all I ask.' He gave her an odd look. 'In three days it will be Our Lord's birthday, and we shall have other guests to entertain. I fancy you will then have no reason to complain of idleness. My cousin Lady Eveline, her husband and his sister have sent word that they intend to spend Christmastide with us.'

Why was he looking at her like that – as if he laughed at some secret jest to which she was not a party? 'That will be pleasant for you, my lord.'

'Will it?' Athelstan's eyes mocked her. 'Perhaps you may not think so when you have met Lady Eveline! But we shall see...' With those tantalising words he went out, leaving her to stare after him in bewilderment.

The next few hours were happy ones for Perdita. Within minutes of the Earl's visit to her chamber she was supplied with a quill, ink and parchment; also a chest containing several lengths of silk and thread suitable for embroidery, together with all the implements a lady might consider necessary for such employment. She seized on them with delight, knowing that she would never need to be idle again.

The servants had also brought a small

harp for her use. Perdita looked at it doubtfully, feeling unsure of her ability to play the instrument. She experimented gingerly, and found that her fingers were not trained to manipulate the strings correctly. It seemed clear that she did not have a natural gift for music. She was disappointed at her lack of skill until she realised that she could ask Gervase to teach her to play. It would be something for them to do together, and instinctively she knew that he would be pleased if she begged him to show her how to coax music from her harp.

Her opportunity arose at supper that same evening. He sat next to her as he had on the previous night, but he was subdued and seemed disinclined to talk. At last, she turned to him with a winning smile.

'Will you not sing your new song for me, Gervase? You promised me faithfully that you would, when we walked together to Father Jonathan's chamber.'

'I might,' he said. 'I thought you would be angry with me, Perdita?'

'Because you tried to make me look at your family's tombs?' She wrinkled her nose at him. 'It was unkind of you to laugh at me because I was frightened, and that was why I ran away when you teased me so unmercifully. I was cross then – but I have decided to forgive you.'

'Oh?' He looked at her suspiciously. 'Why?

Are you sorry for me?'

'Indeed I am not!' she exclaimed. 'You were not kind to me – but you can redeem yourself if you wish.'

'How?'

'By teaching me to play the harp.'

The doubt was almost gone from his face now. 'Perhaps I shall – if you really want me to.'

'Yes, I should like it very much.' She smiled at him. 'Will you not sing for me now?'

'Do you truly wish it?' He relaxed as she nodded, and summoned a servant to fetch his harp. 'Tonight I shall sing songs to make you smile, Perdita. I am sorry I was cruel to you this morning. I – I do not mean to hurt you. Sometimes I cannot help myself.'

'It is because you have had no one to share your love of music, Gervase. From now on you will be too busy, teaching me, to play foolish tricks.'

'If I am unkind, you must tell me to go away. That shall be my punishment.'

'I shall not spare the rod,' she said, shaking her head at him. 'If we are to be friends you must be happy to be with me, then you will not want to hurt me.'

'I am always happy to be with you,' he replied, grinning. 'But I cannot promise always to be pleasant and sweet tempered. I shall often tease you, but you must not hate me for it.'

'I could not hate you, Gervase.'

'No… You are not like her.' A cloud passed across his face and was gone. 'Here is my harp. Watch my fingers as I play – this will be your first lesson.'

He took the small harp from the servant, running skilful fingers over the strings. Perdita watched, entranced by the sweet music he coaxed from the instrument. He sang a soft lullaby just for her, telling of a mother's love for her child as she rocked the cradle and listened to the storm outside her humble cottage. Applause from all round the great hall and cries for more brought Gervase to his feet. He began to walk slowly past the tables, singing a witty tale of a jester and a king. His song told of how the jester always managed to outwit his master, and he was so amusing that soon the room echoed with the sound of laughter.

'That was well done, Perdita,' said Athelstan, leaning forward to murmur in her ear. 'Gervase is now your friend, but take care not to make him fall in love with you. Unless, of course, you mean to have him for a lover?'

'Oh – I would not…' She blushed as he stared at her intently. 'How could you think…?'

'The warning is for your own sake. My brother does not forgive easily, Perdita. In that way, he and I are much alike.'

He turned aside to speak to the priest, and Perdita wondered why he should think it necessary to warn her against trying to make Gervase fall in love with her. She was very much aware of her situation, and she would not dream of abusing his hospitality. Besides, she was not a wanton. Did he imagine that all women were so easily won? It was unfair of him even to think that she might behave so badly! It was another tiny thorn in her flesh. It seemed that, whatever she did, Athelstan was prepared to think the worst of her, and she had tried so hard to please him! She felt upset; then she saw that Gervase was returning, and smiled at him. Athelstan was impossible to understand. At one moment he asked for her friendship for his brother, but when she gave it freely, he seemed to resent it! It was beyond her comprehension, and she would not let his barbs sting her.

Perdita had already thanked him for sending her so many gifts, but he had carelessly brushed her gratitude aside. She stole a nervous glance at his profile, wondering what was in his mind at this moment. What kind of a man was he really? There were so many contradictions in him that she found herself confused: sometimes he seemed to have a real concern for his fellow men, and yet his scorn had sent a young girl to her death. A girl he had first seduced – if

Gervase was telling the truth, and why should he lie?

A little shiver ran through her as she realised that she was allowing her thoughts to be possessed by him. Was that how it had been with Jania? His kisses the previous evening had shown her how easy it would be to let herself be carried away on the tide of his passion, but that was something she must never do!

It was easy to decide that she would not let her mind be dominated by Athelstan, but more difficult to control the wayward thoughts. Alone in her chamber that night, she found sleep elusive. There were no more screams to disturb her, but vivid pictures formed behind her eyelids whenever she closed them. Perhaps because she had no clear memories of the past, the people round her assumed an even greater importance than they might otherwise have done. Perhaps that was why she could still feel the sting of Athelstan's kisses…

As soon as Griselda came to help her to dress three days later, Perdita was aware of a different atmosphere in the castle: a restlessness that had not previously been present. From the expression on the old nurse's face, it was immediately apparent that something was troubling her.

'Why are you cross?' Perdita asked. 'Have

I upset you?'

'Nay, child, it's not you.' Griselda's hand shook, and the girl caught a glimpse of something that might have been fear in her eyes. 'Lady Eveline arrived an hour since – she and that sister-in-law of hers…'

'You– You don't like them, do you?' Perdita stared at her in surprise.

''Tis not for me to judge my betters,' Griselda said sourly. 'But if that woman ever becomes mistress here, it will be time for me to seek my grave.'

'Lady Eveline?'

'No – though her tongue is sharp enough! It's her I cannot abide – Mistress Meredith: Sir Geoffrey Winterburn's sister.' Griselda muttered something inaudible, then on a sharper note, 'She means to have Athelstan, mark my words!'

Perdita blinked as the nurse caught the comb in a tangle. 'Is Is Mistress Meredith very beautiful?'

'Ay, so most think.' The old woman's chin trembled with anger. 'But her beauty is a mask for a jealous heart. It's my lamb I fear for. He hates her, and she would never rest while he continued to live in the castle.'

Perdita concentrated very hard on the tasselled end of her girdle. 'Do you think Lord Athelstan will marry her?'

'Who knows? The master needs an heir, for his brother is not strong – and she has a rich dowry. Lady Eveline desires this match; I doubt not that she has come here to arrange it, if she can.'

Perdita was silent. She wondered what the old woman would say if she told her that Lord Athelstan had hinted that he wished to make *her* his mistress! Surely he would not think of doing so if his intention was to marry quite soon? Yet perhaps it had all been a part of his game: it amused him to tease her. And if he meant to marry, it would certainly be to someone like Mistress Meredith. He would never look at a girl with no name and no fortune – but such thoughts were foolish. She had no desire to be his wife … yet why did she feel a little jealous of a woman she had never met? Perdita struggled to subdue the unworthy emotions Griselda's words had aroused in her. She had no right to feel anything at all. She was simply a stranger the Earl had rescued from the woods. He had chosen to offer her sanctuary within his home, but that might only be until her memory returned.

It was strange how many small memories had begun to slot into place in her mind, although there were still so many blank spaces she could not fill. It was as if she needed one piece of the picture to make sense of all the rest. Sometimes she wondered if she truly wanted to know who she really was. If she discovered the truth, might it not mean that she would have to leave the castle? And she was still so afraid of the darkness that lurked in her past...

'Wake up, girl!' Griselda's sharp tones interrupted her reverie. 'You'll be late for your lessons.'

Perdita got to her feet at once, giving the old woman an apologetic smile. 'Yes. Thank you for reminding me.'

Leaving her chamber, she walked swiftly in the direction of the priest's room. Now that she was becoming accustomed to finding her way about, Gervase no longer came every morning to escort her to her lessons. They had, however, spent the past two afternoons together, and she could now play a few notes on the harp – though it was clear she would never be as skilled a musician as he!

Arriving outside Father Jonathan's chamber, Perdita knocked and waited. Several seconds elapsed before she was invited to enter, and when she did so, it was in time to see the priest rising from his devotions. He looked a little surprised to see her.

'Did you want to speak to me, daughter?'

'Is it not time for my lesson, Father?'

He smiled and shook his head. 'Have you forgotten that today is Our Lord's birthday? You will be expected in the great hall, Mistress Perdita. The Earl has guests, and I am sure he will want you to join in the celebrations.'

'I had not forgotten, but he – Lord Athelstan – has not sent for me. Are you sure I am expected?' She frowned. 'Could I not spend the morning with you as I usually do? We reached such an exciting passage in our reading yesterday that I was looking forward to continuing this morning.'

'Nothing would please me more,' he said, his eyes bright. 'But I, too, am expected to play my part when the Earl has guests. Come, we shall go down together.'

'How did you know I was nervous?' She smiled and laid her hand on his arm as they walked together. 'Was it so obvious?'

'A little, my child. Your eyes are so clear that sometimes they reflect your thoughts. Besides, Lady Eveline makes me nervous, too.'

Perdita's laughter rang out gaily. She had discovered that he had a quiet sense of humour, much less sharp than that of his master, but amusing. She felt that he was a truly good man, and because of his presence her life in the castle was easier than it might have been. Athelstan and his brother had such complex natures that it was a relief to be with this honest man sometimes. While he was there to remind her of her immortal soul, she felt herself protected from the temptations that might otherwise sweep her into troubled waters.

As they reached the gallery above the great

hall, the sound of merriment reached their ears. Pausing at the top of the stairs, Perdita felt a stab of surprise as she watched the scene below. Long, narrow tables were set at one end, loaded with huge platters of cold meats, bread, cheese and fruit; the food was flanked by silver ewers brimming with wine and ale, from which Athelstan's men helped themselves liberally as they watched the entertainment. At the moment a dancing bear was causing much amusement; but there was also a troupe of players who danced, sang and did amazing feats of juggling. Some of the men were playing the ancient game of bob apple, while others indulged in a friendly bout of wrestling or pitted their wits over a giant chessboard with wooden chessmen so large that it took two men to move them. The girl had never seen Athelstan's men at play before, and for a moment she could only stand and stare. Her companion's soft chuckle made her look at him suspiciously.

'Why are you laughing, Father?'

'It is good to see so many happy faces, daughter, but I fear my master suffers. I must go to him before Lady Eveline quite wears out his patience.' He glanced at her as she instinctively drew back. 'You must come with me, or your reluctance will be mistaken for rudeness.'

'I – I should not want that, of course.'

Perdita's gaze was drawn across the room to where Athelstan stood in the midst of his guests. They had their backs turned to her, but even at this distance she could see that his face wore a cold, withdrawn expression and she wondered at it. Did it not please him to have visitors?

Keeping her eyes downcast, Perdita followed one step behind the priest. She did not know why she was so apprehensive of meeting the Earl's guests – it was hardly likely they would take much notice of her!

'Ah, there you are, Father Jonathan,' said Athelstan. 'My cousin has been asking after your health. Please reassure her that I do not use you unkindly. Nor, I think, have I led you astray?'

The priest nodded, his lips curving slightly as he moved to take his place at the visitor's side. 'I am quite well, Lady Eveline. I thank you for your concern – but you must know how generous the Earl has always been to me.'

'My cousin has wealth enough to be generous without noticing it.'

The sharp tones of Lady Eveline's voice brought Perdita's head up. Surprised, she stared at a woman of perhaps thirty who had neither softness nor beauty in her face. Her hair was a dull black, making her skin appear sallow and dry; her body was so thin that she looked almost gaunt, as if Death's shadow already hovered at her shoulder. Except that her eyes had the sharpness of a young kestrel – and they were staring intently at Perdita.

'Why do you gape at me, girl?'

'I – I meant no harm, my lady!' Perdita curtsied hastily, feeling embarrassed. She had been staring rudely.

'I suppose this is the wench you rescued from the forest, Athelstan? A pity she has no manners; but what do you expect when you bring a nameless wench into the house?'

'You are mistaken, Eveline. She is a little shy of you, that is all.' Athelstan's frown made the girl flush. 'Come, Perdita, you shall meet Mistress Meredith now.' He held out his hand imperiously, and she went to him, feeling the clasp of his strong fingers about her arm as he led her forward, past the cold staring eyes of his cousin.

'I am sorry, my lord,' she whispered. 'I did not mean to upset Lady Eveline.'

'It was I who did that, before you came.' Athelstan's face was grim as he glanced down at her. 'I am afraid my cousin is displeased with me. But you must meet Mistress Meredith; you will not find her so ferocious, I think...' There was a flicker of a smile about his mouth now. 'Do not let my cousin frighten you, Perdita.'

'She does not, my lord. I was only sorry to have disgraced you.'

'Indeed? Then you need not repine, Perdita. I have no fault to find with your manners.'

She looked up at him, but now his smile was not for her. Following the direction of his gaze, she saw the woman who could only be Mistress Meredith. A woman so beautiful that she took Perdita's breath away. She was tall and graceful, with pale silky hair that flowed over her shoulders to the small of her back. Her eyes were bright green like emeralds, and her complexion was creamy perfection – though her lips were thin and rather hard. She stood perfectly still as Athelstan brought Perdita towards her, extending a slender hand at last with a smile that was supposedly intended to embrace both of them.

'My lord, how kind of you to bring Perdita to me,' she said, her curiously dark lashes fluttering for one moment as he kissed her hand. Then, turning her bright gaze on Perdita, 'Athelstan knew I was longing to meet you. You poor child, what a wretched time you have had!'

Perdita was gathered into a perfumed embrace, stiffening as she felt the touch of cool lips on her cheek. Instinctively she knew that Meredith's kiss was as false as her words of welcome. This was a pretence of friendship for the Earl's sake! Her lack of response brought a sharp look from Meredith as she was abruptly released, but it was swiftly replaced by a smile.

'Will you not say something to me, Perdita?'

'I – I am happy to meet you, Mistress Meredith.' Perdita felt the words stick in her throat, for she felt an immediate dislike of this beautiful woman and only Athelstan's frowning presence kept her from betraying it.

'Perdita has just felt the lash of Eveline's tongue! You must forgive her if she seems unresponsive.'

Perdita dared not look at him. He had shielded her from his cousin's attack, but he obviously expected her to be at ease with this woman. He would be angry if she spurned Meredith's offer of friendship, even though it was patently false.

'I – I was speechless at your beauty, Mistress Meredith,' said Perdita, knowing that the Earl was waiting for some response from her. Her chin went up as pride came to her aid. She, too, could play this game! 'If I was staring, it's because I have never before seen eyes quite the colour of yours.'

Meredith laughed, her lashes sweeping down to hide the angry glitter in her eyes. 'What a charming child she is, Athelstan! You must leave her with me for a while. I insist on having her all to myself.'

He inclined his head, a smile hovering

about his lips. 'I shall leave you together for the moment. But you have not forgotten the archery contest, Meredith? You will want to watch that, I know.'

'Of course,' she replied, cocking her brow at him provocatively. 'This year I think I have found a champion to beat yours. Will you wager on it?'

'Willingly, lady. Ten silver marks, say, that Balsadare can outshoot your man.'

'Paltry! Come, my lord, is not fifty marks a fairer price?'

'As you wish. I shall rejoin you in a little while, and we shall all watch the contest together.' He nodded to her and then to Perdita. 'Excuse me, I must speak with Sir Geoffrey.'

Perdita watched as he strode away. She had seen the gleam in his eyes as he met Mistress Meredith's challenge, and she felt a twinge of jealousy. It was clear that the Earl enjoyed the company of a woman as beautiful and clever as Meredith. What a fool she had been to think that he might really be interested in herself. No man would want a dowerless child when he could have the wealthy lovely Mistress Meredith! If he had paid her some attention these past few days, it was merely to while away an idle hour.

'Balsadare has won the contest for two years,' said Meredith, as if repeating her thoughts aloud. 'This year, I believe Athelstan will lose his wager. I wonder if I should have made it a hundred marks?'

'You are very confident,' Perdita spoke without considering. 'Supposing you lose your wager?'

'What does it matter?' Meredith shrugged carelessly. 'I shall win the prize I seek no matter what the outcome of the contest, Perdita. If you had hoped to take it for yourself, you have discovered that your cause is hopeless, have you not?'

Perdita looked up into her face. There was no mistaking the venom in those green eyes. Meredith was no longer bothering to hide her emotions now that the Earl had left them. It was clear that the feeling of instant dislike had been mutual.

'I have no idea what you mean...' Perdita began, breaking off with a gasp as the other girl's fingers grasped her wrist.

'You little slut!' Meredith hissed savagely. 'Don't look at me with those innocent eyes – I can see through you! I don't believe you've lost your memory. It's just a convenient trick to lure Athelstan into your bed. You're a lying whore! Jania thought she could trick him into marrying her that way – but he will marry no one but me. Do you understand?'

'Then why should you be jealous of me?' Perdita asked, a gleam in her eyes. 'I have no name and no fortune. How can I be a rival to you, Mistress Meredith? If you are so sure of Athelstan's love, you need not fear anything I might do...'

Meredith's grip tightened cruelly. She gave Perdita a look that was clearly meant to frighten her. 'How dare you speak to me so! I shall have you whipped and turned out of the castle.'

'Not while I have breath in my body!' Gervase's interruption startled them both. 'Let go of her, Meredith. I know what a false witch you are, and if Athelstan were half as clever as everyone thinks, he would too. He must be mad or blind if he believes in those honeyed smiles you give him.'

'Ah, Gervase my sweet, I wondered how long it would be before you arrived. Is your leg paining you? Is that why you're so late? Athelstan sent for you when we arrived.'

'My brother knows why I delayed.' Gervase scowled at her. 'Leave Perdita alone – or I might tell him things you had rather he did not know.'

'You dare to threaten me?' She laughed shrilly. 'When I am mistress here...'

'I shall not stay to witness that.' Gervase took Perdita's arm. 'Come, I want to talk to you alone.'

She went with him willingly, a little shocked at the bitter exchange between the two. 'You– You need not have quarrelled with Meredith on my behalf, Gervase,' she said when they were out of the other woman's hearing.

'It was not just for your sake. I hate her – and she responds wholeheartedly.'

He grinned, and Perdita smiled uncertainly. 'She is very beautiful, though.'

'So is a serpent.' Gervase looked at her oddly. 'Meredith is Jania's sister. She talked Lady Eveline into arranging the betrothal between us, thinking it would push Athelstan into a marriage with her. She blames me for what happened. I should have bedded Jania to stop her whoring with my brother!' His mouth twisted bitterly, and Perdita squeezed his arm.

'Don't let it hurt you, Gervase – the past is over and done.'

'Yes.' He smiled at her. 'You are right. But Meredith shall not sink her claws into your flesh. Especially today. It is Our Lord's birthday, and we must celebrate. I have a gift for you, Perdita.'

'A gift for me?' She felt a thrill of excitement, but then her eyes clouded. 'But I have nothing to give you in return.'

'You can give me a kiss,' he replied instantly. 'Here – I hope you will like it.' He pressed something into her hand.

They had found a quiet spot at the back of the hall, and Perdita sat down to open the little package. Wrapped in a piece of velvet, it felt hard and mysterious as she fumbled with the ribbons. As the covering fell away, she saw a large silver brooch. The mount was intricately worked and surrounded an oval amethyst encircled by tiny pearls. She gasped with pleasure, looking up at him.

'Oh, it is so pretty, Gervase! Thank you for giving it to me.'

'I am glad you approve. You may give me my present now if you wish.'

He sat on the bench beside her, and she threw her arms impulsively about him, her lips brushing his cheek. He caught her to him, turning his face so that their lips met and his dominated hers. She was surprised, withdrawing from the crushing embrace as soon as she could to stare at him uncertainly.

'Gervase, I...'

'It was rude of you to desert Meredith.' Athelstan's shadow fell across them. 'It is time for the contest, Gervase. You should join the others now.'

Perdita looked up at him, flinching as she saw the anger in his lean face. For a moment she felt wretched, then a mood of stubbornness came over her. If he chose to believe Meredith, he was the fool, not she! Turning to Gervase, she took the fine scarf from round her throat and tied it about his arm.

'There! You shall be my champion,' she said with a little toss of her head. 'Good luck, Gervase.'

'You have chosen badly, Perdita. I never win these contests.'

'Today you will,' she insisted. 'My favour will bring you luck.'

'I shall need more than luck,' he smiled wryly. 'But I shall try – for your sake.'

Perdita watched as he walked slowly away. Today the limp was not so pronounced, and she wondered if sometimes he used it as an excuse to avoid duties he found unpleasant, then she scolded herself for the uncharitable thought. Keeping her face averted from the man at her side, she yet sensed the seething anger in him. He was blaming her for the quarrel with Meredith. It was not just, but she could not complain without betraying Gervase's part in it – and that she would not do! There was too much bitterness between the brothers without her making more.

'You will come with me,' Athelstan said coldly. 'And you will be polite to my guests – all of them, Perdita.'

She gazed up at him then, her face proud. 'I shall do as you wish, my lord. I apologise if Mistress Meredith has complained of my behaviour.'

He inclined his head without answering, and she knew he was really annoyed with her this time. Taking her arm, he pulled her roughly to her feet, and as he did so, the brooch clattered to the ground. Before Perdita could retrieve it, he swooped and picked it up, staring at it with a frown before handing it to her.

'Gervase gave it to me,' she said, oddly defensive.

'So you were thanking him just now.' He paused as if in thought, then, 'It belonged to our mother. Gervase treasured it. He must think well of you to give it to you, Perdita.'

'He– He is my friend.'

'Are you sure he thinks of you as a friend?'

'What do you mean?' Surely he did not imagine they were lovers? She felt a little faint as she looked into his eyes and saw the assessing glitter there.

'Now is not the time to talk of this,' he muttered, taking her arm again. 'Come, we must join the others at once.'

Perdita forgot the momentary sensation of dizziness as the Earl led her through the crowded hall to join his guests. It seemed that his action was a signal to all the others present. A buzz of excitement went swiftly round the huge chamber, and everyone abandoned whatever they happened to be doing to follow their lord and his friends out into the courtyard. Judging by the tense atmosphere, Perdita guessed that this annual contest must be a very important one for all concerned.

Outside, the cool, sharp air lent a freshness to the morning that helped build the mounting excitement. Looking about her with interest, Perdita saw that six large round targets had been set up at the far end of the courtyard. A line had been marked across the ground, and a group of some sixty bowmen were waiting for the Earl to appear and give the signal for the contest to begin.

When everyone had found a place to their liking, and the resulting hubbub had finally sorted itself out, Athelstan's voice was heard: 'My friends, it is our custom to welcome visitors to the castle on this day each year, and to hold this contest in honour of Our Lord's birthday. As you know, all those who wish may enter and the prize will be a golden arrow as usual – the winner to be fêted at tonight's feast.'

A rousing cheer greeted his words, and the first six contestants took up their bows. At a command from the Earl's steward, they each fired a series of six arrows at the targets. When the scores had been tallied, another six took their places. Laughter and cheering greeted each succeeding line of contestants as the men urged their fellows on against outside challengers – one of whom was a tall, fair-haired fellow sponsored by Mistress Meredith; but as the contest progressed, the atmosphere changed subtly and a tense hush fell over the spectators as it was eventually narrowed down to the six finalists, who would now each fire three arrows.

Perdita felt a little thrill of pleasure as she

saw that Gervase was one of them. He had scored well, and she was proud that her champion was amongst the finalists, especially when he turned his head to smile at her before taking up his position at the line.

'It seems that your favour has brought my brother luck.'

Athelstan's quiet voice made Perdita glance up at him. His face was expressionless, and she could not tell whether he was pleased or annoyed because Gervase had reached the last six.

'Could it not simply be that Gervase is a skilful archer, my lord?'

'Undoubtedly my brother has many talents, Perdita, but he can seldom be bothered to make the best use of them. It is only because I force him to enter that he takes part in the competition at all. I do not care to see him waste his life in self-pity. I know he cannot fence or train as the others do, but he has a strong back and he can pull a bowstring as well as the next man – as he has proved today.'

The six archers had let fly the first of their three arrows. Balsadare's had pierced the centre of the target, while Gervase and the others could only manage to clip the inner ring. Meredith had been watching the Earl's conversation with Perdita, and now she moved closer, touching his arm to gain his attention for herself.

'You need not think that you have won so easily, my lord,' she said with a provocative smile. 'My champion will recover with his next arrow.'

'Indeed?' Athelstan arched his brow. 'I think Balsadare has the advantage still. What do you say, Perdita?'

'I believe Gervase may surprise you both!' Her chin went up as Meredith laughed mockingly. 'I have no money, but if I had, I would wager it on my champion.'

'Why not wager that brooch against mine?' Meredith's eyes glittered mockingly as she unpinned a large gold and ruby pendant brooch, holding it beside the silver one Perdita wore to compare them. 'It's hardly a fair wager, but I am willing to accept it.'

'I – I cannot! Gervase gave it to me, and it would seem ungrateful to risk his gift so carelessly.'

'Then you do not truly have faith in his ability to win the contest!' Meredith sneered.

'I shall accept your challenge,' Perdita cried, her cheeks flaming. 'Gervase will show you all!' She had gone too far to draw back now.

'Think well, Perdita,' the Earl warned, his face impassive. 'Gervase will not be pleased if you lose the brooch he gave you.'

'It is too late,' Meredith cried. 'The wager is set. Be still now – they are ready to shoot again.'

The archers fired even as she spoke. This time Balsadare, Gervase and Meredith's champion all hit the centre of the target. An excited buzz ran through the crowd as they prepared to fire once more. Balsadare seemed certain to retain his title, and Perdita bit her bottom lip, hardly daring to watch. She had been foolish to stake Gervase's gift, and she knew he would be furious if Meredith won his brooch – but the other girl's taunting had pricked her pride and she had been unable to refuse the challenge.

A gasp of disbelief issued from the watchers as both Gervase and Meredith's champion hit the bull's-eye, while Balsadare's shot went wide. It meant that all three were equal and must shoot again – but this time they would have only one arrow each.

'I told you my champion would recover,' Meredith said excitedly, clutching at the Earl's arm. 'This time he will win the golden arrow.'

'Perhaps,' said Athelstan, an odd smile in his eyes. 'Yet it is rare for Balsadare to miss his aim.'

Perdita was silent. She did not care for her own sake that she might lose the brooch, even though it was so pretty – but she knew it could turn Gervase against her. Crossing her fingers tightly behind her back, she forced herself to watch. This time the archers were to fire one after the other.

Gervase was first to the line. He set his bow, then turned deliberately to grin at Perdita. His smile was so confident that she laughed back at him, feeling a surge of excitement. He was going to win! He knew it, and so did she. His arrow was straight and true, hitting the exact centre of the target. Perdita clapped her hands, feeling triumphant as she swung round to catch the angry gleam in Meredith's eyes.

Her champion was the next to fire. He too hit the centre of the target, but his arrow was much nearer to the inner line and therefore not as true as Gervase's.

'Balsadare has yet to fire,' she said, a bitter note in her voice. 'Gervase has not won.'

'But he will,' Perdita said quietly.

Balsadare took aim as a breathless hush fell over those assembled in the courtyard. His eyes went to the face of his master, and he drew back his arm, holding the bowstring tautly. Was he about to lose his title? A gasp of astonishment issued from Athelstan's men as his arrow clipped the inner ring. Then there was complete silence. The Earl's brother had won, and no one quite believed it. As Perdita began clapping, a tremendous cheer broke from their lips and Gervase was suddenly surrounded by his fellow contestants, who slapped him on the back and congratulated him with great enthusiasm.

'Gervase has won, Perdita,' said the Earl, 'and so have you. Meredith must give you her brooch.'

Perdita's chin went up and her face was proud. 'I do not want it, my lord. Gervase has won, and I am content with that.'

'Indeed? Then you are a singular young woman.' Athelstan held out his hand. 'Give me the brooch, Meredith.'

Meredith unpinned it, handing it to him carelessly. 'Take it. It is of little importance.'

'It was fairly won, Perdita,' said Athelstan, turning it so that it caught the light, the ruby flashing fire in a ray of wintry sunshine. 'It is very fine – would you not like to have it?'

'No, my lord. I do not want the brooch.'

'Then you may keep it, Meredith.' Athelstan gave it back to her. 'Though I am sure it means less to you than Perdita's brooch meant to her. Excuse me, please – I must present the prize to our new champion.'

As he moved away, Meredith's face twisted with anger. 'You think yourself so clever, but you will live to regret this – I promise you that!'

'You do not frighten me, Mistress Meredith! I have done nothing wrong...'

'You tried to make me look a fool. I know you for a false schemer, and I shall prove it. I warn you that when Athelstan discovers you are lying about your memory, he will be quite ruthless.'

'Since I am not lying, I have nothing to fear.' Perdita's head lifted defiantly. 'Shall we watch the presentation now?' She turned aside as the call went out for silence.

The Earl held up his hand to quieten the buzz of excited voices. As a hush fell over the men, he smiled and took a velvet-wrapped package from inside his doublet. Unfolding the coverings, he brandished the glittering prize aloft for everyone to see.

'Every year I am proud to offer this prize to the most skilled bowman amongst us, and often it is to one of our own men – but I have never been quite as proud or happy as I am today. It is my pleasure to award this arrow to my brother Gervase, who has today shown us that he is truly a worthy champion.'

Gervase came forward to receive the prize, his face flushed with excitement. He took it from Athelstan, hesitating as their eyes met for one moment. Mumbling his thanks, he turned his back on the Earl, looking directly at Perdita.

'I won this for you, Mistress Perdita,' he said in a clear voice. 'I give it to you now as a token of my esteem.'

Perdita blushed as all eyes turned on her, feeling embarrassed. She shook her head, knowing what they must all be thinking, and wishing that she could find a way to deny it without humiliating Gervase.

'The arrow is yours, Gervase,' she said. 'Please keep it for yourself. You deserve it, and I – I have no need of such a prize.' An odd silence greeted her words and she knew that Gervase's smile had faded.

'Perdita has just refused a valuable brooch she won wagering that you would be the new champion, Gervase,' said Athelstan, his voice breaking the silence. 'She was content that you had won – and I think you must accept that she has no great desire for worldly treasures, but wishes only the satisfaction of seeing a friend excel. Now, my friends, the hour grows late. We shall return to our feasting – not forgetting that our champion must be suitably fêted!'

His speech had taken the tension from the situation, and a burst of cheering greeted his words. Gervase was once more surrounded by his fellow contestants, who lifted him shoulder-high, carrying him into the great hall with much laughter and jesting. As Perdita turned to follow, she felt her arm caught and looked up into the unsmiling face of the Earl.

'I warned you not to make Gervase fall in love with you unless you meant to have him as your lover,' he said coldly. 'Are you ready to share his bed, Perdita?' His fingers bit cruelly into her arm, and she winced. 'Are you in love with him – or do you simply want to see him begging for favours at your feet like a lap-dog?'

'Y– You are hurting me!' she gasped. 'Please do not look at me like that. I meant no harm when I gave Gervase my favour. It was an impulse, no more than that.'

'You little fool!' he snarled, his face black with fury. 'Can you not see that he is already half in love with you? You should have taken the arrow since he wished you to have it. Such a public refusal will anger him.'

'I meant no harm!' Perdita twisted her hands uneasily at her sides. 'To– To have accepted would have seemed as if...'

'As if you accepted his love?' Athelstan asked with a frown. 'If you humiliate Gervase he will never forgive you. Be careful, Perdita.'

'Gervase is my friend. I would never willingly hurt him. You must believe me!'

'Would you not?' He stared at her intently, the fury gradually fading from his face to be replaced by a strange expression she could not read. 'No, perhaps you would not intentionally hurt Gervase – but love itself can be destroying. If Gervase loves and you do not, it could do more harm than if he hated you. I say again, be careful, Perdita. Do not deny my brother friendship, but give him no reason to hope for more... Unless you mean to have him?'

She blushed and looked down at the floor. 'I think you need no answer to that, my lord.'

155

'Do I not? Am I so unlike other men, Perdita? Or is it simply that you believe I have no heart – no desires to stir my blood?'

His words made her eyes open wide as she gazed up at him. 'I do not understand you, my lord.'

'Do you not? Then perhaps I am answered.' His brow creased in thought as she blinked and looked bewildered. 'You think I speak in riddles, Perdita? Yet were I to say plainly what I mean, I doubt you would believe me. Now is not the time for dalliance. Come, we have guests waiting.'

As he steered her forcibly inside, Perdita's heart was racing wildly. What had he been hinting at just now? Was it possible that he truly desired her for himself as he had seemed to indicate? Surely not! It was Meredith who held his interest.

Inside the great hall, the feasting had begun in earnest. The musicians were playing a cheerful tune, and some of the men were performing a morris dance, with ribbons and bells tied to their ankles and on their sleeves: a fool capered and cavorted at their heels while the hobby-horse followed close behind. Gervase had been crowned with a wreath of laurel leaves, and his companions seemed intent on plying him with quantities of wine.

'It is the custom for the champion to get drunk,' said Athelstan, his eyes narrowing. 'I

156

had forgot that for the moment.'

'Do you think it might bring on one of his attacks?' Perdita asked, sensing his anxiety.

'I shall watch carefully for the signs, but it would be better if you could persuade him to sing for us.' The Earl sighed suddenly. 'I fear what I ask of you is almost impossible, Perdita. Forgive me if I abused you just now. You cannot help it if men find you beautiful.'

'Beautiful?' she echoed, staring at him in surprise. 'Am I so, my lord?'

'Do you not know it?' He smiled, his eyes seeming to caress her for a moment. 'Oh yes, you are very lovely, lady. Gervase is not the only man here to fall in love with you, I dare swear! Now I must attend my cousin before her wrath descends on us both. Do what you can for Gervase, Perdita.'

She watched as he strode away from her, her pulses throbbing. He had said she was beautiful! Oh, how hard it was to keep her head when he looked at her in that way! She felt herself being drawn nearer and nearer to the flame that would consume her if she once let down her guard – but that must not happen.

Fighting the confusion inside her, Perdita crossed the room to join Gervase. As she reached him, he frowned and deliberately turned his back on her. She touched his arm, pulling at his sleeve until he was forced to look at her.

'I knew you would win, Gervase,' she said. 'Meredith was so angry when she lost her wager. I won her ruby brooch, but I would not take it from her – and that made her even more cross.'

'Why did you refuse the arrow? I won it for you, and it means nothing to me if you will not accept it.' His moody eyes pierced her.

'Don't be cross,' she pleaded. 'I am not like Meredith – you don't have to give me things to please me. It made me happy because you won. You are my friend, Gervase. I like you…' Her voice trailed away to a whisper as she saw his eyes take fire.

'But I want more, Perdita,' he said fiercely. 'Much more.'

'Gervase, I…' she was unable to go on.

'Ah, there you are, girl.' Lady Eveline's acid tones cut across the silence. 'Come, sit with me. I want to hear what you have to say for yourself.'

Perdita looked about for Athelstan, but he was in close conversation with one of his men, and as she watched, he walked with him from the hall. Obviously she could look for no help from him, and Gervase was still scowling at her. Resigned to her fate, she gave the youth a little smile as she was almost dragged away by the older woman. Glancing over her shoulder, she saw that he, too, had noticed Athelstan leave, and was following. At least he had ceased to drink tankard after tankard of ale, she thought thankfully.

Her relief was short-lived. Lady Eveline thrust her into an alcove and drew the curtains behind them. As Perdita looked at her uncertainly, she lashed out, striking her across the face.

'That will teach you some manners, girl! Next time you greet a lady, you will behave properly.'

Perdita pressed a hand to her cheek, staring at her with horrified eyes. 'I – I did not mean to offend you, my lady.'

'The very air you breathe offends me! Why my cousin brought you into his house I do not pretend to understand.' Her thin face twisted with spite. 'I suppose you are his harlot. If I had my way you would leave here in the morning, but there is no reasoning with Athelstan. He means to keep you here, and nothing I can do will sway him – at least until he discovers the truth about you. I dare swear that you are nothing but a common slut who has learned to copy her betters.' She leaned forward menacingly, peering suspiciously into the girl's face. 'Just who are you? Where did you come from? Tell me the truth, and you have nothing to fear. If you persist in this deceit I shall make it my business to learn your secret, girl. And when I do...'

Perdita backed away from her, trembling. 'I do not know who I am – I can remember nothing…'

'Lies! All lies.' Lady Eveline's lips pursed. 'Do you expect me to believe that tale? A very convenient way of playing on my cousin's good nature, but not convincing.'

'I swear it is the truth!'

A harsh laugh escaped the older woman and her eyes narrowed. 'If you do not lie, there must be some evil in your past. This affliction is put on you by God, mark my words, wench! I knew as soon as I saw you that you carried the mark of the Devil.' She stared at the girl with intense dislike. The little slut could ruin all she had worked for if she were not got rid of as quickly as possible. Athelstan was clearly intrigued with her. No doubt he would tire of her soon enough and see his duty, but in the meantime there was always the possibility that he would do something foolish.

'Do you really think I am evil?' Perdita stared at her, her head whirling. Was it true that her loss of memory was a punishment for something terrible she had done?

'I have no doubt that you have something to hide. Rest assured that I shall discover who you are – and when I do, you will be returned to wherever you came from.'

'No… You cannot,' Perdita moaned as the fear swept over her. She was afraid of the unknown menace in her past. She could not bear the idea of leaving the castle and the Earl's protection. 'Lord Athelstan will not turn me away!'

'We'll see about that!'

Everything was spinning out of control. She could hear the baying of the dogs and she knew they were close behind her. He was gaining on her! She had to escape or he would drag her back, and then... The fear closed in on her and the room began to spin faster and faster. She gave a little cry as the blackness closed in on her and she collapsed at her tormentor's feet.

CHAPTER FIVE

'Wake up, Perdita! What has that skinny witch been saying to you? If she has harmed you, I swear I'll make her suffer twice as much!'

Perdita's eyelids fluttered, and she gave a little groan as she opened them to find Gervase bending over her, his face anxious. 'What happened – did I faint? I was talking to your cousin…'

'Thank God, I thought you might have lost your memory again!' Gervase grinned at her. 'My cousin was frightened when you swooned. I believe, for a moment, she thought you were dead! I heard her calling for a servant and came to investigate. She pretended you had complained of a headache, but I guessed she had been bullying you. What did she say to upset you so much?'

A cushion had been placed beneath Perdita's head and his cloak was over her. She thanked him for his thoughtfulness, feeling better as she sat up and clasped her knees. 'I – I think Lady Eveline hates me.'

'Nonsense! Why should she? She hardly knows you.'

'She thought I was rude to her earlier.'

Perdita frowned. 'She says I have the mark of evil on me.'

'And she hasn't, I suppose?' Gervase scowled. 'You should not listen to her. She has always had a sharp edge to her tongue. Athelstan will deal with her.'

'I would rather you said nothing to him about what happened, Gervase.'

'If I do not, he will likely discover it for himself. There is not much that escapes my brother!' Gervase saw the distressed look in her eyes, and sighed. 'Very well, if you wish, I shall keep silent, but the hag deserves his censure for frightening you. Just what did she say to you?'

'It doesn't matter.' She smiled as he helped her to her feet. 'Shall we return to the hall? They will be bringing in the wassail soon, and I would not want to miss that.'

'We shall drink from the dish together, Perdita,' he said joyfully. 'I have something to celebrate! I've never won the contest before.'

He had obviously recovered from his sullen mood. She took his arm, leaning on him until her head cleared. 'Perhaps you never tried until today?'

'Do you know me so well? I must take care, or I shall have no secrets from you. How did you know I was capable of winning?'

'It was just something you once said in an

idle moment. I felt that you could do it if you wanted to.'

He glanced down at her. 'You are clever, Perdita! I wonder what else I have told you without knowing it? Somehow, I do not think that even Athelstan yet realises what a prize he has found.'

'Where has he gone?'

'That is something I shall not tell you.' Gervase gave her a sly look. 'He will return soon enough.'

There was some small mystery here, but she forgot it as they returned to the hall just as the wassail was brought in piping hot from the kitchens. It was the climax of the evening as the bowls of hot ale, spices, sugar, eggs, cream and roasted apples were passed from hand to hand in a spirit of fellowship.

Gervase took her hand, pulling her into the midst of a group of laughing men. He received a bowl and drank from it, giving it to her with a chuckle. She sipped it and exclaimed as it burnt her tongue, passing it on hastily. All round her, Athelstan's men were singing carols, their voices slurring as the long day of celebration drew to its end.

'I am so tired,' said Perdita, smothering a yawn. 'Should I bid your cousin good-night before I retire?'

'It is not necessary – especially after the way she behaved to you!' He scowled. 'I'll see you safely to your chamber, though I doubt she will try anything more tonight. It frightened her when you swooned like that.'

Perdita looked up at him then. 'She wants to be rid of me, Gervase. She threatened to do something awful – but she could not have meant it, could she?'

'My cousin is capable of anything! Trust neither her nor Meredith.'

'They would not really harm me?'

'Eveline would have you whipped if she dared; and Meredith's smiles are as false as her heart.'

'Yes, I know you are right.' They had paused outside her chamber. 'Thank you for helping me, Gervase. I am sorry if I hurt you by refusing the arrow.'

'I should not have embarrassed you by offering it so publicly.' He took her hand, looking at her awkwardly. 'You do know that I care for you very much?'

'Yes, I do,' she said, feeling a lump in her throat. Sometimes he could be so thoughtful. 'You know I think of you as my good friend, don't you?'

'I would have more than friendship.' His fingers caressed the back of her hand, making it tremble. 'I would have you as my wife, if you would consent to the marriage? I believe we could be happy together, Perdita.'

She sensed how much it had cost him to

speak those words, and her heart contracted with pain. She did not want to hurt him as Jania had hurt him, but what could she say?

'Please do not ask me such a question yet, Gervase,' she whispered, her eyes misting with emotion. 'I do not know how I feel – I do not even know who I am. How can I marry anyone when I have no past? I may be as evil as your cousin says.'

'Your past does not matter. You are beautiful, and your heart is true. I could love you, Perdita, and I would strive to make you happy.'

'Please do not press me,' she said, withdrawing her hand from his. 'I must have time – time to know myself.'

'But you will consider my offer?'

She hesitated, knowing she should make her feelings clear at once, but the wistful look in his eyes held her back from uttering the words that would strike him to the heart. 'I shall think about it, Gervase,' she whispered. 'But you must give me time…' Smiling at him regretfully, she opened her door and went in alone.

'It was she, Sir Edmund, I swear it. She stood with the Earl and his family to watch the contest, and Gervase dedicated the prize to her – though she declined to take it,' Fulk said, beads of sweat standing out along the line of his brow as he looked into the furious eyes of his master. 'They do not call her Rosamund – but I will take an oath on it that it was her!'

Sir Edmund's fleshy face was blotched with purple as his hands clenched into tight fists. 'You would lie to save your own skin, Fulk! Had I not suspected he had her at the castle, you would have been hanging from a gibbet long since.'

Fulk fell to his knees, wringing his hands in anguish. 'I swear it was her, sir!'

'Get up, dolt! I have not said you are lying. In this instance I believe you, for I knew he had her when he came here. If it had been merely a matter of the men-at-arms, he would have sent a servant to warn me to be ready.'

'Athelstan's men make merry,' Fulk said, looking at his master slyly. 'You know his custom to keep open house at Christmas-tide. Could we not send a small force to snatch her from him?'

'Fool! Would you have us all slaughtered in our beds? We should never be able to sleep easily again. Besides, he never allows all his men to drink at the same time. There will be fifty on guard at any given moment...' Sir Edmund frowned, his fingers toying with a sweetmeat. 'No, we must watch and wait. She will be spoiled goods by now, but I am a tolerant man. I can be patient when I choose. Athelstan will soon tire of her, and then...'

'Supposing he – or his brother – should marry her?' Fulk recoiled as his master's hand struck him across the face. 'I meant no harm, sir!'

Sir Edmund's eyes narrowed. 'So, you have served your purpose at the contest. Why should I not hang you now?'

Fulk trembled, knowing the temper of the man he was bound to serve. 'I – I have more news that might interest you.'

A hand grabbed him by the throat, almost choking the breath from his body. 'What trickery is this? If you dare to hold back from me, you shall suffer for it.' He was thrust roughly away and stood gasping, his face red. 'Well, speak, man, or I'll kill you myself!'

'I – I saw someone arrive at the castle just as I was leaving. He came stealthily, under cover of dusk...'

'So Athelstan meets in secret...' Sir Edmund's face lit up. 'Who was this man you saw?'

'A man I have seen at Court, sir. A man who serves the Duke of Hereford.'

'A messenger from the traitor Hereford!' A gleam of triumph entered his eyes. 'So the great Earl of Athelstan intrigues with traitors, does he? What more does he plot, I wonder? I thought his enquiry about my men an idle question to blind me to the truth, but now I see that there may be more afoot than I first guessed. The King would reward me handsomely for this information, I'll warrant!'

Fulk breathed again as his master sat down, sipping his wine as he stared reflectively into the flames of the fire. He hardly dared to breathe, knowing that his fate still hung in the balance. Sir Edmund's rages were apt to come and go like a spring breeze, and were just as treacherous; often they died away, but occasionally they became a full-blown gale.

'You have served me well,' Sir Edmund said at last, 'so I shall spare your life. You may still be of use to me.'

'You know I would do anything to serve you, sir.'

A little smile played about the Baron's mouth. 'Ay, for I should hang you if you betrayed me. But stay and drink with me, sirrah, while I explain how you may serve me best...'

'Ah, you are already up,' Griselda said with a sniff. ''Tis just as well, since the master is asking for you. Come, let me tidy your hair, girl.'

Perdita smiled and handed her a small square of silk. 'I woke early so I finished sewing this kerchief for you. See, it has your name embroidered in the corner. I am sorry it was not finished yesterday, but it's only one day late.'

The old nurse stared at her and then at the delicate embroidery. Without speaking, she took the gift and tucked it inside the bodice of her kirtle. Perdita sat on the stool obediently as her hair was combed and left to flow smoothly over her shoulders. She had not expected any thanks for her gift, but she sensed that her gesture had been accepted.

'You had best hurry, Mistress Perdita,' Griselda said when she had done. 'The master is waiting for you in the courtyard.'

'Thank you.' The girl glanced at her shyly. 'Did he say why he wanted me?'

Griselda snorted her disgust. 'I am not privy to my master's thoughts, girl!' But there was a knowing look in her eyes as she answered.

Laughing, Perdita hurried from the room. Griselda's tongue was sharp, but she was no longer disturbed by her scolding, knowing that it hid a warm heart. She had seemed to hint at some mystery, but perhaps that was imagination? Perdita's feet seemed to fly as she scurried through the draughty passages. Last night, when Lady Eveline had threatened to have her removed from the castle, she had realised how hard to bear that would be, and she knew it was because its master had assumed so much importance in her life. It was not only her fear of the past that made her want to remain close to the

Earl! Realising that she was foolish to allow herself to become dependent on his good humour, she could not altogether still the rapid pulsing of her blood at the mere mention of his name. She did not know why he should have such an effect on her, but it made her happy because he had sent for her. Perhaps she was a fool – but she could not help it!

As she reached the inner courtyard, she saw the Earl standing with his grooms and Balsadare. Several horses were saddled, their harnesses jingling as they stamped their hooves impatiently. Balsadare was wearing a thick leather gauntlet, and a hooded kestrel perched on his wrist. It was obvious that they were about to set out on a hunting trip – but was she expected to accompany them? She halted abruptly, her heart pounding as she wondered what to do.

Her question was soon answered as the Earl led a milk-white palfrey forward, greeting her with a smile that was tinged with impatience. 'So, you are here at last, lady. This horse is my gift to you. I had another, but you seemed not to care for jewels or gold. I sent my servants in search of something special I had seen in a neighbour's stables and made my purchase last night, but when I returned, I learned that you had retired.'

There was a hint of censure in his voice, and she flushed. He had thought her churlish to retire without bidding him good-night, but she could not have known he had meant to surprise her. She moved towards the horse, hiding her confusion as she put out a tentative hand to stroke its nose. It snickered and nuzzled her as if in greeting, and her nervousness eased. It was clearly a gentle creature and had a mane as soft and fine as silk threads. She felt a little thrill of pleasure, her hand beginning to stroke the creature with more confidence.

'His name is Dioscuri – son of Zeus.' Athelstan watched her petting him with an indulgent smile. 'I thought that might appeal to you?' His brows went up and he waited expectantly.

Her eyes sparkled at his wit. 'How beautiful he is, and how well the name suits him! I thank you for your gift, my lord, but – but I do not believe I know how to ride him.'

He seemed taken aback for a moment, and then he laughed. 'Well, I had not bargained for this. It seems that I must teach you at least the elementary skills. Come, give me your hand.'

She obeyed, her flesh tingling as his cool fingers clasped hers. He drew her forward, gazing down into her anxious face with mischief in his eyes; then his hands encircled her tiny waist and he lifted her bodily into the saddle, showing her where to place her heel and how to hold the reins. Then, taking a leading-rein, he walked horse and rider up and down the courtyard, while the grooms looked on with impassive faces and the other horses chafed impatiently at their bits.

Her first sensation was of distinct unease as she felt herself in danger of sliding from the saddle; but an instruction from the Earl showed her how to sit more securely, and as her first anxiety died away, she found the swaying motion was not unpleasant. She was not sure that she would ever enjoy it, but she was more frightened of making a fool of herself than she was of the horse. Besides, the palfrey had been chosen for his docility, and was perfectly behaved. After a few turns about the courtyard, she was beginning to feel a little more confident when the Earl glanced up at her.

'Are you ready to accompany us, or shall I cancel the ride today?'

She saw the challenge in his eyes and was determined to accept it. 'I am ready, my lord.'

'Good.' His look was approving, tinged with a hint of malice. 'Stay close to me, and you will come to no harm.'

Leaving her, he vaulted into the saddle of his own horse – a great, black, snorting beast with fiery eyes that warned of its temper. He brought it back to Perdita and took up the leading-rein once more, clearly intending to keep her under his control. His action was a signal to the others, who mounted hastily and followed behind their master and his lady.

Perdita firmed her lips, determined to show no sign of nervousness as she kept her palfrey at the Earl's side, responding to his instructions as best she could. The horses walked sedately through the courtyard, pausing for a moment before crossing the drawbridge. The clatter of hooves on the heavy wooden bridge sent a little shiver down her spine, but she trained her eyes straight ahead, not allowing herself to look down at the murky waters of the moat. The forest loomed dark and forbidding before them, and she bit her lip, feeling reluctant to enter it. Her nightmares always began with the forest, and she was afraid of betraying her fear of it in front of the Earl and his men. To her relief, he turned away, following a narrow path that wound round the castle and eventually descended to a wide sweep of open grassland.

Overhead, the sky was patchy with white, floating clouds, but the air had temporarily lost the bite of winter. Gradually the horses had increased their pace to an easy canter. In the distance the shine of water caught Perdita's eyes and she gasped with pleasure as they rode closer to the small lake, forgetting to be nervous when the Earl slackened his hold on the leading-rein. She looked up, startled by the loud fluttering noise that filled the air. All at once the sky was dark with birds of many kinds; they rose from water, tree and bush in sudden panic as Balsadare loosed the kestrel, letting it soar into the air. For a while it hung almost motionless, its wings seeming barely to move before swooping with deadly accuracy on its prey.

Following its majestic flight, the girl experienced both pain and pleasure. The hawk was magnificent, its kill clean and swift, yet she felt pity for the songbird it had caught in its sharp talons. It was the law of nature; the weak were always at the mercy of the strong. It was cruel and yet beautiful; sad and yet somehow right. A part of the mystery of life.

'Do not look so sad, Perdita,' said Athelstan, seeing the expression in her eyes. 'It was meant to be. The songbird feeds on the worm, and in its turn becomes food for the kestrel. In death there is also life. Only God can say why the one should serve the other; we ourselves are but one small part of his plan.'

'I know…' Emotion caught at her throat as she looked at him, sensing that his words had a deeper meaning for her alone. She felt her heart quicken with a strange emotion she could not yet identify. 'Am I wrong to feel sorrow for the victim?'

'No. You have a gentle soul, Perdita, and I would not have you otherwise. Do not grip your reins so tightly – see how I hold them.' He smiled as he censured her, making her heart flutter wildly. 'Forget the bird, lady. This outing was intended to please you.'

'And it does, my lord, though I fear I am a poor equestrian. Your gift is most generous. Already you have given me so much…'

'It pleases me.' He seemed to dismiss her gratitude. 'You ride well enough for a beginner. You must learn to relax, Perdita. Let your body move with the horse instead of straining against it. We shall go on ahead of the others for a while. I have the rein and you will come to no harm.' He made a sign to Balsadare, then turned to her with a commanding gesture. 'Do exactly as I tell you.'

She nodded, her pulses throbbing as he jerked on the leading-rein and the palfrey increased his pace to a gallop. Her heart rose in her mouth as she clung precariously to the reins, finding this new sensation terrifying. There was no time for pondering the mystery of life – or the nature of this strange, fascinating man – all her attention was given to simply staying in the saddle. Yet as their horses raced side by side, surging far ahead of the others, she became aware of an affinity with her horse. It was almost as if the instinct had always been in her, that to blend with the motion of her mount was as natural as breathing to her. She became aware of a singing in her veins as the fear left her, and she knew only the pleasure of being alive and happy.

At last he called a halt. Dismounting, he came to help her to slide from the palfrey's back, holding out his arms to receive her. She was panting, shaken by the thrill of the chase and the unaccustomed exercise, her legs wobbling as she touched the ground. He laughed as she trembled, catching her against him with a look of triumph.

'What, out of breath, lady? I see I must take you in hand...' The laughter left his face abruptly as he gazed down at her. Bending his head, he touched his lips to hers, his kiss caressing, yet demanding her response. As he felt her mouth soften and open beneath his, he held her tighter, his hand curving into the small of her back to press her firmly against him so that she could feel the sinewy hardness of his lean frame as their bodies seemed to fuse into one. Looking up at him, she felt herself bending to the mastery of his will and recoiled, shocked by the wild responses the contact had roused in her. He withdrew slightly, gazing down at her with a mocking smile. 'Why so, Perdita?' he asked softly. 'Will you not thank me properly for my gift?'

'You– You ask too much of me, my lord,'

she whispered breathily. 'I fear you would have more than a kiss from me.'

His hand stroked her throat, making her pulses leap and the colour stain her cheeks. 'And if it were so?' His eyes seemed to scorch her flesh as they devoured each flicker of her betraying emotion. 'Supposing I would have all, lady – could you deny me? Speak honestly, for I shall be merciless if you lie.'

Perdita lowered her lashes, her heart beating so wildly that she could hardly breathe. She knew she was in terrible danger at this moment – danger of surrendering her will to his. For one second in his arms, she had been tempted to let herself be swept away by the swirling tide of his passion. Why should she resist him, when her whole body was on fire with the longing to return his kisses a hundredfold? She knew instinctively that she would find in his embrace pleasure such as she had never known, so why should she deny herself and him? Yet there was that in her that would not let her yield. Call it pride or obstinacy – it was there, and it stood between them like a wall of stone.

'I am not Jania, my lord!' She raised defiant eyes to his. 'I know well you would not take a nameless wench to wife – and I shall not play the wanton in your bed. If you will have me, you must take what you desire by force, for I shall not give it willingly.'

'So, you hold out against me still?' An odd smile curved his mouth. 'You have both pride and spirit, Perdita. I could tame that pride and teach you to understand me better, but we have time. I would not have you come to me believing me a heartless monster. We shall return to the castle. I have something to show you – something that may earn your good opinion.'

She looked at him curiously, but he shook his head, leading her back to where the horses were quietly grazing. His hands took possession of her waist, and she trembled as he seemed momentarily to hesitate, half fearing that he would begin yet another assault on her already crumbling defences; then he smiled and lifted her on to the palfrey's back, standing for a moment to mock her with his eyes. She felt again that he enjoyed the conflict between them, that it was a battle he did not want to win too swiftly.

He was silent as they rode back to join the others. Perdita glanced at his stern profile occasionally, not daring to question him. Was he angry because she had dared to repulse his advances? He had not seemed so at first. Rather, she had thought him amused by her defiance. It was as though he knew he had her caught fast in his net, and was playing with her like a cat with a mouse, letting her escape for a moment before reaching out to deliver the final blow. And did she truly wish to escape? Would she leave him if she could? Knowing the answer, she wondered again at her own stubbornness. Why did she not simply submit her will to his? He had already shown his willingness to be generous and he would not be less so when he tired of her, but that was the truth of it. How could she bear to be cast aside when he had done with her? If she gave up that inner self to him entirely, she would cease to exist. Had it been so with Jania?

Sanity returned as she remembered Jania's fate. She had taken her own life when Athelstan spurned her. It was difficult to believe that he could be so cruel, especially when he smiled at her – and yet she had seen Jania's tomb for herself. The stonemason had portrayed an innocent girl, hardly more than a child. It was a terrible end for one so young. Why should she, Perdita, expect to be treated differently? Both Griselda and Gervase had hinted at danger, and she knew she would be a fool to lose her heart to this man. A man she had met only a few days ago…

They had reached the castle. As the horses' hooves clattered over the drawbridge, Perdita's thoughts turned at last to the reason for their return. The Earl had something to show her that he thought would please her. What could it be? She knew that he had many treasures; jewels, books, strange icons brought from foreign lands, pictures, tapestries and many more wondrous things. Father Jonathan had told her about some of them, and she had sensed that there were other, more sinister secrets that the priest would not speak of to her. Gervase, too, had hinted at his brother's secrets. Was she about to learn more of them? She was not sure that she cared to know why Athelstan disappeared into the bowels of the castle when everyone else was sleeping. He had said that it was on an errand of mercy – but could she believe him? He had told her his enemies believed he was in league with the Devil. What did it mean? Could it be true? she wondered. Was that why his kisses turned her limbs to molten fire. Had he bewitched her?

So many questions to torment and confuse her! He came to help her to dismount, his grey eyes so serious that she felt he had read her mind. Chiding herself silently for her foolishness, Perdita forced a smile to her stiff lips. There was no evil magic to this feeling inside her. It was the natural urging of her flesh – sinful, but no more than any girl might feel for a man as powerful and compelling as Athelstan. It was her own weakness that might betray her, not his intriguing with the Devil!

She smiled at her thoughts and his brow went up. 'Why do you look so, lady?'

'I smile at my own foolishness, sir.' She shook her head at him. 'No, I shall not tell you. What have you to show me?'

His lips twisted wryly. 'In another I might think that urgency was desire for a pretty trifle, but do not fear I mean to insult you by trying to buy your favours. I told you of a boy the other night, and I believe you thought I had been torturing him. Would it please you to see how well he recovers from his ordeal?'

'Yes, indeed it would.' She was pleasantly surprised, and he laughed as he saw it in her face. 'You said his leg had been crushed beneath the wheel of a cart, did you not?'

'Yes, but I led you to believe it had only then happened. It was not so. The accident occurred some weeks ago; his wounds had healed, but he was a cripple and in some pain. I persuaded his parents to let me try to cure him. I broke his bones and reset them; it was then that he woke and you heard his screams – an occurrence that I much regret. He was fortunate, however, that the delay was not too long. I have been successful, and I believe he will walk again in time.'

Perdita stared at him. 'You have done something similar before, haven't you?'

'Yes.' Athelstan frowned. 'Gervase was one of my first patients. I fear I was only partially successful in his case, though his leg is straighter than it was. I should like to try

183

again, but he will not permit me. The treatment is painful, and he dislikes being confined to his bed.'

'Sometimes I wonder if he limps more than he needs to, but perhaps I am being unkind?'

'No, you are right.' He sighed deeply. 'Gervase resents me for trying to help him. I have attempted to find a cure for his sickness, but too often he refuses to take the medicine I prepare. He prefers the foul concoctions Griselda brews for him – and since I do not know that my remedies will work any better than hers, I cannot force him to take them.'

Perdita nodded, a little in awe of his knowledge of such things, which seemed to border on the art of sorcery. She held back the impulsive words that sprang to her tongue. Gervase might not want to suffer physical pain because of his brother's attempts to straighten his leg, but she believed the cause of his resentment ran much deeper. Surely Athelstan must know how bitter his younger brother was over the way his betrothed had died! Surely he must feel some remorse! Yet he had expressed none, even though she had twice reminded him of his culpability…

He had taken her arm and was leading her to a wing of the castle that she had not yet been inside. Entering through a small arch, Athelstan guided her past rooms that were clearly occupied by his men. She heard laughter and deep voices issuing from behind the doors; then they halted outside one of them, and the Earl knocked.

The voice that bid them enter belonged to Father Jonathan. As they went inside, he rose from his seat beside the bed and came forward, greeting them with a smile of welcome.

'Ah, you have come, my lord. This lad has been asking for you, and I said I would beg you to visit him when you had time.' His twinkling eyes turned to Perdita. 'Our patient is impatient to be up and about again.'

A young boy of perhaps fifteen was sitting propped up against a pile of pillows. He looked rosy-cheeked and obviously healthy, except that one leg was bound between thick wooden splints and covered with linen bandages that had been soaked in some foul-smelling stuff which moulded them to his leg.

Athelstan approached the bed, his face grave. 'You wished to see me, Ewan. Are you still in pain?'

'I feel it a little now and then, my lord.' The boy's eyes met his urgently. 'Father Jonathan says that I will walk again. Is it so, sir? He is not just saying it to comfort me?'

'I believe my work has been successful. You may have a slight limp, but the bones will knit and you will certainly walk again in time.'

'God bless you!' Ewan seized his hand and kissed it. 'When– When shall I walk, my lord?'

'Soon! You must be patient for a while.' Athelstan laughed as he removed his hand from the boy's eager grasp. 'Here is Mistress Perdita come to visit you.' He beckoned to her. 'Come, lady, say something to Ewan.'

'Are you feeling better?' she asked, approaching the bed diffidently. 'I hope you are not in too much pain?'

'Oh no,' he assured her cheerfully. 'I was in more pain before I came here, and I don't mind that. I shall walk again, and help my father on the land as I did until the accident. It is a miracle, Mistress Perdita. Except that it was the Earl and not God who cured me.'

'It has been done with God's help,' said Father Jonathan, with a hint of reproof. 'Never forget that all we do is through Him.'

'Listen to the priest, Ewan,' said Athelstan, a slight smile curving his lips. 'I would not have you led astray. Some might take your words as blasphemy. Come, Perdita, we shall leave him to rest now.'

She felt his hand on her arm, propelling her from the room. Outside, she looked up at him curiously. 'Is it because of your healing powers that some say you are in league with the Devil?'

'That – and other things.' He frowned at her as if he would prevent her from dis-

186

covering more, then he sighed. 'Do you believe that what I have done is the Devil's work?'

'Oh no, my lord! How can it be wrong to help others?'

'There are those who condemn me for my work, Perdita. They believe that my experiments go beyond what is natural and must therefore be evil.' He smiled oddly. 'Some say that I have sold my soul to Satan in return for a secret beyond price.'

'And have you, my lord?'

His laughter was deep and infectious, making her laugh with him. 'Oh, Perdita, what a witch you are! Do you not know that men would kill for the answer to that question you ask so innocently? They believe I have learned to turn base metals into gold – that I am an alchemist.'

'Such a secret would be dangerous indeed.'

'How wise you are, my little one. If I knew the secret, it would be one I must carry to my grave. Such knowledge could never be allowed to fall into the wrong hands.'

'Then pray do not tell me the answer, my lord. I have no wish to know it.'

'But think what it could bring you, Perdita,' he said, his eyes gleaming. 'You would have unlimited wealth – and the power that goes with such riches.'

'I do not wish for either!' she cried indignantly. 'If this is meant to test me, you waste your breath, sir.'

'Indeed, I know it,' he said, half ruefully. 'You have made it plain I cannot buy your favours, so what would you have of me, Perdita?'

'You mock me, my lord?'

'No, I am curious. What do you most desire of life, lady? What would make you truly happy?'

'I – I am not certain.' Her brow creased. 'Perhaps to know who and what I am, and yet...'

'And yet?' he asked softly. 'Why are you afraid? I do not frighten you still?'

'No...' She blushed beneath his intent look. She was not afraid of him, only of herself. 'I – I think I could be content if you were my friend. I am frightened of life outside the castle. Out there is only darkness...'

'Then you need have no fear; I have no intention of casting you out.' He studied her face thoughtfully. 'So you would have my friendship? You intrigue me, Perdita. I would swear there is passion in you, but you keep me at bay. Why? I do not think you prudish.'

'Nor am I a wanton!'

'No?' he chuckled at her outraged face. 'I believe I could change your mind, my sweet innocent – but nay, I shall not tease you. You shall be my friend since you wish it, Perdita.

There, I have done tormenting you. We must join our guests, or Meredith will come to search for us.'

'Is Mistress Meredith still at the castle?'

The disappointment in her tone was so obvious that his eyes lit with malice. 'My cousin and her family intend to stay for at least a week. Does that not please you?'

'If – it pleases you, my lord.'

'So meek, Perdita? Why do you not say that you wish Lady Eveline would go to the Devil?'

'My lord! I would not be so rude.'

'Would you not?' He sighed heavily. 'Unfortunately, neither would I – what a burden politeness is at times! Perhaps I should let Gervase do his worst? He seems to have no such scruples where our cousin is concerned.'

Her laughter rang out, making him look at her sharply. 'You have a wicked enough tongue, my lord. If you cannot send her packing, I doubt Gervase would fare better.'

'Ah, you grieve me, lady. I had thought you were beginning to revise your opinion of me.'

'You are not quite as stern as I first believed,' she admitted, looking away to avoid his burning gaze. 'But I do not quite trust you, my lord. I think you like to make fools of us all. You let your cousin say what she pleases, because it amuses you. If it did not, you would banish her for once and all.'

'Those innocent eyes see more than some might think.' Athelstan quirked his brow. 'This becomes interesting. Tell me, what do you…' His teasing expression changed as they entered the hall and Meredith came purposefully to meet them. 'Confound it! We shall continue this conversation another time, Perdita.'

'You did not tell me you meant to ride,' Meredith cried accusingly, her eyes flashing as she glanced at Perdita's face. 'I would have come with you had you asked. You know how I love to fly the hawks!'

'It was remiss of me,' he said easily. 'As you have no doubt heard, I chose to give Perdita her first riding-lesson. I do not believe you would have cared for it – I know your taste for a hard gallop. We kept to a gentle canter for most of the morning.'

'Oh, how dull!' Meredith pulled a wry face. 'No, I should not have cared for anything so tame, but, of course, with Perdita you had no choice. Tomorrow you will take me with you, won't you?'

'Yes, if you wish.' His brow furrowed as he saw the flush in Perdita's cheeks. 'But you must not disparage our guest's skill, Meredith. Perdita has a natural flair for it. I have seldom seen anyone with a better balance. It is true that she has much to learn, but she is a born horsewoman.'

Perdita tingled with pleasure as she looked at him and saw that his compliments were sincerely meant. He had not said a word of this to her!

'Indeed?' Meredith glared at him. 'She is a paragon of virtue!'

'Perhaps.' He smiled oddly. 'Excuse me, I must speak with my cousin. Perdita – Gervase is looking for you.'

Perdita nodded, watching as he walked away with Meredith hanging on his arm. For a moment she felt bereft, as if his going had somehow betrayed her, then she scolded herself mentally. She had no right to expect all his attention, yet their conversation just now had seemed to promise so much. Even so, she knew her emotions now were unworthy. She was jealous of the way he smiled at Meredith, and of the promise he had given to take her riding tomorrow. It was ridiculous. She had no hold on him. She wanted only that… What did she want? He had asked her what would make her happy and she had had no answer to give him – no answer she dared give! There was something she wanted, but as yet she was afraid to name it even to herself.

It had made her happy when he praised her efforts to Meredith just now. Thinking about what he had said, she knew within herself that it was true. After her initial nervousness had worn off, she had felt an instinctive confidence in her own ability. She knew that as yet she was unskilled and awkward, but time and practice would bring her a better understanding – and she was swift to learn. She wanted to learn how to ride really well, so that Athelstan would be proud to take her with him...

'Did you enjoy your ride?'

Gervase's question brought her wandering thoughts to heel. She heard the slightly bitter note in his voice and she knew that he, too, was jealous – of Athelstan. What a tangle it all was! She shook her head at him chidingly.

'Yes, I enjoyed it very much. It was my first time on a horse, you know, but your brother says I have a good balance. Why did you not accompany us? You would have liked to see the hawk fly, would you not?'

'I was not asked to accompany you,' Gervase said slowly. 'I've told you before that Athelstan orders and we must obey.'

'But that isn't quite true,' she exclaimed. 'Why are you always so bitter where he is concerned? I believe he allows you far more freedom of choice than you claim.'

'You take his part, Perdita. Has he ensnared you so swiftly? Will you follow blindly where he leads?'

She blushed, avoiding the accusing look in his eyes. 'You are unfair, Gervase. I do not forget your warning – but is it not time to forget the past?'

'I shall never forget! I thought you were different – but it seems all women are faithless harlots.'

'Gervase!' she cried, but he glared at her and turned away, leaving the hall without a backward glance.

She watched him go, her thoughts in turmoil. She was being forced to choose between the two brothers, and it was as though she stood poised on the edge of a precipice. If she were to lose her balance, it might send her crashing to her death? Whom could she trust? Was there no one to guide her to a safe path?

Seeing Father Jonathan enter the hall, she felt a surge of relief. At least there was one person here she could talk to who demanded nothing from her. Smiling, she went to greet him.

Perdita was preparing for bed when she noticed that the brooch Gervase had given her was missing. She had worn it pinned to the shoulder of her gown at supper, and it must have somehow worked loose. She frowned, knowing that its loss would annoy Gervase. He was already displeased with her, and had hardly spoken a word to her at table. Once she had seen him looking at his brother with something akin to hatred in his eyes. It had frightened her, and she felt vaguely guilty at being the cause of further bitterness between them. Had she been at fault in allowing Gervase to believe that she might marry him? Yet to have refused him outright would have seemed so cruel!

Her conscience would not let her rest. She decided that she must go back and look for the brooch, even though the hall would probably be deserted by now. Dressing hastily, she took a lighted taper and left her bedchamber, her soft-slippered feet moving noiselessly over the stone floors. In the great hall some of the torches were still flaring brightly in iron sconces on the wall, but it was completely deserted, Athelstan's men having already sought their beds. Making her way to the dais, she knelt to search for her brooch, finding it at last beneath the rich cloth that overlapped the table. As her fingers closed over it, she heard a loud noise and stiffened. It had sounded like a heavy door being opened, and as she got cautiously to her feet, she was in time to see Athelstan disappearing behind one of the fine tapestries that adorned the walls. Her heart pounded as she stared at it, realising that she had witnessed something that was meant to be private. Whatever went on in the dark hours was Athelstan's secret, and she had no right to be inquisitive – yet she could not help wondering. He had spoken of his work, hinting at strange experiments that were thought by some to be instigated by the Devil. Was it possible that the Earl was Satan's servant?

Suddenly Perdita knew that she must discover the truth for herself. It was important to her – more important than she had so far dared to admit, even in her own mind. She was not sure why Athelstan's slightest look aroused such strange feelings inside her, but she feared the vulnerability of her own heart. Could she but decide what kind of a man he really was, she might be able to control her emotions. If her immortal soul was in danger, she would ask Father Jonathan to help her to fight the terrible temptation she felt whenever the Earl touched her.

Kissing the silver crucifix the priest had given her, Perdita walked slowly towards the spot where Athelstan had disappeared. She was nervous, her knees trembling as she tried not to think about what she was doing. It was wrong to spy on the man who had rescued her from the forest and given her a home. Hesitating uncertainly, she considered returning to her chamber, then her lips firmed to a determined line and she drew back the tapestry, revealing an opening in the wall. It was obvious that the stone had been cunningly contrived to slide back when a hidden lever was operated. Had she not seen Athelstan enter, she could never have discovered the secret chamber for herself. Just as clear to her was his conviction that he was unobserved, for he had not bothered to close the entrance behind him. Perhaps he felt safe in the knowledge that none of his men would dare to follow him?

Taking a firmer grip on her chamber-stick, Perdita stepped inside the opening. A narrow stair spiralled downwards, just as she had expected. It was very dark and cold, and she shivered as the chill struck into her. At the bottom of the steps was a long passage; ahead of her was only darkness – a darkness that seemed to enfold her, reminding her of the dreams that haunted her sleep. She wanted to run away, to hide in the safety of her own chamber and forget this madness. Yet she could not turn back now. She was drawn on by something stronger than her own will; like a moth to the flame of a candle, she was caught by the fascination of Athelstan's mystic charm. She had to know what he did down here, even if she risked discovery and his anger.

Approaching the end of the passage, Perdita could see a glimmer of light. Hastily she blew out her own taper, feeling her way forward cautiously. All at once the passage opened out into a huge cavern. In the middle was a glowing furnace, over which was set a huge black cauldron. An acrid smell filled the air, causing her to choke and hold a kerchief to her lips. Athelstan was standing with his back to her; and as she watched, he filled a heavy ladle from the pot and poured a white-hot liquid into a small container. He seemed to concentrate on the contents for several minutes, then he removed the thick leather gauntlets he was wearing and turned towards her.

'Why don't you come in, Perdita?' he asked, his icy tones making her quake with fear.

'How– How did you know it was me?' She moved slowly forward and raised her eyes fearfully to meet his. In the red glow of the furnace, he had the appearance of a demon standing at the mouth of Hell, his eyes seeming to burn like fire. For a moment she felt faint, her limbs turning to water as she gazed into his angry face. 'I am sorry, my lord. I should not have followed you.'

'No, you should not.' He stared at her coldly. 'Why did you, Perdita? You said you had no wish to learn my secrets, but were you lying? Have you been deceiving me all this time? Was the charade in the forest a plot so that you could come here to spy on me?'

'Oh no!' she cried, holding out her hand as she moved nearer, wanting to convince him. 'I truly have no wish to know your secrets, my lord.'

'Then why did you follow me?' His eyes seemed to pierce her, and her head swam.

'I was looking for my brooch, and when I saw you, I wanted to know … what manner of man you really are,' she faltered, knowing that her impudence could bring down his wrath on her at any moment.

'You wanted to discover whether I am truly a servant of the Devil, is that not so?' His eyes gleamed with sudden laughter. 'At least you have courage – many men would not dare to venture here! Well, now that you have seen my secret place, what do you think of me, Perdita? Does this seem like the pit of Hell to you?'

'I – I do not know, my lord.' Her tongue moved over dry lips and she took a half step backwards. 'I shall go now…'

He moved swiftly towards her, grasping her wrist. 'No, you shall not go yet, sweet innocent. You have come where few others dare. Now you shall see for yourself what I would show to no one else. Look about you, lady; discover the secrets others would learn if they had your courage.'

His fingers were pressing cruelly into her flesh as he dragged her deeper into the cavern. He seized a torch, holding it aloft so that she could see more clearly.

'Let me go, my lord! I beg you, do not punish me for my foolishness. Pardon me and let me go.'

'No!' he said angrily. 'You are here, and you shall see. Then, perhaps, I shall set you free.'

Knowing there was no escape for her, Perdita let her eyes travel around the huge chamber. The walls were of uneven stone, as if they had been clawed out of the earth by some ancient force; but everywhere she looked there was evidence of the work that went on here. There were strange charts with drawings of the moon and the stars; others of the sea with mythical beasts and demon-like creatures; yellowed scrolls in some unknown script that seemed to her to have an evil significance, and mysterious instruments that she found somehow threatening.

'What are all these things, my lord? I do not understand them.'

'These writings are ancient Arabic teachings – many of them cures for the ills that afflict us.' He smiled wryly as he saw the doubt in her eyes, and pointed to various instruments. 'This is an astrolabe – and this a quadrant. This sphere is a device for plotting the celestial longtitude and latitude. They are instruments of *scientia*, Perdita. Men of learning all over the world use them to discover the secrets of the sky, and to forecast the destiny of mankind – if they can. Not one of them is a sinister device to conjure up the Devil.'

'Oh…' She drew a deep breath. 'They seem so strange to me, I am but a foolish woman. What do you keep in all these jars?'

'Powders, crystals, horn, herbs – various ingredients I need for my work. No, do not look inside, Perdita. Some have contents that might distress you.'

She trembled, drawing back her hand from the lid of a stone jar. Her eyes fell on a chart depicting the human body, but drawn in such a way that it seemed to be opened to her gaze; she looked away quickly, not wanting to see such things. She knew that his work must entail much that would seem unpleasant if she allowed her thoughts to dwell on it, yet she had seen the welcome results of some of that work: Ewan's mangled limbs were whole again because of it. So what right did she have to question what he did? Even so, she was a woman of her time, and she found it hard to accept all that he had shown her. She did not believe that he himself was evil, but was he dabbling in things that were better left undone? Was not what he did an offence against both God and man?

Athelstan sensed her doubts, and was angered by them. What right had she to question him? He had tried to make allowances for her innocence, explaining more than he would consider doing for anyone else. And still she dared to reproach him with her eyes!

She was the same as all the others – blind, ignorant fools who feared what they did not understand! Those who wanted to interfere with his work did not know of all the wondrous things he had discovered, for in their stupidity they would condemn him as a sorcerer. He had been mad to hope that at last he had found a woman with whom he could share his dreams. He should tell her who she was and send her back to her home – but there was something about her that stirred his senses. She was lovely, but it was more than mere beauty...

Her eyes were liquid pools that drew him down into a whirling current of desire, heating his blood to fever point. She seemed to stand in judgment on him, like an accusing goddess at the gates of Paradise, her lips soft and inviting even as she cast him back down to Hades. His desire for her was robbing him of rational thought, sweeping before it both anger and common sense. He wanted her more than he had ever wanted any other woman – and he wanted her now! It had amused him to play a waiting game, but she had followed him – she had spied on him. She dared to show her doubts plainly where another woman would simper and hide behind smiles. She was a temptress and a witch, and she belonged to him. Why should he not ease this fever in his blood and take her to his bed?

He reached out, pulling her roughly against him. His hand tangled in her long hair, forcing her head back as his mouth fastened hungrily on hers, bruising her with the fierceness of his demands. She uttered a feeble protest and was silenced as his lips covered hers, then slid down the white arch of her throat, scorching her flesh. He encountered the silken barrier of her tunic; and pushed it aside impatiently, tearing the fine material in his urgency to taste the sweetness of the soft flesh nestling beneath.

Perdita was near to swooning. She felt herself unable to resist this determined assault on her defences. Tonight his kisses were so different from those he had given her earlier. Then he had seemed to invite her response; now it was as though he meant to take her, whether she would yield or no. The touch of his flicking tongue between her breasts was like the burn of hot irons, making her flinch from him. She was being consumed by flames – the flames of Hell! He was the Devil, who would own her, body and soul, if she did not fight him with all her strength!

Giving a cry of terror, she wrenched herself away from him. He tried to catch her arm, but she avoided his grasp, running from him blindly, knowing that she had to escape before it was too late.

'Come back, Perdita! I'm sorry – I did not mean to frighten you…'

She heard him call, but she would not stop. If she hesitated now, she was lost. He would bend her will to his, making her his slave – and when she no longer pleased him, he would cast her aside, as he had Jania. And she could not bear that!

The passage was long and dark. Without a light, she stumbled unseeingly from side to side, scraping her hands on the rough walls and stumbling over the hem of her gown. She was breathing heavily, fearful that he would come after her – would force her to return with him. She had made him angry, and his patience was at an end. It was her own fault for daring to follow him!

At last she had reached the opening leading back into the hall. Her feet moved faster as a gleam of light appeared ahead. The torches were beginning to splutter in their sockets, but she could still see sufficiently well to make her way swiftly through the hall and up the stairs.

She did not stop running until she was inside her own chamber. Bolting the door behind her, she stood with her back pressed against it, trembling, her breasts heaving as she fought to recover her breath. Then, as the panic gradually subsided, the tears began to flow – slowly at first, and then in deep sobs that shook her whole body. Creeping to the bed, she lay on it, stiff with misery as the realisation came to her.

Whatever the Earl of Athelstan might be, she was caught fast in his net. She had escaped from him tonight but he would not let her go – and the terrible truth was that she was in love with him...

CHAPTER SIX

'You look tired, girl.' Griselda looked at her suspiciously. 'Did you not sleep well, Mistress Perdita?'

'No, not for most of the night.' Perdita avoided her penetrating gaze. 'I – I had bad dreams.'

'Then you should let me give you something to make you sleep, as Gervase does.'

'I thank you, no.' Perdita stood up as the nurse finished her work. 'Please do not be offended, but I would rather not take anything. Now I must hurry or I shall be late for my lessons.'

Leaving her chamber, she walked thoughtfully in the direction of the priest's room. There had been no summons for her to accompany the Earl out riding this morning, and she felt a pang of regret as she realised he must still be angry with her. He had taken Meredith instead, and she was left behind as a mark of his displeasure. It was another bright morning and she was wistful as she remembered how pleasant the outing had been yesterday; then her eyes clouded as she understood the price she must pay for Athelstan's favour. It was too high! She blinked away the sharp, pricking tears as Gervase approached her.

He looked at her awkwardly, a hint of sullenness about his mouth. 'You do not ride with my brother this morning, lady?'

'He has not sent for me. I believe Meredith goes in my stead.'

Gervase's eyes narrowed. 'So you are discarded for her sake! Have you offended Athelstan?'

'You– You should be pleased,' she said defensively, her cheeks hot. 'You warned me to take care, and...'

'And now you have discovered how dangerous he can be?' There was both mockery and amusement in his smile. 'Poor Perdita, but perhaps you have not learned before it is too late?'

'I am no wanton, Gervase, so you need not look at me like that!'

'Then my brother is to be pitied; it is not often his wishes are thwarted. If you are telling me the truth?'

'I have not lain in his bed, nor shall I!' she exclaimed indignantly. 'You are unkind to think so ill of me.'

'But I do not, Perdita,' he said quickly, seizing her hands tightly. 'I love you and I want to wed you. If you were my wife, you would then be safe from Athelstan.'

'Jania was not!' she cried, and then regretted it as she saw his face twist with pain.

'Forgive me, Gervase, I should not have said that. I did not mean to hurt you.'

'What you said was true, but you are not like her. I know that once your promise was given you would not betray me – and Athelstan, too, would know it. Once we were wed, he would leave you in peace. We could go away from here if you wish.'

She shook her head, too choked with emotion to answer him at first. 'How I wish I could be sure that he would leave me in peace, but I think it is already too late. You must not press me, Gervase. I do not know what I feel, and you promised to be patient.'

'And so I shall, but do not keep me waiting too long, or you may find yourself trapped. If Athelstan means to have you, you will not long keep him at bay. Be warned, and choose while you can.'

He left her then and she continued on her way, her thoughts confused and tangled. She knew that she should leave the castle before it was too late, but to do that would break her heart. She was still quiet and thoughtful when she reached the priest's room.

He greeted her cheerfully, and they talked for a while of Ewan's progress before beginning their reading for the morning. Perdita struggled to concentrate, but she stumbled over the words, her mind drifting away as Father Jonathan explained some detail that had puzzled her. At last he called a halt, frowning at her sternly.

'This is not like you, Perdita. Why do you waste my time? If you do not wish to study...'

'Oh, but I do,' she assured him, flushing guiltily. 'Pray forgive me. I did not sleep well last night, and perhaps that is why I am so stupid this morning.'

His bright eyes studied her face, seeing more than she realised. 'Is there something you wish to tell me, daughter? Would it help to unburden your soul by confessing?'

'I have nothing to confess,' she said, looking up at him defensively. 'I have committed no sin.'

'Perhaps not with your body; but the sin is in your mind, is it not?'

She bit her lip, knowing that it was useless to lie. 'I have tried to fight it, Father. I am not a wicked girl, but – but it is very hard to resist, because I...'

'Because you love him?' The priest nodded. 'Do not think I cannot understand your feelings, child. I serve God but I am also a man with all a man's failings. I know how a good soul can be tormented by the sinful urgings of the flesh – but you must fight them with all your strength. Remember that I am here to help you whenever you have need of me.' He smiled at her gently. 'Let us go on with our reading, and later we shall pray together. If you ask him, God will give you the strength to do what is right.'

'Thank you,' she whispered, bending her head over the book because she could not bear to meet his gentle, reprimanding gaze. 'I shall try to obey you.'

Summoning all her will-power, she devoted herself to the Latin prose, pushing the troublesome thoughts to the back of her mind. The priest was right. She must not let herself be haunted by the pictures that would keep crowding into her head despite all her efforts to dismiss them… Athelstan looking down at her with such a hungry desire that her very bones seemed to melt. No, she would not allow him to dominate her thoughts! No doubt he was looking at Meredith in exactly the same way at this very moment.

The morning seemed to drag in spite of her attempt to concentrate on her work. Even while she prayed, Athelstan's face haunted her thoughts, and she knew that he had won. If prayer could not help her, she was lost. Her whole body was on fire with impatience to see him again. How could she fight him when her heart and mind betrayed her? At last the priest set her free, and she hurried out, hoping that the Earl would have returned from his ride.

Reaching the hall, she saw that it was empty save for Lady Eveline and her husband. About to turn away, Perdita was halted by Sir Geoffrey's gentle command. She looked at him curiously. It was the first time he had spoken to her, except to greet her formally at supper, and she had thought him a quiet, unassuming man who lived in the shadow of his dominating wife; but now he was smiling encouragingly at her, beckoning her towards them.

'Do not leave us, Mistress Perdita. It would please us if you would sit beside the fire and talk with us.'

Perdita advanced slowly, glancing uncertainly at Lady Eveline before sitting on the stool he indicated. 'I – I did not wish to intrude, sir.'

'Nor have you.' He gave her a genial smile. 'Such a pretty child. Athelstan is fortunate to have your company! It would please my wife and me if you could visit us one day. We have no children of our own, and when Meredith is married we shall miss her sorely. It would be comforting to have a bright face about the house.'

Seeing Lady Eveline's sour look, Perdita realised that this plan was all her husband's; but the fact that she was willing to accept it made the girl wary. Why were they being kind to her when Lady Eveline had made her dislike plain the other evening? Their threats had not worked, so did they now mean to try bribery? Was it just another plot to lure her from the castle?

'You are generous, Sir Geoffrey,' she said uncertainly. 'I am honoured by your invitation, but I could not consider a visit without first asking Athelstan's permission.'

'I am happy to hear it, Perdita!' The Earl's soft voice startled her and she looked up quickly, her heart pounding. He had come upon them so silently that she had not heard him. 'For the moment, I could not give that permission. You are under my protection and you will stay here with me until I bid you go.' His look was stern and set her limbs trembling.

'Yes, my lord,' she said submissively, not missing the sharp glint of humour in his eyes as he heard her meek tone. It was easy to obey when his commands exactly suited her own wishes! 'I shall do as you say.'

'Would that you were always so obliging,' he said, and was satisfied as the hot colour stained her cheeks. 'I would ever have your obedience, lady. I did not send for you this morning, since I knew that your rest was disturbed by unquiet dreams. However, I am ready to give you further instruction now, if you wish it?'

'Oh yes,' she cried, standing up eagerly. 'Are we going out with the hawks again?'

'No...' He frowned. 'I did not think it pleased you to hunt, so I took Meredith earlier. I had it in mind to show you some of the finer points of the equestrian art. We shall stay within the castle grounds.'

He held out his hand, and she went to him obediently with a tentative smile for those she left behind. Lady Eveline's scowl told her that Athelstan's actions displeased her, but it mattered little. She was to be with him for a while, and he was not angry with her. Nothing else was of any consequence.

Since they were to remain within the courtyard, in full view of Athelstan's men as they went about their daily tasks, there would be no chance to be alone with him. Perdita was not sure whether she was glad or sorry that her virtue was thus safeguarded for the moment; it would certainly keep her from temptation, but now that she was with him again, her blood was already singing in her veins. Last night she had been terrified, perhaps because of the sinister atmosphere of the cavern, but in the daylight, her fears had faded. Having admitted in her heart that she loved him, Perdita knew it was only her pride that stood between them now. She could not bear to be used and then cast aside, but need it be that way? Was there not a chance that he cared for her? Sometimes, when he looked at her, she believed that this feeling between them was more than the casual lust of a man for a woman. If he truly loved her, she would be a fool to refuse all that he was offering. But how could she be certain?

'I am sorry if I frightened you last night,' he said when they had left the hall. 'I was clumsy and impatient. You were right to run from me, Perdita. In my anger I might have destroyed what may yet be a joy to both of us.'

She looked up at him shyly, her heart leaping. 'It was my fault. I had no right to spy on you, or to doubt what you do. I have no understanding of these things, but I should be glad if you would teach me. If I knew why you do what you do, I might not fear your work.'

He smiled, nodding as if her words had struck a chord within him. 'I have a dream, Perdita. I dream of a future where men do not die in terrible pain because no one knows what ails them. I dream of a world where all men are equal, and suffering can be controlled by the dedicated work of a few; where knowledge is not frowned upon, and God is loved, not feared.'

She looked up at him, her eyes shining. 'I think you dream of Paradise, my lord. Can life ever be as you describe it? Will there not always be those who scoff at new discoveries, and fear them?'

'Perhaps. I know that my own work can be only a tiny candle flickering in the darkness of man's ignorance, but I am driven to do what I can.' His mouth twisted. 'You find my dreams foolish, I think?'

'Oh no, my lord,' she whispered, her throat catching with emotion. 'I find them honourable, and I am ashamed of my suspicions. I was wrong to doubt you. I shall not do so again.'

'Will you not?' he asked softly, a light of mischief dancing in his eyes. 'Do not give me a martyr's crown, Perdita – I doubt not that I shall plague you for many a day.'

She did not dare to answer him. Her heart was beating so wildly that she could scarcely breathe. He spoke as if he meant to keep her with him; and she held the precious thought, guarding it jealously within her. She knew that she was very close to surrendering that inner self. He had broken down her defences one by one, and now she could hold out no longer. She was his whenever he chose to reach out and lay his hand upon her. She knew her capitulation was sinful, but somehow that did not seem to matter. In the space of a few minutes he had wiped away her fears, and with them went the need to resist. She loved him, and she must accept whatever fate had in store for her.

If Athelstan guessed what was in her mind, he gave no sign of it as he helped her to mount the palfrey. His hands did not linger about her waist, perhaps because he knew that it was not necessary to tease or taunt her. Indeed, he proved a stern taskmaster as he made her ride up and down the courtyard for over an hour.

'Keep your back straight,' he commanded. 'No! Your hands are wrong. Hold the reins as I showed you. That's better. Do not forget again!'

Over and over he shouted instructions at her until she was ready to scream at him to stop. It seemed that nothing she did was right, and he would be satisfied with nothing less than perfection. Only her pride kept her from giving way to tears, and her expression grew tight with temper. What did it matter if she rode well or not? He was impossible, and she... Her lips thinned in determination. If this was meant to test her, she would die before she allowed him to best her! All at once, laughter bubbled up inside her as she understood the nature of the man she loved. Damn him! She would show him she could take whatever punishment he chose to give her.

At last he called an end to it, coming to help her down with an approving nod. 'I shall make a horsewoman of you yet, Perdita.'

'If I do not die in the attempt!'

He laughed at the disgruntled note in her voice. 'You would not have Meredith outshine you when we go to Court?'

'Are we going to Court?' She looked at him with startled eyes. 'I think you tease, my lord!'

'Should I go, and leave you here to pass your time with your sewing?' His expression was grave. 'Since you do not care to come…'

'You would not leave me behind!' she exclaimed, rising to his bait. 'You are wicked to mock me so.'

'I told you not to give me a martyr's crown.' His soft laughter sent little tingles shooting through her. 'Perhaps I shall take you if you please me…'

'And what must I do to please you, my lord?' She tipped her head provocatively to one side, her eyes challenging him.

'Witch! Be careful, Perdita, you play with fire.'

'Indeed?' She tossed her mane of thick hair. 'Then I must make sure I do not burn myself.'

'Have done, wench, or I'll not answer for my actions.'

She laughed as she saw his frustration, and knew that she had scored a hit. 'We should go in, my lord, or someone will come to look for us.'

'Damn them all! Perdita…' He was left standing as she ran, looking back over her shoulder to send him a mischievous smile. 'You shall be called to account for this, wench.' He followed more slowly, a gleam of satisfaction in his eyes. She was learning fast, and not just how to be an excellent horsewoman! The promise in her eyes had set his pulses racing, and it was only the curious stares of his men that kept him from running after her like a green youth. The years had taught him patience, but not how to control this leaping in his blood. He quickened his pace, his lips curving in a smile of anticipation.

'Ah, I was just coming to look for you.' Meredith's approach took him by surprise. She arched her brow at him. 'You have been neglecting me this visit, my lord. I had hoped that perhaps we might have more time together. I know my brother expects us to make an announcement soon.'

Athelstan frowned, the furious retort that sprang to his lips held back as he acknowledged privately his own part in this. He had considered marriage with Meredith; she was beautiful and of suitable birth, but something inside him had kept him from saying the words that would bind him to her. Yet he had given her some cause to believe an offer would eventually be made. In confusion, he realised that he could not insult her by spurning her too openly – there was no telling what she might do. No, he must go carefully. She was an intelligent woman, who would see for herself which way his thoughts were moving.

'Your brother has had no word from me, Meredith,' he said coldly. 'Nor, I think, have you.'

Her cheeks flushed and she gave him an angry stare. 'It has been understood for some time.'

'Considered, but not spoken.' He looked straight at her. 'I would not have you cut short your visit, Meredith, but you should not expect anything. Do you understand me?'

'It is because of that wanton!' she cried, gasping at the sudden fury in his face. 'Does she share her favours equally between you and Gervase?'

His fingers curled about her wrist, bruising her. 'They are friends. You will not speak of her again like this, or I shall oblige you to leave my house! You would not then be welcome here again.'

The colour drained from her face, and her green eyes darkened with spiteful anger. 'Gervase does not think of her as a friend! He wants to marry her, and she has said that she will consider his offer.'

'If it is true, it is because she does not want to hurt him.' He flung her hand away with a snarl of disgust. 'You cannot understand that, can you? She is worth six of you, Meredith. Be careful that you do not push me too far! I have not forgotten your wanton sister...'

'And I have not forgotten what became of her,' Meredith flashed. 'I wonder what would happen if I told everything I know?'

His lips curled scornfully. 'If you did that, I think you know what would happen to you. I should be a merciless enemy, Meredith.'

'You dare to threaten me?' Her hand flew to her throat as she saw the ice enter his eyes. 'I – I did not mean it, Athelstan. You know I would never betray you.'

'I am sure you would not.' He smiled unpleasantly. 'Come, let us not quarrel over what cannot be undone. The past is buried, so let it lie for both our sakes.'

She looked at him uncertainly, shaken by this new harshness in him. He had never been less than charming to her before – and she knew who to blame for the change. It was that dark-eyed wanton! The scheming vixen who had wormed her way into his house – and, she dared swear, into his bed! Perdita should pay for what she had done. Somehow, there would be a way to be rid of her. And then Athelstan would remember his duty. Smiling at him with a pretence of her old confidence, she took his arm.

'Why should we quarrel?' She pouted at him prettily. 'We have always been friends, have we not?'

Reluctantly, he smiled. He could not blame her for her flash of temper. He knew himself at fault, and accepted this attempt at peace. 'Yes, we are friends, Meredith,' he said, his lips twisting wryly. 'Forgive me if I have hurt you.'

All was not yet lost, she thought with satisfaction. He still cared for her a little and, with that wanton gone, she could persuade him into marriage yet. 'You did but tease me, as is your way, my lord,' she said, smiling at him intimately.

It was then that Perdita saw them enter the hall together. She turned away, the feeling of expectancy dying within her. For a short while she had believed Athelstan truly cared for her, that there was something special between them... But now he was smiling at Meredith, and everyone said he would marry her. Blinking back her foolish tears, she took a step backward, bumping into someone. Swinging round with a swift apology, she found herself looking into Sir Geoffrey's mild blue eyes.

'I beg your pardon, sir,' she said, blushing.

'It was my fault for coming up behind you.' He glanced towards Athelstan and his sister. 'They make an attractive pair, do they not? It is my guess that they will marry in the spring.'

'Oh...' Perdita swallowed with difficulty. 'Is it certain that they intend to wed?'

'It has been understood for some time. He will not break his word to her, Mistress Perdita.'

'No, I suppose he could not.' She clasped her shaking hands behind her. 'Excuse me, sir. I – I must see if I can find Gervase. He is teaching me to play the harp.' She walked calmly from the hall, her head high. What a fool she had been just now in the courtyard – and how Athelstan must have laughed at her!

Perdita tossed restlessly in her bed as the nightmare deepened. She was running through the forest, fleeing from the man whose face she could not see. He was coming after her, and when he caught her he would drag her back to face the horror that had caused her wild flight.

'No, don't touch me!' she moaned, her head turning from side to side on the pillow. 'I shall not submit to you no matter how much you beat me. Murderer! I saw... Ahhh!'

She woke suddenly, screaming, her eyes staring wildly in the darkness, terrified by the glimpse behind the curtain in her mind the dream had given her. Sitting up, she clenched her knees, shuddering as the nightmare refused to leave her, feeling again the horror she had known as she witnessed a murder. The woman she had called her mother had been mercilessly robbed of life as she herself watched hidden in a closet near by.

'No...' she cried, fear sweeping through her. 'No, it cannot be true! It cannot...'

At that moment her door opened and Athelstan came in, carrying a lighted taper. He had heard her cry and now he saw the stark terror in her face. Setting down his chamber-stick, he approached and sat down on the edge of the bed. He looked at her in silence before reaching out to draw her gently into his arms, holding her pressed against him and rocking her as she wept.

'Hush, my sweet,' he whispered, his lips brushing the hairline at her brow. 'What has upset you so – was it the old dream?' He held her back to smile at her tenderly, smoothing the damp hair from her cheeks. 'You are safe now. Nothing can harm you while I am here.'

'It was the same dream,' she whispered chokily, 'and yet it was not. I saw ... something that was so horrible.' She looked up at him pleadingly. 'It cannot be true, my lord. Surely it was only a part of the nightmare?'

'What did you see, Perdita?' he asked, frowning. 'Can you not tell me?'

She shuddered, closing her eyes as though to shut out the memory of her dream. 'I – I saw a woman being murdered. A woman who was dear to me. The room was lit only by a small candle, and I was hidden in a dressing closet, watching through a crack in the wooden panelling. I saw someone come in and place a pillow over her face. She struggled for a while, but she was weak from illness and it was soon over. I – I tried to cry out and stop him, but I could not move.' She gazed up at him desperately. 'Oh, why did I not do something to stop him? Why did I let him kill her?'

'It was but a dream, Perdita. Dreams are often so. It could not have happened thus.' He touched her cheek, making her shiver. 'You would not have watched and done nothing. I know you too well to believe that.'

She gave him a watery smile. 'Was it just a dream?'

'Yes, I am sure of it. A part of the nightmare, but only that. Try to forget it. I shall leave you to sleep now.' He moved as if to depart, but she caught his hand, holding it tightly. 'Do you want me to stay?'

'Yes...' She gave him a shy smile. 'If you want to.'

'If I want to stay with you, Perdita – surely you know the answer?' He bent his head to touch his lips to hers, so softly that it made her sigh for more. His hand smoothed her cheek, tracing the slender line of her throat, to move caressingly downward to the firm mound of her breast. 'How much I want to lie with you, sweet temptress!'

She felt a spasm of desire as his hand cupped her breast, his fingers kneading the rosy nipple, and her lips parted invitingly for the kiss that followed. This time his mouth searched hers, demanding an answering response. Suddenly the barriers inside her gave way before the surging tide of her longing for him. She slid her arms up round his neck, pressing herself against him with mounting urgency. Her fingers dug into his shoulder, bringing him down with her as she lay back against the pillow, abandoning all restraint. Her breasts rose and fell as her breath came faster, and she looked up at him, her eyes wide and slightly scared.

'Do as you will with me, my lord,' she whispered. 'I shall not resist you.'

She heard him groan and felt the deep shudder that went through him as he gathered her against him. His kisses were soft and tender, drawing a wild response from her. She clung to him almost desperately, arching her body to meet his. It no longer mattered to her that what she did was sinful. Her pride had been banished to a forgotten corner of her mind. Now all that was important was the clamouring of her body for his; the heady sensation that swept her on to such sweet madness. The caress of his searching hands sent spasms of sharp desire snaking through her, making her body jerk as she tried to hold back the little cries that came unbidden from deep within her.

'Oh, Perdita, my love,' he murmured, his body trembling with the need to possess her completely. 'I want so much to make you mine.'

'I am yours, my lord.'

'Are you sure? You are so lovely...'

'I want to belong to you.'

His eyes glowed with hot desire; for a long moment he looked down into her innocent face, and then a strangely tender expression twisted his lips to a rueful smile. 'You shall belong to me, Perdita, but I cannot take you like this. I shall not snatch greedily like a thoughtless child. You deserve more – much more.'

She felt an aching loss as he left her. What had she done wrong? 'Did I not please you, my lord?' she whispered.

'Oh yes, you please me – more than you can guess,' he said, tracing the line of her cheek with one finger. 'Do not tempt me to stay; this costs me dearly as it is. Be patient, my Perdita. Soon you will know what I plan for you. Sleep now, and let your dreams be of nights to come, when we are together.'

She sighed as he went quietly from the room. The change in him was puzzling. He had been determinedly battering her defences almost from the first, yet now that she was willing to surrender to him, he had refused to take all that she offered. What a strange, wilful man he was, she thought, her eyelids fluttering as she turned her face to the pillow, inhaling the masculine scent that still lingered tantalisingly beside her. She had not wanted him to leave her, even though he had promised that there would be other nights. She did not understand what he planned, but it did not matter. She was his now, and she would be waiting whenever he chose to come to her...

'Wake up, girl! Will you lie abed all day?' Perdita stirred as she felt Griselda's hand shaking her shoulder. 'The master is asking for you – you must get up.'

Perdita opened her eyes, smiling sleepily as she looked at the old woman. 'I have not slept as well as this since I came to the castle.'

'Ay, I know it.' Griselda stared at her suspiciously. 'What have you been about, girl? I hope you have not been foolish!'

A faint flush stained Perdita's cheeks. 'I have done nothing that shames me!'

''Tis none of my business,' Griselda muttered crossly. 'I warned you once. If you choose to ignore my words, I am not responsible.' She sniffed, holding out a silken wrap as the girl got out of bed. 'Come, let me help you to dress. The master is impatient. I have not seen him act in this way since he was a lad!'

Perdita smiled to herself, feeling a surge of happiness. If Athelstan was impatient to see her, he could not be more impatient for their meeting than she! She wanted to see that look in his eyes once more and tell herself that she had not been dreaming. A slight sound made her turn her head to see the door opening. She held her breath, half expecting it to be her lover, but her smile faded as Gervase entered. He stood on the threshold, his face cold and sullen.

'Leave us, Griselda. I want to talk to Perdita alone.'

'No, do not go,' Perdita said quickly, not wanting to risk a quarrel with him. 'I cannot talk to you now, Gervase. I must hurry. Athelstan has sent for me.'

Gervase came towards her. Pushing Griselda aside, he pulled Perdita to her feet, gripping her shoulders cruelly. His face was tight with anger as he gazed down at her and saw the sudden flash of alarm in her eyes.

'Send her away! I want to speak with you in private.'

Sensing his urgency, she looked awkwardly at Griselda. 'You had better go, but come back in a moment or two.'

Griselda shuffled from the room, muttering beneath her breath. 'There'll be trouble ere this day is out... Mark my words, it will happen again...'

'Well?' Perdita's head went up proudly as she met the youth's accusing eyes. 'What is so urgent that you must speak to me at once?'

His fingers bit deeply through the fine material. 'I saw Athelstan leaving your room late last night. Can you deny that he had been with you?'

She felt the hot colour in her cheeks and dropped her eyes. 'I do not deny that he was with me...'

'You wanton bitch! You swore to me that you would not lie with him.'

She brought her head up sharply. 'It was not as you think...' Her words trailed into extinction as she met his glaring condemnation, and knew that it was by Athelstan's choice and not hers that she was still innocent. 'Do not look at me like that, Gervase! I made you no promises.'

'You promised to consider my offer, and all this time you were scheming to get Athelstan into your bed. How clever you have been! Keeping him at bay until he is so mad for you that he...'

'It was not like that,' she choked. 'N-Nothing happened between us. I did not want it to be this way, but I cannot help the way he makes me feel.'

'You would not lie to me?' He stared at her wildly. 'Then it is not too late. I shall save you from yourself, even if you hate me for it!' He laughed oddly and released her, turning to walk away.

She stared after him as he reached the door. 'Where are you going?'

He glanced back at her, his face tight and cold. 'To do what I should have done days ago.'

'Gervase, come back. This is nonsense! Tell me what you intend to do.'

She followed him to the door, calling his name, but he refused to stop or even look back at her. Realising she could hardly go after him in her wrap, she looked impatiently for Griselda, signalling to her to hurry as she emerged from a door further down the passage.

'Help me quickly! I must go to Athelstan before Gervase can tell him some foolish story he has in mind. He thinks I will marry him, but I have never said so.'

'Hurry, hurry… Make up your mind, girl! I have other work to do. I cannot be always at your beck and call.'

'I am sorry, Griselda. I did not want to send you away just now.'

'You are to blame. You made my poor boy fall in love with you. And you knew what he had suffered before on account of that Jania. It was a cruel thing to do if you do not care for him.' Griselda's tone was harsh and her hands were rough as she began to comb the girl's hair. 'You have hurt him by your carelessness.'

'Oh, I know I am to blame in part,' Perdita said miserably. 'Gervase is my friend. I did not want to hurt him. I know I should have told him I could never marry him when he first asked me, but it would have seemed so cruel.'

'Not as cruel as allowing my brother to believe you might have him.' Athelstan's swift arrival surprised them both. Giving a cry of protest, Perdita swung round to face him, trembling as she saw the glitter of anger in his eyes. 'I was impatient to see you, and I met Gervase on my way here. He has told me you have promised to wed him. I warned you not to make him fall in love with you, Perdita. He will never forgive you for this.'

'But I did not try to engage his affections,' she said, rising to her feet. 'Please, you must listen to me...'

'Leave us, woman!' Athelstan jerked his head at Griselda. 'We would be alone.'

'Come, go – always do this, do that,' she grumbled, looking at him sourly. 'There's no peace for a body in this accursed house...'

'Be silent, or I shall have you beaten,' he said sharply. 'Your place is to serve your mistress, not to question her orders.'

'Oh, please do not be angry with her,' Perdita cried. 'It is I who am at fault.'

He came to her then, ignoring Griselda who was shuffling from the room. 'I have told Gervase that he cannot have you. You are mine by right, and I shall not give you up to him or to any other man.'

'You know I am yours, my lord. Surely you cannot doubt it after last night? I would not have it any other way. If I have hurt Gervase

I am sorry for it, but it was not my intention.'

'It is too late for regrets now,' he said curtly. 'I warned you to be careful. Well, you have made an enemy of him and we must both live with it. It is no longer important. You will be my wife, or go to the nunnery and plague neither of us again. Choose now, for I shall not ask again.'

His wife! He was saying that he meant to have her as his wife! She was stunned, hardly able to credit his words. She had thought that he intended to make her his mistress. She saw his impatience, and her heart thundered in her breast as she answered quietly, 'I have made my choice, my lord. You knew that last night.'

'Then it is settled.' His eyes were colder than she had ever seen them. Why did he look at her like that? It was not the look of a man in love. 'I shall expect duty and obedience from my wife, Perdita. If you give any other man cause to hope for your favours, I shall kill you. In my wife I shall not tolerate any loose behaviour.'

Why was he saying such things to her? Surely he must know that she belonged to him body and soul? She was white-faced as she gazed at him. 'Would you not have more of me, my lord? Is duty all you require of the woman you would honour with your name?' Why did he wish to marry her if that were all? Was it simply to thwart his brother? Surely not!

'What more would you give me?' He studied her pale features in silence, his expression stern. 'Are you offering me your love, Perdita? Is that what you would have me believe? How can I be sure of you – when you lied to Gervase?'

'It is unfair of you to doubt me,' said Perdita. 'How could I have behaved otherwise than I have? I am a stranger in your home, knowing little of either you or Gervase – nor even my own name...' Her voice cracked a little, but she recovered and faced him straightly. 'I have been forced to walk a precipice – I was not betrothed to your brother, I made him no promises. I sought only a kinder way to refuse his offer.'

'You are right,' he answered at last, sighing. 'The damage was done a long time ago. You have been thrust into a precarious situation that was not of your making. Forgive me, I have been harsh with you.'

'You were angry – and perhaps I deserved your reprimand.'

'No, you did not.' He smiled slightly. 'Give me the comb, and sit down, Perdita. I shall finish dressing your hair. Today you will wear it loose for me. I like to see it like that – as it was spreading on your pillow last night.'

She obeyed him shyly, trembling as she

felt the touch of his hands on her hair. 'You should call Griselda, my lord. It is not fitting that you do this for me.'

'I shall decide what is fitting for my future bride,' he said, easing the comb gently through the tangles. 'There, I have done. Now you may send for your woman, and I shall wait for you below. Do not keep me waiting too long, or I may send Beelzebub to fetch you! After all, it was he who first caught you for me.'

She laughed, glancing up at him before he left the room, and receiving a mocking smile. She had already begun to dress herself when Griselda returned, still grumbling. The girl's happiness was such that she ran to the old woman, hugging her in a burst of excitement.

'Will you not wish me happy, Griselda? I am to be wed to Lord Athelstan.'

The nurse looked startled, then gave a harsh cackle. 'So you have bewitched him with those innocent eyes! 'Tis a miracle, no less. And what will Mistress Meredith say when she hears, I wonder?'

Perdita's head went up. 'I do not care what she or Lady Eveline may say. My lord has chosen to wed me, not Meredith.'

'And I thank God for it.' Griselda's words brought a look of surprise to Perdita's face, making the old woman laugh again. 'If there's to be a mistress here, at last, it is better that it should be you than her.'

'Then you have forgiven me for upsetting Gervase?'

Griselda sniffed. 'It was she who cut him to the heart, not you. He is angry now, but the pain will pass in time. It was the other one who committed an unforgivable sin.'

'Jania.' Perdita frowned. 'How can I blame her for loving Athelstan – when I have found it impossible to resist him?'

'She loved the wealth he could give her, not the man.' Griselda scowled. 'Go to him, mistress – or he'll have me beaten as he threatened!'

Perdita nodded, smiling as she left. Her feet seemed hardly to touch the ground as she hurried to meet her lord, mindful of his threat to send the dog to fetch her if she tarried. As she reached the head of the stair, her heart missed a beat as she saw the activity going on. Servants were scurrying about, and Athelstan was deep in conversation with Balsadare and Sir Geoffrey. He did not even turn his head as she approached. Glancing at his stern profile, she knew at once that something was seriously wrong. Her heart jerked painfully and she felt a stab of fear. What had happened to make them all look so concerned?

'You should refuse to go, my lord,' Balsadare was saying as he came up to them. 'Make your stand here at the castle, where you can defend yourself. I know the men will support you to the last.'

'Would you have me play the coward, cowering in fright behind these walls?' Athelstan's tone was chiding. 'No, my friend, I shall answer the charges against me...' He became aware of Perdita standing silently at his side, and turned to smile down at her. 'I fear we must postpone our wedding, my lady. The King has summoned me to Court, and I must attend him with all speed.'

'You will take me with you?' She laid her hand urgently on his arm. 'You would not go, and leave me here?'

'You would be safer here, Perdita. This is not at all as I planned it. I am summoned to face a charge of high treason.'

'But you were to be given a month to pay the fine,' she said, her eyes anxious. 'Why this summons now?'

'It seems that fresh charges have been laid against me.'

'If you are in danger, I demand my right to be at your side. If you will not take me with you, I shall follow you.'

'Does it mean so much to you?' he asked softly as their eyes met and held. 'Then I shall not deny you, my love. We shall face our destiny together.' He took her hand and kissed it, holding it firmly as he turned to look at his cousin's husband. 'I would have your promise that you will guard and protect this lady if anything should happen to separate us. Will you so swear, Sir Geoffrey?'

'You know you have my loyalty, Athelstan. I swear to abide by this trust you place in me.'

'Then I thank you.' His fingers clasped Perdita's so tightly that she almost winced. 'Now, Balsadare, my most constant friend, swear always to protect this lady who has honoured me by consenting to be my wife.'

Balsadare went down on one knee before her, his face serious as he lifted his head to look her straight in the eyes. 'Before God, I swear that my life shall be spent in protecting yours, my lady.'

'Thank you,' she whispered, her eyes misting with emotion. 'But your first loyalty must be to my lord – for without him, my life means nothing.'

'How touching!' Meredith's scornful tones brought all eyes to her. She stood watching at a distance, her mouth twisted with anger. 'So I am to wish you happy, Athelstan? So be it. I give you my blessing freely. May you and your bride receive all that you so richly deserve.'

Athelstan's eyes were flinty as he bowed his head to acknowledge her. 'I thank you for your – generosity – Meredith,' he said. 'I know just how sincerely it is meant.'

She flushed, giving him a bitter look. 'When shall I have the pleasure of seeing

236

you wed?'

'Perhaps at Court, if you still intend to accompany us.'

'I see no reason to change my mind.' Her emerald eyes fixed on Perdita with a touch of spite. 'You will need new clothes if you are to appear at Court. I shall be happy to lend you anything you may need.'

'You are generous, Meredith, but I am well provided for.'

'Perdita will have whatever she desires,' Athelstan said harshly. 'I have ordered all that is necessary. A score of sewing women have been working for a week to prepare, and the clothes await us in London. My wife will have no need of borrowed finery.'

Sensing his anger at Meredith's effrontery, Perdita tugged at his sleeve. 'When arc wc to leave, my lord?'

'Within the hour – two at the most. I would be well on our way before nightfall. Go to your chamber, Perdita, and rest while you can. It will be a long and tiring journey.'

'Is Griselda to come with us?'

'No. She is too old to travel so far. We shall engage the services of a suitable woman from the village.'

'Mistress Perdita is welcome to share my tiring-woman,' said Meredith. 'You will have more chance of securing a suitable dresser in London. These village women are clumsy fools! Remember that it will be your wife's first appearance at Court. You would not have her shamed by her woman's lack of skill?'

Athelstan frowned as if he meant to refuse, but Perdita pressed his arm. 'I thank you for your offer, Meredith. I shall accept it gratefully until alternative arrangements can be made.'

'Perhaps it is for the best,' Athelstan agreed reluctantly, 'since we have little time to waste. Your offer is accepted, Meredith. I thank you for it.'

He turned away to confer with Sir Geoffrey, and Perdita left him, realising that for the moment she was only in the way. There were plans to be made, and many arrangements for the journey. All the servants were hurriedly packing household items that their master and his companions would need for the journey. Accommodation on the way could not be relied upon to provide the necessary comfort, and it was the habit of all important men to travel with a large accompaniment of servants, baggage and men-at-arms.

Meredith joined her as she made her way upstairs, and Perdita held her breath, half expecting a bitter attack from her rival. Instead, Meredith spoke only of the journey and the reception they might receive at Court.

'My brother will stand by Athelstan at the

hearing,' she said. 'He is our kinsman – and besides, the King would have us all arraigned as traitors if he could! He wants all power for himself, and his nobles are to be made merely puppets.'

Perdita nodded, feeling anxious. 'I – I have heard something of this from others. You don't think Athelstan will be found guilty, do you?'

Meredith laughed shrilly. 'Are you frightened that he may not be able to marry you after all? He will demand his right to wager of battle, and he will win. There is no one who can defeat the Earl of Athelstan in hand-to-hand combat.'

'But supposing the King will not grant his right to trial by combat?'

'He would not dare to refuse!' Meredith sneered at her. 'Do you not know anything? Already the barons are restless at Richard's tyranny. It needs only a spark from the tinder to start a rebellion in England.'

'You mean there will be civil war?' Perdita's cheeks paled as she remembered the stranger she had seen on her first day at the castle. Could this new charge of treason be in some way connected with that man's visit? Was it possible that Athelstan was actually engaged in plotting to bring about the downfall of the King? If so, he would be in grave danger at Court.

'If Richard goes too far, the people will

rise against him,' Meredith said with some satisfaction. 'Now that John of Gaunt is dead, the King has seized his lands despite his promise that they should pass to his son. If Hereford comes back to claim his inheritance, think you Athelstan will stand quietly by? They are friends who have sworn to be faithful one to the other.'

'I – I see...' Perdita licked her dry lips. 'Thank you for telling me this, Meredith.'

A scornful smile curved her lips. 'If you are to be his wife, it is right that you should understand the situation. You may be a widow sooner than you think.' Her eyes glinted. 'I must leave you for the moment, but here comes Gervase. I think he would speak with you.'

Perdita sighed as Meredith departed with a spiteful glance over her shoulder. It was obvious that they would never be friends, and no doubt she would lose no opportunity to prick her with sharp darts whenever she had the chance. Yet they were forced to travel together, and she could do nothing but accept it. Seeing Gervase bearing down on her, she knew that he, too, had only harsh words for her.

'Are you coming to Court with us, Gervase?' she asked, smiling at him tentatively. 'You know that we are to leave at once?'

'I have heard,' he said, his eyes sullen. 'But I have no wish to come. Besides, someone must stay here in case an attack is made against the castle.'

'Do you think that the situation is so serious?' she asked, feeling a pang of fear.

'Who knows?' He shrugged carelessly. 'My brother has many enemies, and it may be that one of them will take the chance to strike at him while he is at risk. He will leave the castle well defended, for without it half his power would be gone.'

She looked at him uncertainly. 'Are you still angry with me? You must know that I never meant to hurt you, Gervase.'

'You have made your choice,' he told her. 'Now you must accept the consequences.'

'Yet could we not still be friends?'

'Perhaps.' His eyes seemed to look through her. 'I have duties to attend to, Perdita. When you return, we shall talk again.'

He nodded curtly and walked away, leaving her to stare after him sadly. He was so much like Athelstan in so many ways that she could not bear to be at odds with him; he had been her first friend when she discovered that she had forgotten her name, and she was sorry that they must part in anger. However, it seemed that there was no help for it. She pushed the niggling anxiety away as she hurried towards her room. There would be things she must take with her – and she wanted to say goodbye to Griselda.

CHAPTER SEVEN

'Look, Perdita, yonder lies the Abbey of Athelone.' The Earl pointed to an ancient grey stone building nestling in the lee of a hill. 'If ever you should need sanctuary, the Abbess will take you in.'

Perdita felt chilled, her heart filled with fear as she looked at her lord's serious face. Why was he taking all these precautions for her safety? Surely he would not do so if he were as confident of victory as Meredith seemed to think? She knew that she must hide her anxiety on his behalf, however, for they had come scarcely twenty miles and if she wavered, he would send her back to the safety of the castle. Smiling, she nodded acknowledgment of his advice.

'I shall remember, if I have cause, my lord.' She tilted her head at him provocatively. 'But I do not think I shall have cause to seek out the good lady. Unless you mean to cast me out when you are tired of my wifely nagging?'

Athelstan's eyes gleamed with appreciation. 'Do you mean to be a scold, Perdita? Remind me to buy a stout stick to beat you with! Since I am forewarned, it would be as well to be prepared.'

She laughed, feeling a surge of renewed confidence as she looked at him. This was a man of great wit as well as wiry strength. No matter how cunningly his enemies worked against him, he would triumph; but because he cared for her, he had tried to cover all eventualities. The knowledge of his solicitude warmed her inwardly, helping to ease the pain of aching limbs. They had travelled such a short distance, but already she was feeling the strain. She glanced across at Meredith, envying the ease with which she rode. A sharp glance from those bright green eyes made her straighten her back. If it killed her, she would let no one guess how much she was suffering!

'Are you tired, Perdita?' Athelstan's gaze fell on her proud face. 'In another hour or so we shall stop to rest the horses and ourselves.'

'Pray do not break your journey on my account, my lord. I know you wish to reach Nottingham before nightfall.'

'And so we shall,' he said, smiling at her stubborn look. 'But have you no pity for our horses? They must be given a short rest, even if we do not need it.'

She made no reply, knowing that even in his concern he must always taunt and tease her. It was the nature of the man she loved, and she would not change him if she could.

She was filled with pride to be riding at his side, her doubts subdued or forgotten altogether. Now that she had accepted her love for this man, it was growing rapidly. Somehow she understood that this was her destiny. All that had gone before was a part of God's plan for her. She would be Athelstan's wife, his companion for life, sharing all that Fate held in store for them, whether it be happiness or sorrow. It did not matter that she had forgotten her own name, for she could not bear a prouder one than that he would bestow on her.

She smiled across at him, and suddenly her tiredness fell away. She was aware of the cold and the biting wind, but also of bird-song and the beauty of rolling hills, winter brown fields and starkly bare trees. No matter what happened at Court, she would always have this memory of happiness to hold inside her...

Dusk was falling as they neared the city gates, and Perdita sighed with relief. Athelstan's servants had gone on ahead to prepare his town house for their arrival, and she would be glad to sleep in a comfortable bed at last. These past few days had been a testing time: forced to ride mile after mile for what seemed an endless journey, she had learned to control her mount out of sheer necessity, knowing that she could no longer rely on her lord to watch out for her constantly. At night she was so weary that she ached in every limb, her flesh bruised and painful from the unaccustomed motion, but she had kept her misery to herself, refusing to let anyone see how hard it was for her merely to stay in the saddle. She might not yet have the studied grace of an accomplished horsewoman like Meredith, but she had given her lord no cause to be ashamed of her.

The journey had taken several days, and their accommodation had varied from the none too clean inn bed-chamber she had shared with both Meredith and Lady Eveline to a tiny, bare cell in a nunnery that had been blessedly hers alone.

Lady Eveline's sharp tongue had made the last few days harder to bear than they need have been; for she complained constantly, finding all manner of fault with the beds, food and service provided wherever they rested, even though the Earl's servants and her own had done their best to provide her with every comfort. Her scolding had driven Meredith to call a truce with Perdita, the two girls finding a mutual need to unite in the face of the older woman's tyranny.

Only Athelstan remained unaffected by the hardships of their journey, presiding over the sizeable cavalcade of men, servants and baggage with his usual urbanity; and showing courtesy to fellow travellers, whether itinerant tinkers, friars or wealthy noblemen. If Perdita had not known it previously, she saw now that he was a man of great power and importance. Everywhere they went, he was greeted with deference, from both the ordinary folk and his peers. She began to see what Meredith had meant when she insisted that the King would not dare to refuse Athelstan a fair hearing. His influence was far greater than she could have dreamed among the lesser gentry and the common folk of England. As they passed, people would lay down their tools in the fields to watch him ride by, and sometimes they cheered him. At first this had puzzled her, for though she loved Athelstan, she did not know why the ordinary folk should seem so affected by his progress. Seeing her curiosity, Sir Geoffrey had brought his mount alongside to explain the reason for the Earl's popularity.

'They have heard of his reputation for fairness, Mistress Perdita. When he sits at the Sessions, he often gives judgment in favour of the poor, sometimes against his fellow nobles. It is one of the reasons he has so many enemies among those Barons who would bleed their own peasants dry.'

'I see.' She frowned thoughtfully. 'Gervase told me he had many enemies. I – I thought that it was because of his wealth and power?'

'There is that, too, but Athelstan was always a champion of the common folk. Like others in England, he believes that the time must come when all men are free, with a right to speak their mind through Parliament.'

'And are you one of these men, Sir Geoffrey?'

'Ay, in this I stand with Athelstan. It is time the King was made to listen to reason.'

His words gave Perdita much to occupy her thoughts during the journey. It was becoming increasingly clear to her that England was fermenting with discontent, among not only the nobility but also the great majority of freemen and the peasants. It seemed inevitable that the unrest would culminate in an armed struggle against the Crown – and Athelstan's trial might be the spark that set the rebellion alight. Surely the King would be aware of this, and give him the chance to deny the charges of treason brought against him?

Clearly, her lover was prepared to risk his life for the ideals he believed in, and she could not but honour him for it; but she was a woman and she wanted peace, a home, children and a husband by her side. As they neared London, the anxiety inside her had become a stone, making it more and more difficult for her to laugh and hide her fears.

When they entered the city, a dread chill

struck her heart. She was seized with a terrible premonition of disaster, and her fear was so great that she felt physically ill. Athelstan came to help her to dismount, and she made a determined effort to smile at him, but her head was aching and she swayed dizzily as her feet touched the ground.

'You are ill?' he said, his face grave as he looked at her pale cheeks. 'The journey has been too much for you.'

'No – I am just a little tired, my lord.' She tried to stand alone, and almost fell. 'It is nothing. My head aches…'

'Foolish girl,' he scolded, bending down to sweep her up in his arms. 'Why did you not tell me you were ill?'

Her protests were pushed aside as he carried her into the house, past the startled faces of the servants, to the chamber he had had prepared for her. Laying her gently down on the bed, he stooped to brush his lips against hers, smiling chidingly.

'Sometimes stubbornness is painful, my Perdita. You will be better when you have rested. I shall send Meredith's woman to you in an hour, then we shall sup together.'

'And when must you go to Court?' she asked, gazing earnestly at him. 'When shall you answer the charges made against you?'

'Tomorrow or the next day. I shall ask for a private audience with Richard first – but if he will not listen, I must appeal to the Court of Chivalry for my right to trial by combat.'

'I shall pray that the King will listen to reason.'

'In either case, my cause is just and I must triumph!' Athelstan's eyes were glowing with an inner conviction. 'Do not be anxious, Perdita. Right is with me, and I cannot fail.'

'You will not fail, my lord,' she said, knowing that she must not seem to doubt his strength. Yet as the door closed softly behind him, her eyes clouded with fear. He was brave and proud, but he was also mortal. The King was powerful and Athelstan had many enemies – and she was so afraid that they would combine to strike him down.

Sliding to the floor beside the bed, she knelt in prayer, knowing that the outcome would be decided by a power greater than that of any man...

The palace courtyard was overflowing with opulently-dressed nobles and their ladies. Perdita had never seen so many people gathered in one place, and had she had time to spare a thought for vanity, she would have been glad of the richness of her own clothes and jewels – jewels that had been given to her earlier that morning by Athelstan. When he handed her the casket stuffed full of precious gems in the form of rings, brooches and strings of pearls, she had drawn back with a little shake of the head.

'I have no need of such gifts, my lord,' she protested.

'Nevertheless, you will wear them to please me, Perdita,' he said with a wry twist of his lips. 'My wife may not shame me before the Court, even though she has no love of finery. You would not have Meredith pity you?' She had laughed as he intended, accepting his gifts with a shy glance and some reluctance that had set his brow quirking. 'What an odd creature you are, lady. What may I give you that would please you?'

'Do not think me ungrateful,' she said hastily. 'It is not that I spurn these beautiful gifts, but I already have so much. All I want is to be beside you, my lord.'

'Is it so indeed? Then I am the most fortunate of men.'

Something in his tone made her flush. 'Do you not believe me, Athelstan?'

'I am almost afraid to believe you,' he replied, his eyes strangely troubled. 'The gift you offer me would demand too much in return. I should be weakened by my fear of losing such a prize.'

'Then you must laugh at my foolishness, my lord! I would not be a burden to you, especially at this time.' She gave him a challenging smile. 'Help me to choose a jewel that will make you proud of she who is soon to be your wife.'

'Perhaps I am the fool,' he said quietly. 'But we shall pander to the vanity of a world that sees only the outward signs of glory, Perdita. Wear these pearls – and this ring.' He wound a long string of large, creamy pearls about her throat and looked at her appraisingly. 'Yes, that should serve to satisfy both the pride and the curiosity of those who will look at my future bride and envy her all those things for which she has no use.'

There was mockery in his voice, hiding the emotion he could not quite keep from his eyes. He felt a fierce desire to sweep her up in his arms and carry her off to safety, where they could live in peace and forget the world; but then he knew that he would never be at peace if he turned his back on the struggle to come. He had chosen his path long ago, and he could not waver now, even though it might cost him more dearly than he had expected.

Smiling, he took her hand. 'Come, we must visit the Court and pay our respects to Richard. I shall present you, and then seek an audience. If I succeed, you will stay with Sir Geoffrey and the others until I come for you. If not, we shall leave immediately together.'

'You do not fear arrest, my lord?'

He shook his head. 'No, I think not. I have received word from the King's uncle, the Duke of York, that I might present my case in safety. Richard respects York as much as any man in his kingdom, and I have no fear that I shall receive anything but a just hearing.'

Knowing nothing of politics or the powerful men who had once almost managed to control the King's excesses, Perdita could only accept what she was told. Riding through the streets at Athelstan's side, she had been glad of all that he had taught her on that afternoon when she had found him such a hard task-master. Especially when they rode into the outer courtyard of the palace, and she found herself the object of much attention. She was still a novice at the equestrian art, but she was learning all the time.

They had left their horses in order to mingle with the courtiers in the huge open galleries of the palace until the King arrived with his attendants. He was a fair-faced man with soft hair that curled above the ermine collar of his rich robes, but Perdita thought that there was a certain weakness about his mouth that was almost petulance. Had she but known it, her judgment was a fair one. Richard had been flattered and pandered to in his youth, his chance of being a great king spoiled by the doting women who had taught him that his will was supreme.

For a time his wife, the good Queen Anne, had helped to restrain his selfish, indulgent nature, but after her death there had been no one to deny him. The few who tried were imprisoned or banished – or foully murdered by those who wished to earn his favours. Then he had taken another wife, a young French princess who was still a child when he wed her. This marriage with a daughter of France had angered the people, who remembered the wars with their old enemy across the Channel, and the nobles who found glory and riches on the fields of battle.

Yet, from the resentful pride in his face, it was clear that he believed himself omnipotent. He received Athelstan coolly, his eyes dwelling for a moment on Perdita before moving on to Lady Eveline and Meredith. His welcome was a mere movement of his stiff lips and a glance as cold as the icy winds whistling about the palace towers.

Athelstan remained as the others moved on; and risking a look over her shoulder, Perdita saw that the King appeared to consent to a request for a private audience. The small group of men walked away to an antechamber, and she held her breath, fearing some treachery. Would they seize the Earl once he was out of the public view and drag him down to some secret dungeon beneath the palace?

'You must not let Athelstan see how afraid you are,' said Meredith. 'He would be ashamed of your weakness.'

Perdita's head went up at the spiteful thrust, but she knew that it was no more than the truth. Athelstan must not be allowed to see how much she suffered for his sake. He had already hinted that he would find too much devotion a burden, and she wondered if it was only her determination to hold out against him that had first caught his interest.

'I am not afraid,' she lied now. 'I know my lord will persuade His Majesty to see reason.'

'Indeed?' Meredith's eyes seemed to strike at her heart with a dagger's blade. 'Then he will achieve what others have tried and failed before him! I believe he will be forced to demand his right to appear at the Court of Chivalry.'

Perdita felt the cold hand of fear clutch at her heart, but she struggled to keep a smile on her lips. It was almost as though Meredith wanted Athelstan to risk his life in personal combat – as though she would rather see him dead than married to another! But he would not die! He must not!

They were strolling in a gallery that overlooked an inner courtyard, and Perdita paused to look out of the window at the activity below. Some newcomers had arrived, the sound of their voices harsh in the chill of the winter air. She saw one of the men look up and point excitedly at something, urging his companion to do the same. At that moment, Meredith's voice brought her hastily from the window.

'Here comes Athelstan. He looks angry,' Meredith said, a hint of triumph in her tone. 'Did I not tell you? The King has refused to listen to him.'

Looking at the Earl's face, Perdita saw that she was right. It was clear even before he spoke that the audience had not gone well. His eyes were hard, and he was very angry. He held out his hand to her imperiously.

'Come, Perdita, we are leaving at once.'

'Yes, my lord.' She went to him obediently, feeling chastened even though she knew his fury was not for her, and holding back all the questions that sprang to her mind. She must not plague him with her worries; he had enough to occupy his thoughts, and he would tell her anything he wished her to know.

Athelstan was silent as he strode through the corridors, his face cold and tight with rage. At his side, Perdita was aware of the curious glances towards them, some grave and thoughtful, others smirking in secret triumph at the Earl's apparent humiliation by the King. He himself seemed oblivious to anything but his own thoughts, walking so determinedly that she was forced almost to run to keep up with him. Thinking only of him, and the certainty of the danger he now stood in, she did not notice the men who had arrived a short time earlier, nor did she see the gleam of excitement in one man's eyes as she passed him – but he saw her!

'You will go back to the house with Sir Geoffrey and the others.' Athelstan spoke to her at last as the groom brought their horses. 'I have something I must do... People to see...'

'Yes, my lord.' She looked at his stern face, wanting to reach him in some way, to put her arms about him and hold him close. But what could she do? There was nothing she could say that would change what must be, and to offer her love at this moment would only distract him from his purpose. Her tears must be kept inside, away from his impatient eyes and Meredith's scorn.

Taking her palfrey's reins firmly in her hands, she followed the others from the courtyard, resisting her desire to look back. And so she did not see how long he gazed after her, nor the twist of pain about his mouth before he turned to ride in the opposite direction.

'I knew he would bring the strumpet with him!' There was triumph in Sir Edmund Mortimer's face as he looked at his servant. 'I'll have her yet, you'll see! Athelstan will have no time to guard the wench when he answers the charges I laid against him.'

Fulk looked at his master, basking in the Baron's unaccustomed good humour. 'And once she is yours, you will have a rich reward, sir.'

'What do you know of that?' Sir Edmund's eyes narrowed. Conscious of the curious glances of the courtiers milling about in the palace grounds, he kept his itching hands from striking out in sudden temper. 'If you have heard more than you should, you shall lose your ears for it!'

Fulk cursed the slip that had brought the gleam of fury to his master's eyes. He was fully aware of the cause of Sir Edmund's determination to recapture the wench. She was comely enough, but there were village sluts to ease the Baron's lust when the heat was on him. No, there were other reasons why he needed to get his hands on the runaway – and one of them might hang him. Knowing as much as he did, Fulk had considered using his cunning to gain some reward from his silence, but as he looked into the murderous eyes of Sir Edmund, his courage failed him. The Baron would kill him instantly if he guessed what was in his mind.

'Why, sir, the wench is pretty. I thought you wanted to bed her...'

Sir Edmund looked at him suspiciously. 'Is that all, sirrah? If I thought you lied to me, you should pay for it with your life!'

'What else could there be, sir?' Fulk felt the cold sweat trickling down his spine, and wondered why he served the master he hated. He was bound by law as well as fear, but others had broken free of the yoke of serfdom. Sometimes he thought that he would rather starve by the roadside than live in the shadow of this man's wrath, but as yet he had not found the courage to leave him. Few had done so and lived long enough to know the pangs of hunger.

'What else?' Sir Edmund's face grew red with temper. 'Why, revenge, man! I'll be paid for what she did to me before she ran away. You would do well to remember, Fulk. It may take me some time, but I always repay my debts...'

Fulk swallowed his saliva, feeling it stick like a hard lump in his throat. For the moment the Baron seemed prepared to accept his ignorance, but what if he used torture to force the truth from his unwilling lips? The thought of pain made the sweat break from his brow. Would it be wiser to pass the dangerous secret he carried in his head to someone else? To the Earl of Athelstan, perhaps? Yet surely the girl would have told him as much as she knew? If he already knew and was not interested in justice, he might send the luckless informer back to certain death. He had heard that the

Earl was a fair master, but there were also other tales that chilled his blood. Was there really any difference between the proud men who made up the core of the English nobility? Were they not all blood-suckers, living off the backs of the downtrodden people? There was no way out for him, Fulk accepted despairingly. He was born to live and die in servitude – and he could never be free.

'I'll remember, sir,' he said, fighting down his bitterness. 'How could I forget? You are my master.'

'Good.' It was fortunate for him that Sir Edmund's attention had wandered and he did not notice the look of resentment in his servant's eyes. He was looking closely at a man who had come into the courtyard, his eyes glittering with excitement. 'Stay here, sirrah, and wait for me. I must speak with his lordship the Bishop of Nantes. I have heard that he has no love for Athelstan. It would be as well to make sure that there is no way of escape for our respected neighbour...'

Fulk's eyes turned towards the stout, velvet-gowned figure of the Bishop, who greeted Sir Edmund with a look of haughty disdain. As they talked, however, the Bishop's expression gradually changed, and at last he smiled, nodding his head as if in perfect agreement with the Baron's plan.

Whatever they plotted together, it would bring harm to Lord Athelstan; of that the servant was quite certain. Sir Edmund was too much afraid of the Earl's wrath if he should ever discover just who had whispered in the King's ear. Fulk wondered again whether to pass his information to the Earl, but he could not quite find the courage. After all, why should Athelstan listen to him?

Perdita could no longer bear the silence of her chamber. She had supped alone since Athelstan had not yet returned from wherever his business had taken him, and Lady Eveline had complained of a headache as soon as they came back from the Court. Meredith had begged her brother to take her to visit some friends, making it quite plain that Perdita would not be welcome to accompany them. Left to herself, the girl had spent her time in embroidering a silk belt for Athelstan, but the afternoon had passed slowly and she was tired of her own company. Surely he must have returned by now!

Pulling on a thick mantle to keep out the chill of a winter's night that had turned bitterly cold, she picked up an iron candlestick and went out into the corridor. The town house was much smaller than the castle, its walls covered with thick tapestries or sometimes panelled with oak that had been deeply carved with scenes that bore witness to the wood-cutter's art, and it took her only a few minutes to reach the head of the main stair. Hearing the welcome sound of Athelstan's voice coming from the great chamber, she prepared to go down to him, pausing as he emerged into the hall and his words reached her.

'It has been agreed for the morrow,' he said clearly. 'I shall spend this night in a vigil to prepare myself, Balsadare. You know what to do?'

'No one shall approach your door, my lord.'

'It is well…' Athelstan seemed to hesitate. 'And my lady – where is she?'

'She has spent her time alone in her chamber.'

'She will be resting, and I shall not disturb her. It would be too stern a test, my friend. Those who accuse me have chosen Simon the Wolf to be their champion. I shall need all my strength to defeat him, and dare not spend it in a woman's arms.'

'Is she to know that you fight tomorrow?'

'I would not wish to have her there for her sake, Balsadare. You know what I would have of you?'

'I think so…'

Their voices were coming closer. Frightened of discovery, Perdita turned and fled back to her own room. Athelstan did not wish to see her; he was apprehensive of her love, fearing that it would weaken his purpose. He meant to spend the night in a lonely vigil, preparing himself – for what? Death or glory in combat! The pain twisted inside her like a knife. This might be his last night alive, and she had hoped he would spend it in her bed, holding her close until the dawn. She wanted so much to feel the burn of his kisses and the strength of his arms about her. If he should fail tomorrow... But he must not fail! She could not bear it if he died. She loved him so much ... so much.

Lying on her bed, she felt the useless tears slide silently down her cheeks, wetting the pillow. Oh, why had she fought against him so hard at the start? If she were never to know the completeness of his love ... never to bear his child... In the darkness, her heart was crushed with the pain of her fear. Tomorrow he must fight with the man they called Simon the Wolf – and she would be there! Her tears dried as the determination hardened in her mind. She would be there to witness her lord's victory, or his death, if she had to find her way through the streets alone! With that thought her pain eased, and she slept.

Athelstan had already left the house when she went downstairs in the morning. Meredith was pacing about the small chamber like a caged vixen, her face white with temper. She rounded on Perdita as she entered, spitting out her words in an angry rush.

'We are not to be allowed to watch the contest! My brother agrees with Athelstan that we shall be better employed here with our needlework.'

'Do you know when it is to take place?'

'In two hours, as near as I can tell.' Meredith scowled. 'What does it matter, since we are barred from attending?'

'I shall not stay here while my lord's life is in danger,' Perdita declared. 'I intend to follow him, even if I must find my way there alone.'

'I know where it is to be held,' Meredith said thoughtfully. 'We could go together, if you wish. We shall be quite safe if my groom accompanies us.'

Perdita had been prepared to go alone if she must, but to have the other girl's company and the protection of a groom would be so much better. She smiled at Meredith gratefully, accepting this offer of a truce between them.

'Will you send for the horses, Meredith? I shall fetch a mantel and slip out by the side door to join you. I know Balsadare will try to stop me if he guesses what I mean to do.'

'So that is why he did not go with Athelstan and my brother. He was left here to watch over you. Take care that he does not discover your plans! I have no mind to be thwarted by his interference!'

'Nor I,' said Perdita, feeling in sympathy with her for once. 'I shall not keep you long.'

She turned and ran upstairs, her heart beating wildly as she thought of the adventure before them. It would be risky to go to the tilt in disobedience of Athelstan's orders, but she was determined to be there when he defended his honour. Reaching her chamber, she delved frantically into a coffer for a thick mantle, and turned. Seeing Balsadare standing in the open doorway, she hesitated, realising that he suspected her intention to disobey Athelstan.

'You are to stay here, Mistress Perdita,' he said, eyeing her warily. 'It is the Earl's wish that you remain in the house until he returns.'

'May I not even walk in the garden, Balsadare? I am weary of being cooped up in this house.'

'I suppose it could not hurt – but I shall accompany you, my lady.'

'As you wish.' She smiled at him innocently as she advanced towards the door. 'Where is my lord?'

'He has business elsewhere.'

'Then I must be patient until he returns.' She paused at the threshold and glanced back. 'Oh, I have dropped my kerchief. Will you pick it up for me, Balsadare?'

He took a half step inside the room and hesitated, suspecting a trap. His hesitation cost him dearly. She gave him a little push in the small of his back, thrusting him off balance. Before he could recover, she slammed the door to behind him and locked it swiftly. He wrenched at the latch, calling out as he realised he had been tricked.

'Do not be foolish, my lady! You do not know what danger you may face if you leave this house without protection.'

'I shall have the protection of Meredith's groom,' she said. 'It is my lord who is in danger, and I must be near him. Forgive me, Balsadare. I do not like to serve you thus, but you gave me no choice.'

'Let me out, and I shall take you to the tilt.'

She laughed merrily, delighted at having outwitted him. 'Oh, you will not catch me that way, my friend! I know that you serve Athelstan, and he has ordered that I shall stay here. Do not be anxious, Balsadare. I shall not permit him to beat you for letting me escape.'

'My lady, I beg you...' he began, but it was already too late; she was on her way to meet Meredith. He began to hammer at the door, shouting at the top of his voice. 'Let me out... Someone unlock this door...'

Perdita fled, frightened that one of the servants would appear and forbid her to leave the house, although she knew that Balsadare was the only one who shared the Earl's confidence. In the courtyard, Meredith was waiting impatiently, but her frowns turned to laughter as she listened to Perdita's story.

'I did not think you had the cunning for it,' she said with a wry twist of her lips. 'Perhaps I have underestimated you. I shall have to take more care in future!'

'Nothing shall keep me from being there if Athelstan needs me,' Perdita said, ignoring her taunt. 'You are sure you know your way, Meredith? Shall we be there in time?'

'You must trust me in this,' Meredith said. 'I want to watch the fight as much as you do. It will be exciting! Athelstan will win, of course, but I want to see him acquitted of these false charges.'

Perdita nodded her agreement, allowing the groom to help her to mount. She hated the thought of the contest as much as Meredith seemed to relish it, but though she dreaded seeing the men fight, she knew she must be there. If Athelstan were wounded, she must be with him!

Meredith led the little cavalcade, apparently confident of her ability to find her way through the city streets, and it was clear that she had visited the capital many times previously. Perdita followed trustingly, the groom at her back as they rode between the close-spaced houses that seemed to lean drunkenly inward, almost touching where they overhung the narrow road. It was a cold, dark morning, the sky overcast with threatening clouds that carried a hint of rain. Once the most thickly populated district was left behind, Perdita could see the turrets of the White Tower, and the silver gleam of the river as it wound its way past houses, palaces and hovels to the open countryside and onward towards the sea. It was becoming clear that Meredith was heading towards the city wall.

As they passed through the Ald Gate, Perdita could see a steady stream of people moving in the direction of Tower Hill. On a field beyond, the bright colours of tents and banners waved boldly in the breeze. From the laughter and general comments of the good-natured throng, it was clear that word had spread of the contest. It was a rare treat to have such an event in midwinter, for the tournaments were usually held in spring or summer; but the rumours had spread quickly and the people were in a holiday mood. Women were selling apples and meat pies from the baskets they carried at their hips, while pedlars displayed trays of ribbons, pretty trinkets and beads to catch the ladies' eyes.

Athelstan's colours of green and black stood out boldly from the myriad of scarlet, yellow and gold banners. As Meredith and Perdita dismounted at the edge of the ground, leaving their horses with the groom, they saw that the King and his attendants were already seated beneath an awning of silver cloth. With a wary glance at the royal party, they merged with the crowd, moving to a less prominent position where they could watch the contest without being seen themselves.

'My brother is going into Athelstan's tent,' Meredith whispered. 'We must have arrived just in time.'

Perdita nodded, looking around at the large and mixed crowd; there were nobles and their ladies, friars, bishops, urchins in their rags, men and women from all ranks of life. Their faces were flushed from the cold and the thrill of the occasion, and it was clear that some form of tournament had already taken place. It must have been hastily improvised, but a broken lance and a discarded gauntlet lay in a corner as evidence of what had gone before. It seemed to indicate that they had indeed arrived only just in time.

A sudden blast of trumpets made her jump, then a figure in full armour emerged from the black and green tent, and she held her breath. He wore a short surcoat of green over a body of mail, with leg coverings, gauntlets and elbow pieces of plate armour;

his basinet was plain with the visor pulled up to reveal his face. For a moment Perdita saw him quite plainly, and her heart jerked. He looked so grave, and yet there was pride and determination in his grey eyes.

One of his attendants helped him to mount his horse, handing him a long lance, and his shield which was painted with the heraldic devices of his arms: a sword being consumed by flames. He rode to face the King, lowering his lance in acknowledgment of his sovereign, and then raising it so that the tip pointed skyward.

'My liege, I am come to answer the charges against me, and to prove my innocence by wager of battle. Is there any among you who would take up the challenge?'

For a moment there was silence, and Perdita's pulses raced. Perhaps no one would answer his challenge! Her hopes were short-lived, for another burst of trumpets announced the emergence of a knight from a scarlet and gold tent. From the bold crest on his pennant, it was clear that this was Simon the Wolf. He mounted his charger and came to salute the King, turning to Athelstan at last with an insolent sneer.

'I have come to take up your challenge, Athelstan, as the champion of those who accuse you of vile treason.'

The King held up his hand as a roar of anger issued from many of the common folk who had gathered to watch the contest. 'You are accused of treason against the Crown,' he said in a loud voice. 'Since you deny the charges and claim your right to trial by combat, it will be a fight to the death. Is this understood by you both?'

'It is understood, Sire.' The two spoke as one.

'Then let the contest begin. And may God defend the just.'

As his words died away, there were cries from the crowd, cries of protest that became a chant. 'Athelstan ... Athelstan ... Athelstan...'

The King's face was tight with anger, but there was nothing he could do to quiet them. It was obvious whom the people believed. He was forced to sit with seeming indifference as the two contestants parted and rode to opposite ends of the arena. The Earl Marshal raised his baton, waiting until the knights indicated that they were ready; then it was lowered, giving the signal for the contest to begin.

Meredith gripped Perdita's arm as the two horsemen thundered towards each other. Her eyes gleamed with excitement, and her fingers dug deeply into the other girl's flesh.

'Isn't it thrilling?' she whispered. 'How brave they both are. A fight to the death, and neither flinched!'

Perdita could not answer. The drumming

of the horses' hooves was like a pounding in her brain. She felt sick in her stomach, but she could not look away as the first clash of lances sent a moaning sigh through the crowd. Neither knight was unseated, and they both checked their snorting mounts, turned to face each other and lowered their lances once more. This time the awful crunch of shattered metal brought a cry of terror from her lips; but as she swayed on her feet, the roar of approval from the watchers told her that it was Simon the Wolf's lance that had broken in the fierce contest. Athelstan's had found its mark, unseating his opponent.

'See, I told you he would win,' Meredith cried, but even as the words left her lips, the knight was on his feet, calling for a weapon. His squire ran up with a heavy iron-studded mace and a shield. 'Strike him down, Athelstan! Oh – the fool...'

Her protest was because the Earl had dismounted. Discarding his lance and shield, he accepted a two-handed broadsword from his attendant. Immediately the other knight charged at him, growling deep in his throat like the wolf he was named. They clashed in the centre of the arena, mace and sword striking against armour and shield, the force of the blows sending each man reeling on his feet. Yet neither gave ground as blow after blow followed, until, at last, Athelstan stumbled, seeming to falter.

'Oh no!' Perdita cried, her nails digging so deeply into the palms of her hands that blood spurted. 'God give him strength!'

As if in answer to her prayer, Athelstan steadied. Throwing himself forward, he wielded the heavy sword with such ferocity that the other man was forced to give way, using his shield in an effort to fend off the terrible blows. It was struck from his hand, sending him staggering back. He recovered briefly, striking out to catch Athelstan a glancing blow on the shoulder, but it was to be his last triumph. He retreated before the superior skill and power of the two-handed avenger, breathing heavily, his body jerking as the heavy blade sliced through his body mail. Suddenly the mace fell from his hand and he sank to his knees, clasping his side as the blood surged through his fingers. It was obvious that he was vanquished, though perhaps not mortally wounded.

'Kill him!' Meredith screamed, and her cry was echoed by a hundred voices.

Athelstan stood over his defeated opponent, glancing towards the King. 'I have proved my cause is just, Sire. Would you have me spare him as a proof of my loyalty?'

'Kill me and have done with it,' Simon said bitterly. 'I would not have spared you.'

'I have no grudge against you,' Athelstan stated. 'You were duped by others into a cause that was not just.'

'Spare him if you will,' the King said, his eyes angry. 'His life is yours.'

'Then I give it to him freely.'

'Spare me, and I shall be your enemy,' the knight growled.

'So be it…' Athelstan said, and turned his back to walk away. The Wolf looked for his weapon, grasped it as if to strike, then sank back as the weakness overcame him.

Wild cheers were echoing round the field as the people saluted the victor. It was clear that his popularity had not suffered from his magnanimous decision to spare the vanquished knight. Hearing the people's acclamation, Richard's face twisted with fury.

'Am I to be mocked by this rabble?' he muttered beneath his breath. 'Is there no way to be rid of the traitor?'

The Bishop of Nantes leaned towards him. 'I know a way – if you will permit me?'

'Is it certain?' Richard's eyes narrowed craftily. 'He has many friends…'

'He will have none when I have spoken.'

'Then do as you will, and bear the blame for it if you fail.'

The Bishop nodded. It was no more than he had expected. Getting to his feet, he walked to the front of the dais and held up his hand for silence. The cheering died away and an odd hush fell, as if somehow they sensed the blow before it struck.

'I say this was no fair test,' he cried. 'The combatants were ill matched – for one used sorcery against the other.' There was a gasp of horror from the crowd. 'Athelstan, I accuse you of the crime of witchcraft.'

'No!' The cry came from the crowd and was taken up by a hundred voices. 'Shame on you! It was a fair fight.'

The Bishop's eyes glittered as he surveyed them, knowing well the superstitious minds of the people. He waited until they quieted, falling strangely silent. 'Beware all those who would defend this servant of the Devil! For if you are touched by his evil, you will pay for it in the fires of Hell. From this day on the Earl of Athelstan is excommunicated, together with those who serve him or offer him succour.'

'No! It cannot be!' Perdita whispered, her face ashen. 'He cannot do that! Surely not?'

Meredith was stunned. 'I don't know. I must speak with my brother.'

She began to push her way through the crowd towards Sir Geoffrey. Perdita could not think clearly. Everything seemed to be happening somewhere far away, and her head was spinning. She could not take her eyes from Athelstan. What would he say to this new charge? What could he do in the face of excommunication?

'On what evidence do you make this charge, my lord Bishop?' His voice rang out loud and clear as he faced his accuser.

'Several charges of sorcery have been laid against you.'

'They are false! I have no evil powers. What I do is in the hope of a better future for all. My experiments are similar to those carried out by men of learning everywhere.'

'Is it not true that you have sold your soul to the Devil for a secret beyond price?'

Athelstan threw back his head and laughed mockingly. 'Surely you do not believe such foolish tales, my lord? Can you see Satan at my back? Are you so riddled with superstition that you fear anything you cannot understand? Do not fear the Devil! He will be waiting at your deathbed to carry your black soul to Hell!'

'Seize him!' The Bishop's face was purple with outrage. 'He condemns himself as a blasphemer and the servant of Satan!'

At a signal from the King, a score of armed guards moved to surround Athelstan. He was still carrying his sword, and he doubted they could take him alive, but he saw at once that any resistance would be foolish. He had brought only a handful of men with him to the contest; they would support him if he gave the word, and all would die uselessly. He threw down his sword, looking so proudly at the men who came to arrest him that they fell back, strangely subdued.

'I deliver myself into your hands, my lord

Bishop,' he said, his mouth twisting with wry humour. 'In the certain knowledge that I shall be given a fair hearing.'

'No, you must not,' Perdita mouthed. The Church would not give him a chance to prove his innocence in a trial of arms – they would have him tortured to make him confess! She took a step forward as if to stop him, and found her path barred by the body of a thick-set man. 'Please, you must let me pass! I must go to him...'

'I cannot allow that,' the man said harshly. 'I have come to take you home, Rosamund. Are you not pleased to see me?'

She looked up then, staring at the fleshy face of the man who had spoken. At first there was only a strange coldness seeping through her; then the nightmare began to take shape before her eyes. The terrifying pictures crowded into her mind, forcing her to remember all the pain and horror that had culminated in the struggle between them. He had been trying to force her to submit to his bestial lust... The man she had always believed to be her father until that terrible night when she had seen him murder his own wife!

'No! I shall not go with you,' she cried. 'I hate and despise you! Stand out of my way. I must go to Athelstan.'

'He cannot help you now,' Sir Edmund sneered. 'Once the Bishop has him imprisoned, he will be forced to confess to his wickedness. And he will die, like all witches, in the fire.'

'No...' she whispered, her face turning pale at the terrible scenes his words conjured up in her mind. 'I must be with him... I love him...'

Everything was whirling about her, spinning faster and faster until she was so dizzy she could scarcely stand. She knew she had to reach Athelstan, but there was no strength left in her. She took a step forward, gave a gentle sigh and crumpled at his feet.

Sir Edmund scowled as a woman from the crowd tried to reach her. 'Stay away from her,' he growled. 'My servant will attend her. She is mine! Yes, she is mine at last...'

'Where is Mistress Perdita?' Balsadare asked, looking beyond Meredith to the door. 'I was on my way to find you. I have only this moment been released.'

'I have no time to speak with you now,' said Meredith. 'I must talk with my woman. We have to leave this house at once.'

'What has happened?' Balsadare barred her way. 'I know she went with you. What have you done with her?'

'She was lost in the crowd after Athelstan was arrested for sorcery,' Meredith replied angrily. 'I told her to follow me, but she stayed behind to watch what was happening. When Geoffrey realised we could not help Athelstan without being excommunicated by the Church, he hurried me from the field at once. We cannot stay here now. We must go home, or risk the eternal damnation of our souls.'

Balsadare's mouth twisted with scorn. 'Will you run away in fear and do nothing to help him? You know these charges are false! Surely your brother has influential friends who could help to expose the Bishop's lies?'

Sir Geoffrey came in at that moment. 'I shall speak to the Archbishop of Canterbury, but it will take time. We shall need to discover the nature of the charges before they can be refuted. For the moment, it would be wiser to leave Athelstan's house. You, too, would be well advised to leave here and find a refuge until something can be done.'

'By which time the Earl will be dead.' Balsadare frowned. 'I must return to the castle and rouse his men for an attack. Do you know where they have taken him?'

'To the Tower, I think, but you would need to storm London itself to free him by force.'

'If need be, I shall do it! The country is rife for an uprising.'

'Against the King and his tyranny, yes. But this charge is damning. It will raise doubts in the minds of the very men who would have rallied to this cause. Few will risk their lives if they die excommunicated.' Sir Geoffrey frowned. 'The only way is to appeal against his arrest – to the Pope himself, if necessary.'

'Do as you think best,' said Balsadare. 'I cannot wait so long – but where is Mistress Perdita? Have you no idea what has happened to her?' He saw a flicker of something in Meredith's face and grasped her wrist. 'You do know something, don't you?'

'I am not sure…' She tried to pull free of him, then relented. What did jealousy matter now? If it were not for Perdita, she might even now be Athelstan's wife and forced to share his disgrace. 'I shall tell you what I saw. Just after Athelstan's arrest, I noticed her talking to a man, who might be one of Athelstan's neighbours. I have seen him but once at a fair, but I believe it was Sir Edmund Mortimer.'

Balsadare nodded. 'It was as my lord feared – Sir Edmund planned it all! He wanted her to stay here so that she would be safe. The foolish wench!'

'As you say, she is naught but a foolish girl,' Sir Geoffrey said. 'Forget her, and your master. There is nothing you can do for either of them.'

Balsadare watched as brother and sister hurried away, his eyes dark with anger. He at least would not abandon his lord – but Mistress Perdita was also in danger. He had sworn to give his life for hers, but if he did not try to rescue Athelstan, he would never leave the Tower alive. He could go to the aid of only one of them – which one must it be?

CHAPTER EIGHT

Athelstan's face was impassive as he was led to the dank cells beneath the Tower. The waters of the river lapped against the steps down which he had been brought, and there was an unpleasant dampness in the air as he and the warder descended deep into the bowels of the fortress. The unhealthy atmosphere had destroyed the spirit of many a man incarcerated in these dungeons, but the Earl doubted that he would be held long enough to feel the bite of winter agues. He was too dangerous an enemy, and once he had been forced to confess, he would die at the stake.

He had already endured an hour of fierce examination by the Bishop of Nantes and other important Churchmen, who appeared to believe the charges brought against him, even though he had countered all their arguments. The charges were laughable: that he had bewitched some dogs, raised a dying boy from his deathbed, and sent a travelling friar out to preach the Devil's words. In other circumstances they would not have dared to arrest him on such trumpery, but he was an enemy of the State, only escaping a traitor's death because of his superior skill with the sword. His enemies would combine against him, denying him an open trial and forcing a confession by torture – only then could they be sure that his friends would be too late to secure his release.

A warder was unlocking a cell, standing back with a show of respect to usher him inside. 'The examiner will come soon, sir. I advise you to rest while you can.'

Athelstan inclined his head, a slight smile playing about his lips. 'I thank you for your concern, sir. May I ask how long I am to wait for this feast of entertainment you plan?'

A harsh laugh escaped the gaoler's lips. This show of bravado from the prisoner would not last long once the examination began. He had seen too many come and go. Some of them held out until their agony became unbearable, others wept at the first touch of a hot iron – but they all broke in the end, confessing eagerly to any crime that was put to them. He doubted not that many an innocent man had gone to his death rather than face more pain. And if they did not confess, they died anyway.

'Master Lorenzo is at his dinner, sir. He likes a good meal before he starts his work, see? It should be an hour or more.' The warder faltered as he looked into Athelstan's steady eyes. 'I'm sorry, sir. Lorenzo and me

– we only do our work. He mostly asks you to forgive him before he starts…'

'Indeed? I see that you are both Christian men. If I die, will you have my body decently buried? My servants would pay you well for it.'

'If it is in my power, I shall be glad to, sir.'

'Thank you.' Athelstan took a large emerald ring from his finger. 'Please accept this as a gift – and I forgive you and Master Lorenzo for what you must do.'

The turnkey's eyes gleamed at the sight of the precious jewel, and he stuffed it inside his doublet. Any possessions the prisoners had were usually taken by the examiner after their deaths, unless they could be persuaded to part with them earlier for some comforts in their cell. It was unwise to steal, however, for just occasionally the family of the condemned man would succeed in securing his release – though it was often too late for the unfortunate victim to do more than die in his own bed.

The half smile left Athelstan's lips as the cell door was firmly shut and locked, what light there was in the cell fading as the warder's torch was carried with him. He had an hour at most in which to prepare for the ordeal ahead – an ordeal that no man could hope to survive intact. Even if a reprieve came, it would be too late; he would be broken in body and perhaps in spirit. Yet there was one way in which he might defeat his enemies and escape the terrible agony of the examination. It was dangerous – so dangerous that it would lead to certain death if he failed. Strangely, death did not seem so fearful set against the alternative of torture and lingering pain. His regret was only that he might never see her again.

'Sweet Perdita,' he whispered in the darkness. 'Forgive me for my stupid pride, my love. I put what I considered my duty before our love. You offered me a prize beyond all others. I should have accepted your promise of happiness and gone with you to a place where we could live in safety. Better a life in exile in France or Burgundy than that you should suffer the grief our parting must bring you. I pray that you will find happiness...'

For a moment the picture of her sweet face rose in his mind, almost destroying him. He felt the weakness within him as his longing for her drove all resolution from his mind. Like other men before him, the realisation of his situation made him desperately aware of all that he had lost, bringing him to the darkest moment he had ever known. Until this moment his work and his beliefs had been the driving force in his existence, but now at last he understood that a man is nothing without the woman he loves. She had become so much a part of him that he had not realised his need of her. He wanted to live! To hold his woman in his arms and feel the sweetness of her soft flesh beneath him as they lost themselves in one another. He had prided himself on being stronger than other men, of needing no one – but now he acknowledged the frailty of his own nature. Yet how could it be a weakness, when it made him more determined than ever to cling to life? For a moment he had come close to knowing despair, but now the memory of her smile gave him strength to do what must be done. Surely he would succeed. He must! He must live for her.

There was but one choice to make that could perhaps save him. He had prepared carefully for the eventuality of his imprisonment, confiding his plans to Balsadare. So much depended on the loyalty of his friend. The threat of excommunication was enough to make most men turn aside in fear. If Balsadare deserted him, he was lost. There was no other way. He must put his trust in his faithful servant and take his chance...

Perdita sighed and stirred restlessly. She was conscious of a swaying, jolting motion that jarred her aching head, and she realised she must be lying in a wagon. Something thick was covering her face, making it difficult for her to breathe. She tried to reach out and remove it, but discovered that her hands were bound. Why was she a prisoner, she wondered dazedly. What had happened to her?

All at once memory came flooding back. She had been at the contest, watching Athelstan fight for his honour; then when he was arrested, she had been prevented from going to him by the man she hated above all others. The sight of his detested face had torn away the curtain in her mind, revealing all the horror she had tried so hard to keep at bay. Now she understood why she had blocked out those memories. She had been afraid to face them.

Throughout her life she had always mistrusted the man she had believed to be her father. He was a cruel bully who delighted in hurting his gentle wife and the girl he called his daughter. Many a time Perdita had felt the sting of his hand when he was in his cups, and she had often seen the bruises on Lady Mathilda's arms and back. In childhood she had been forced to watch his cruelty in silence, but as she grew older, her conscience would not let her stand aside, and she had received several beatings because she stood between him and his wife. For some reason, however, he had always restrained his brutality with her, and she had not suffered as much as her mother. Perdita still thought of the woman she had loved as her mother, even though on the night she died, Lady Mathilda had told her that she was adopted.

'Mother – forgive me,' Perdita whispered, tears sliding down her face as she lay beneath the blanket, unable to move. 'I wanted to help you, but I could not stop him. He locked me in the closet…'

Now that Perdita could no longer block out the memories, they crowded in on her thick and fast. Lady Mathilda had been ill after being beaten yet again by her husband; unknown to him, she had written to her brother to ask for help, her years of suffering finally driving her to break the silence she had steadfastly maintained. She had done so because of her growing fears for the daughter she loved. Unfortunately, Sir Edmund had intercepted the letter.

He had come to his wife's bedchamber, finding Perdita at her mother's side. Thrusting the girl into the closet, he had locked her in there and proceeded to suffocate his wife. Perdita had beaten her fists against the door until they were raw, screaming at him to let her out. After it was over, he had taken the girl to her own room and locked her in. For almost three months she was allowed to see no one but him, existing on the meagre meals he brought her twice a day. He had thought to break her spirit, and he had almost succeeded; but on the morning of her escape, his suggestion that she should become his wife had driven her to a desperate defiance.

'I would rather die than marry a murderer!' she had screamed at him. 'You– You are a depraved beast, and I despise you!'

'You will wed me once I have bedded you, for no man will marry you when I have done with you.'

He had grabbed her then, forcing his hateful kisses on her. She had fought him wildly, scratching his face and hitting him with the first weapon that came to hand. Her attack stunned him, giving her time to escape. It was then that she had fled to the forest where Athelstan had found her.

'Athelstan…' She whispered the name, the pain twisting inside her. Where was he now? She did not know if he was still alive, and her fear for him made her sick with misery. She was at the mercy of a cruel beast, but what did her own fate matter if she lost the man she loved?

She felt the jolting of the wagon as the wheels turned in a deep rut in the road. Where was Sir Edmund taking her? She believed it would be back to the manor, for he was a creature of habit, and he would think himself safe enough now that Athelstan was imprisoned. Somehow she had to find a way of outwitting him. If she could escape, she could make her way to the Abbey of Athelone. Then she could send word to Gervase at the castle. Surely there must be a way of freeing Athelstan? There had to be!

Frustration at her helplessness swept over her. For the moment, she could do nothing but lie here and endure the torment of her thoughts...

'Where is he, then?' Lorenzo wiped his greasy hands on his shirt, his eyes glittering from the drink he had taken. A man needed something inside him for this work, even if he had as strong a stomach as the chief torturer. 'Fetch him out. We'd best make a start, or his lordship will be here afore we've loosened his tongue.'

The warder nodded, jingling the great bunch of keys at his waist. 'He's a real gentleman, this one. He told me he forgave us both for what we must do, and promised us a rich reward if we deliver his body to his servants.'

'Depends what his lordship decides to do with him.' Lorenzo sniffed. 'You ain't going soft over this one, I hope?'

'Nay, but it might be worth the trouble, Lorenzo.'

'We'll see. Get that door open.'

Lorenzo watched as the warder inserted the key and disappeared inside. He was not about to tell his workmate, but the Bishop of Nantes had promised him a rich prize for breaking this one gradually.

'Keep him alive until I come,' the Bishop had said. 'There is something I must learn from him. Afterwards, you can finish him.'

'Here, Lorenzo! You'd best come quick!'

The warder's shout broke into Lorenzo's thoughts, startling him. He went just inside the cell, frowning as he saw the turnkey kneeling on the ground beside the prone body of the prisoner. 'Be careful, fool! He's probably feigning sleep to trick you in a bid for escape.'

The other man's face was ashen as he glanced up. 'I think he's dead. Have a look for yourself.'

'Come here, then, and guard the door. I've seen this trick before! He's likely holding his breath to deceive you.'

They changed places. Lorenzo bent over the prisoner, peering into the grey, staring eyes. The man did look dead, he had to admit it. He held his torch closer, knowing from experience that the fierce heat and the light would cause the eyes to blink if there was still even a bare thread of life remaining. Nothing happened; there was no movement, no reaction of any kind, even when he touched the torch against the prisoner's bare shoulder. Feeling bolder, he pressed his ear against the man's breast, straining for the slightest heartbeat. Nothing. He could see no sign of life, and the Earl's skin felt cold and clammy to the touch. It was clear that he was dead. As the realisation came to him, he was suddenly fearful for his own life. The Bishop could be generous when he chose, but he was also a ruthless enemy in defeat. If somebody was going to be blamed for this, it would not be Lorenzo!

'What did you do to him when you put him in here?' he demanded, his tone threatening. 'Did you hit him?'

'I swear I never touched him!' The warder's face was beaded with sweat. 'Look at him! You can see I never laid a finger on him. He must have died of fright.'

Lorenzo examined the body for bruises that might prove the warder was lying, but apart from one on his shoulder that he had sustained in the contest, there was nothing. No blood on the back of his head, and no sign of discoloration that might suggest poison. He stood up, frowning as he faced the prospect of conveying the news to the Bishop.

'There'll be Hell to pay, and no mistake! We'll have to stick together in this. You'll testify that we found him like this, and I'll stand by you.'

The warder nodded, swallowing hard. He had heard tales of sorcery, and his blood ran cold at the thought of it. Something strange was afoot, he felt it in his bones, but if he put his thoughts into words, Lorenzo would laugh at him.

'It's queer, though. He seemed in good health when I locked him in... Even asked me how long it would be before you came. That seemed important to him. You don't suppose...'

'Suppose what?' Lorenzo frowned. 'You think he took his own life, but I've checked for poison and there's no sign. 'Sides, he looks so peaceful, almost as though he's asleep.'

'I expect you're right. He didn't seem the sort to go off quick like that, though.'

'Maybe he was hurt worse in that fight than anyone knew. Lock him in anyway while I fetch his lordship. It's best to make sure – though I know a dead man when I see one.' Lorenzo laughed harshly. 'I've seen enough in my time.'

'That's true.' The warder nodded, locking the door securely before following Lorenzo to the upper chamber. 'You'll stick by me, then?'

'We'll stick by one another,' Lorenzo promised. 'I'd best fetch his lordship at once.'

Balsadare paced the floor of his chamber restlessly, torn by indecision. His situation was impossible. He had taken a vow to protect Perdita with his life, and that vow was sacred to him, but there was also the promise he had made to Athelstan just before he left for the tournament. Whatever he did, he was damned. Why could the foolish girl not have remained within the house, where she would have been safe? If anything had happened to her, his master would never forgive him, yet the Earl's instructions had been precise.

They made little sense to Balsadare. His own inclinations were to send for Athelstan's men and storm the Tower. He knew it would be a desperate attempt and likely doomed to failure, but what good could come of keeping a solitary vigil at the gates of the Tower? And what of the other duty his master had laid on him?

His pacing ceased abruptly as he realised what might have been in Athelstan's mind, and he tried to recall the exact words his master had used. He had been speaking about the possibility of death and Balsadare had brushed it aside, not wanting to consider it. He had not fully understood at the time, but now, as the words came back to him, he began to grasp the cunning behind the plan his master had formed. If he was right, it was a desperate measure, perhaps the only one with a real chance of success. Suppose he was wrong? The Earl had not disclosed all the details of his plan, perhaps because he could not be sure in advance of the circumstances he might find himself in. His careful instructions had seemed but a riddle to Balsadare, but now he saw that they were the kernel of a very clever escape plot.

Was it possible that a man would take the kind of risk he was envisioning? Balsadare wondered, shivering. He was not afraid of death, but what his master planned would require nerves of steel, and an unquestioning faith in his own loyalty. He would not want to take such a risk himself, but then he was not the Earl of Athelstan. Suddenly, he was sure that his master would dare where another might draw back, and he knew for certain what he must do. He would follow the Earl's instructions to the letter, strange though they might seem.

'I am coming, my lord,' he said aloud. 'Have faith. I shall be there when you need me.'

The Bishop of Nantes looked up from his supper with a frown. He disliked being disturbed at table, especially in such a case. Touching the napkin to his lips, he laid it aside, deliberately taking his time. Inside he was fermenting with anger, his rage ice cold as he contemplated the fate of the clumsy fool before him.

'You are an oaf, Lorenzo! Did I not tell you that I must speak with him before he died? Have you no skill that you allowed him to slip away from you too soon?'

'I swear he was dead before I saw him, my

lord. I think he died of fright.'

'Indeed? Why so?'

'Because he looks as if he sleeps, my lord. There is not a mark on him, save the bruising from the contest.'

'Are you sure he has not tricked you? Is it some plot to make us think he is dead and then he will seek to escape?'

'I thought of that in the first instant, my lord, but I am sure he is dead. Will you not come and see for yourself?'

'I suppose I must.' The Bishop felt cheated, disappointed at losing the chance to learn Athelstan's secret. He knew the tales were more than likely just superstition – but suppose the Earl really did know the secret of turning base metals into gold? His eyes gleamed with greed at the thought, then turned to glare at the luckless Lorenzo. If Athelstan had known the secret, he had carried it to his grave, thanks to this fool! 'If I find you are lying, I shall have you flogged! Do you understand?'

'Yes, my lord. But will you not come and see for yourself that it was a natural death? I swear there's not a mark on him but for those that were clearly sustained in the fight.'

The Bishop stood up. 'We shall go now. I must report to His Majesty at once if Athelstan is dead. At least he will be pleased with the news.'

Lorenzo went out and the Bishop followed. His chambers were conveniently placed, for this was not the first time he had been called upon to examine a prisoner. There was too much wickedness in the world, and he was a fanatical member of the Church, dedicated to the saving of souls – quite often praying at the side of a sinner who had been put to the test and repented of his evil. It was harrowing work, and he had thought to have some reward for it this time. His eyes bored into the back of Lorenzo's head. If that dolt was lying...

The air was growing more fetid as they descended deeper into the underground passages. The Bishop pressed his scented kerchief to his nose, feeling a little surge of disgust. How anyone ever managed to live down here! It was no wonder that the victims of royal displeasure were often only too eager to die.

He stood back as the warder opened the cell door, noticing his nervousness. Depend upon it, one or other of them was to blame for what had happened! He waved his hand in a gesture of irritation.

'Bring him out. You do not expect me to go in there?'

They obeyed with alacrity, dragging Athelstan's body out between them. The Bishop glanced down, feeling the fury rise in his breast as he saw the man's colourless features and the limp limbs that lay as they were dropped. He bent over the corpse, looking for signs of torture, but there was none. His face twisted with frustration. For once, it seemed, his victim had escaped justice.

'He must have died of fear, as you said – 'tis strange. I thought him made of sterner stuff. Very well, you can dispose of the body.'

'Shall we send for his servants to collect it for burial?' Lorenzo asked, hoping to save something from the fiasco.

'No...' The Bishop smiled slightly. 'Throw it in the river. If there is trouble from his friends, we shall say he died trying to escape.' He saw the disappointment in Lorenzo's face and pressed a coin into his palm. 'There, that is for your trouble.'

'Thank you, my lord.' Lorenzo bit the coin as soon as his master's back was turned, grinning at the warder. 'At least we've got some good out of it!'

'It's a shame not to see him decently buried, though.' He stared at Lorenzo uncertainly. 'While you were with his lordship, I had a call to the gates. It were one of the prisoner's servants, and he asked me if I would contact him if his master died.'

'You didn't tell him he was already dead?'

The warder squirmed under his furious look. 'I didn't see the harm in it. He promised me a purse of gold if we let him take the body.'

'We dare not! If his lordship finds out, we're dead!'

'That's the curious thing. This servant said we was to throw the body in the river and he would see to the rest of it. He promised to bring the gold in the morning if we did as he asked. He told me exactly what to do, Lorenzo.'

'You sure he ain't making a fool of you?'

'He gave me ten silver marks as a sign of his good faith.'

'Show me!' Lorenzo's eyes gleamed as he saw the coins on the palm of the warder's hand. 'I'll take charge of them for the moment. If your friend comes in the morning, we'll split it all between us. I don't suppose it makes much difference where we throw him. His lordship only said he was to go in the river.'

The warder thought of the Earl's ring secreted in his doublet, and smiled. Tomorrow he would be a rich man! 'He'll be waiting on the bank opposite the Traitor's Gate.'

'Come on, then, we might as well get it over with. After all, it's not our business what happens after he goes in the river.'

Between them, they half carried, half dragged the Earl's body through the dank passages and out on to the river steps. Taking him by the arms and legs, they swung him outwards and let go. There was a loud splash, and they nodded at each other before turning to go back inside.

Swiftly a shadowy figure slipped into the water from the opposite bank. He swam strongly to where he had seen the body sink, diving beneath the surface to catch it as it drifted slowly towards the bottom. It was like a stone in his arms as he swam with it to the bank, hauling it on to dry land.

In the moonlight Balsadare could see the dead-white features of his master. They had killed him! He was too late. He had failed. He had not properly understood the message Athelstan had given him before he left for the tournament. Yet surely he had done everything exactly as his master had instructed? But wait — there was something more he must do, though of what use it could be now he did not know. Reaching inside his doublet, he took out the tiny silver phial, staring at it in bewilderment. Then he undid the top and held it to Athelstan's lips, opening them to allow the contents to fall on to his tongue. Then he sat back on his heels to watch.

Nothing happened. It was as he had feared: his master was dead and there was nothing more he could do for him, except see him decently buried. Something had gone wrong with Athelstan's plan to deceive his captors into thinking he was dead. Tears spurted from his eyes and he began to cry noisily. A choking sound made him glance down in sudden suspicion at the body.

'Don't be a fool, man…' It was scarcely more than a whisper, so soft that he thought he was dreaming. 'Get me some dry clothes. I'm freezing!'

Balsadare stared, his eyes widening in a mixture of fear and dawning delight. Was it possible? Had the Earl managed to deceive them all? He did not see how it was possible, but now there were signs of a change in the pallid features. The colour seemed to be returning very slowly to Athelstan's cheeks – and there was some movement! First the flicker of an eyelid, followed by the twitching of his right hand. Kneeling at his side, Balsadare instinctively began to rub the cold hands. He administered sharp slaps to his cheeks and shook him hard. A soft chuckle made him sit back to watch the miracle of the Earl's return to life.

'I thought you were dead, my lord!'

'And so I should have been, had you not been here, my faithful Balsadare. In an hour or less I must have died. I swallowed a poison that simulates death. It is so effective that all the vital signs are slowed down to something that is indeed almost death. However, I could not judge exactly how long my captors would take to dispose of my body. I could only pray that you would succeed in administering the antidote in time.'

'A poison that simulates death?' Balsadare

echoed. 'I have never heard of such a thing. It was a terrible risk you took, my lord! Supposing I had not come?'

'Then I should have died. Better to drown than to roast in the fire. I asked for a decent burial, knowing that the Bishop would need to deny me something since I had cheated him of his revenge. Besides, I knew you would not fail me.'

'I almost forgot the antidote,' Balsadare said with a wry look. 'Why did you not tell me exactly what you had planned?'

'You might have thought me entirely mad.' Athelstan smiled. 'It is a secret I discovered, known only to a few. I owe my life to you, my friend.'

'As I owe mine to you.'

'Then we are equal – the debt is paid. You are no longer bound to serve me.' He sat up, grimacing. 'I feel sick, and I ache all over. Those charming fellows you bribed could have been a little gentler, I think.'

'It is as well for us both that they were greedy rogues.' Balsadare grinned. 'You know the bond between us was never one of debt, my lord. I serve you because you are my friend.'

'Then fetch me some dry clothes before I catch my death of cold! I suppose you did bring some?'

'I brought all I thought you would need for a journey. You will go to France to speak

303

with Hereford?'

Athelstan began to strip as his friend went to fetch the dry garments. 'Yes, I must go the Duke. He will stand with me. I must appeal to Rome against the excommunication.'

'And then? Even if you succeed, Richard will never let you rest in peace.'

'Richard may not rule long in England. Hereford has inherited his father's lands and the title of Lancaster now. He will not stay in France to be robbed of all that is rightfully his. When he returns, Richard will be forced to listen. England has lain too long beneath the tyrant's heel!'

Athelstan finished dressing, and Balsadare led his horse forward. 'You have other enemies, my lord.'

'None so powerful that they would dare to move against me once I have the Holy Father's blessing – and it will be mine, doubt not.'

'Then I wish you God-speed and a safe journey.'

'I shall send you word when I return.' Pausing with his foot in the stirrup, Athelstan looked at him gravely. 'You will guard my lady and care for her until I return?'

'I shall do all that I can.' Balsadare did not quite meet his eyes. Athelstan must not suspect that the woman he cherished above all others was in danger, for if he did, he would not think of his own safety. 'I shall keep my promise to you, my lord – and if I fail, no man shall see my face again in this life.'

'Then I am satisfied. No more could be asked of any man.' Athelstan touched his shoulder, and smiled. 'Farewell for now, my friend. God willing, we shall meet again soon.'

Balsadare stood back as the Earl rode away. He made the sign of the Cross in blessing, his heart strangely heavy as he turned to mount his own horse. For the first time in years he was not to ride at his master's back, but now he knew his duty. He must search for Perdita; and if he was too late, he knew what he must do. If she had been harmed, his life was forfeit...

Perdita stirred as the wagon halted. She realised she must have slept for a while, but now her nerves were tingling as she sensed that something was happening. The blanket was suddenly whipped from her and someone bent to touch her cheek. She blinked, trying to see his face clearly in the gloom.

'Is it Fulk?' she asked, frowning. 'Where are we?'

'At an inn. Be careful, Mistress Rosamund. I shall help you if I can. Hush, my master is coming.'

He had called her Rosamund. She hated

the name, for it belonged to a life that she had left behind her. She would not accept it. She was Perdita, and her life belonged to Athelstan.

She said nothing as Fulk released the ropes round her wrists and ankles, rubbing them to restore the circulation. He had said that he would try to help her, but what did he mean? Surely he would never dare to assist her escape? Knowing how much he feared his master's wrath, the faint hope died in her almost as soon as it took shape. He had merely been trying to comfort her.

'That will do, Fulk. She can stand now.' Sir Edmund came to the side of the wagon, glaring down. 'We shall rest here for the night, Rosamund. Behave yourself, and I might be lenient with you when we get home. Do anything to shame me, and I shall make you pay for it!'

'My name is Perdita,' she said proudly. 'You have no rights over me: you are not my father, and I owe you no duty.'

'No, I am not your father, but I intend to be your husband.'

'I would rather die!'

'If you deny me, I shall have you tried for my wife's murder.'

'But *you* killed her,' Perdita cried, her face white. 'I saw you.'

'Yet for three months you said nothing!' Sir Edmund sneered. 'A ring you took from her hand was found in your room after you fled, so who would believe you? You stole from her, and then you smothered her with a pillow. I have a dozen witnesses who will swear to it.' He gave her his hand, pulling her roughly from the cart, his fingers squeezing so tightly that she almost cried out with the pain. 'Oh, I think you will wed me, Rosamund.'

'Do not call me that,' she said, her eyes smoking with resentment. 'Threaten me as much as you will, I shall never submit to you.'

His flabby cheeks twitched with fury. 'I have endured enough of your insolence, wench! I'll show you who is the master once and for all. When I have bedded you, you will beg me to marry you.'

'No!' Perdita cried despairingly. She struggled wildly, trying to break away from him as he began to drag her towards the stables. Everyone seemed to have retired for the night, and there was no doubt in her mind of his intentions. She kicked at him, screaming, 'Let me go, you brute. If you do this, I swear I'll kill you for it!'

'You tried once, vixen, and I mean to be paid for the scars you gave me.' His thick lips curved. 'I shall learn to watch my back … at least until I've broken you.'

Her hatred of him was so intense that she knew no fear. She would fight to her last breath rather than submit. Death would be preferable to lying with him. As he reached towards the latch of the stable door, she kicked him hard on the shin, wrenching away from him. He swore and lunged at her, grasping her long hair and dragging her backwards into the darkness of the stables. She cried out in pain, unable to do anything as he thrust her down into the straw. As she immediately tried to rise, he slapped her across the face, the force of the blow stunning her. She lay gasping for breath, half conscious as he fell on top of her, his hands pawing at her breasts.

She cried out again, despairingly. 'Help me – for God's sake, someone help me!'

There was a sudden rushing sound and rustling in the straw, then a shrill scream issued from the lips of the man lying on top of her. For a moment he jerked horribly, but as she watched in awful fascination, blood bubbled from the corner of his mouth and he slumped on her. She felt a thrill of sheer terror, her breath catching in her throat. Then she heard a grunting sound, and the dead weight of his body was pulled off her. She found herself staring into the frightened eyes of Fulk as he bent over her.

'Are you harmed, mistress?'

He took her hand, helping her to her feet. Glancing at Sir Edmund's body, she shuddered as she saw the hilt of his own sword protruding from his back. It had been driven deep, and there was no doubt in her mind that he was dead. Fulk had killed him, and now he was shaking with terror.

'I had no choice but to kill him,' he said in a choking voice. 'If I had merely tried to stop him...'

'He would have killed you. Yes, I know it, Fulk, and I am truly grateful.' Her face hardened as she looked down at the body of the man she had hated for so long. 'He deserved to die! He murdered my mother. She was as dear and good a lady as ever lived. I hope his soul burns in Hell for ever!'

'Now I have slain him, and they will hang me for it!'

Perdita looked at him, her expression resolute. 'I shall swear that he was trying to murder me and that you saved my life. Stop trembling, Fulk, and fetch your master's horse. It must carry us both. When we reach the Abbey of Athelone we shall be safe.'

'But supposing we are followed?'

'Cover his body with straw. It may not be discovered until the morning. Besides, who will care that a stranger has been killed? Sir Edmund had few friends. I doubt that anyone will bother to enquire about him for weeks – and by that time you could be in France. I shall ask Athelstan's brother to give you money if you help me to reach the Abbey.'

He seized her hand and kissed it. 'Would that I had come to you sooner, lady! It was my master who laid the false charges against the Earl.'

'I suspected as much when he appeared and snatched me at the tilt. He would not have dared to think of such infamy if he had not believed himself safe from retribution!' She smiled at him, drawing on that inner strength that must sustain her now. 'Come, Fulk, we must be on our way before we are discovered. Only when we reach the Abbey can I try to help my lord.'

Fulk looked at her and nodded. He had made his choice when he plunged the sword into his master's back. For once he had not taken the coward's path, and somehow he gained courage from the young woman he had saved. Besides, there was no turning back now.

'So my brother lives? I had heard that he was drowned trying to escape.' Gervase gave a hollow laugh as he stared at Balsadare. 'I might have known he would outwit those fools! But you say there is no trace of Perdita. Where could Mortimer have taken her?'

'I do not know. I went first to the manor, expecting that he would run for home.' Balsadare looked grim. 'His servants could have been lying, but I do not think so. It is clear from the way they all neglect their work that he is not at home.'

'Then where has he gone? The fox has more cunning than I gave him credit for! Has he found a secure hiding-place to keep her a prisoner?' Gervase banged his fist against the wall in sudden fury. 'We have to find her, Balsadare!'

'That is why I have come to you. Alone, it could take me weeks to search every inn from here to London. You must release some of the men to join in the hunt.'

'Very well, you may take ten men – but I can spare no more. The castle is vulnerable to attack at this time. If my brother's enemies believe him dead, they may well seize the opportunity to move against us.'

'Ten will suffice. I shall pick those most suited for the task.'

'Choose Will Turner,' said Gervase. 'He's a good man, and he knows how to hold his tongue. We do not want a scandal.'

'Yes, Will is a good man. Excuse me, I must delay no longer. Every hour that passes makes our task harder.'

'Go, then – I shall wait to hear from you.' Gervase watched him walk away, his features hardening to stone. 'To hear from you, faithful Balsadare,' he murmured softly. 'Or from Will that you are dead. Now that Athelstan is gone, I shall be master here. And when I have everything that was his I shall hold it – even if he comes to take it back.'

'The Abbess will see you, lady.' The nun smiled at Perdita. 'Will you please follow me?'

'Thank you. I shall be grateful if you will give my servant food and a place to rest. He will be quite content with a blanket and a corner of the stable.'

'Something will be arranged, I'm sure.'

Perdita followed her through the narrow passages to the Abbess's room. A discreet knock was answered with an invitation to enter; and as the smiling nun turned away, Perdita went in. The room was small and sparsely furnished, containing only a table, stool and narrow bed against the wall; but there was a large wooden cross set above a kneeling stool, also a bible and writing-materials. It was clear that the Abbess was a devout woman with simple tastes.

She rose and came towards Perdita with hands outstretched. 'So you are the babe I gave to Mathilda! Welcome, my dear child. Welcome...' Opening her arms, she embraced the girl warmly. 'I have long wished to see you.'

'Thank you.' Perdita felt a lump rise in her throat. 'My mother said that you would give me sanctuary if I had need of it – and I do most sorely need both a place to stay and the help of someone I can trust.'

'You are at liberty to remain with us for as long as you wish. I have been expecting you before this. Mathilda swore to tell you the truth when she felt her death was close.'

There was a note of enquiry in her voice as she released Perdita, and the girl nodded. 'On the night she died, she took a ring from her finger and gave it to me. She told me that it had been found on a chain round my true mother's neck...'

The Abbess looked thoughtful. 'And was that all she told you, child?'

'I – I believe my mother died unwed. She was a poor woman you found wandering in the forest.'

'That was the story we told to the world, but Mathilda knew the truth. Your mother was a gentlewoman. She came here to hide her shame from her family. Her lover was already married and she could never hope to be his wife, but she entrusted to me the ring he had given her as a token of his love.'

'Then that was the ring Mathilda gave me?'

'Yes...' The Abbess hesitated uncertainly. 'After your mother died, a man came to see me. He asked about you, and I told him you had been adopted by a good woman. He asked me to send him word if ever you were in need of help. Would you have me send to him, child?'

Perdita frowned, thinking for only a

moment before she shook her head. 'No, I do not believe it would serve my purpose for the moment, but one day I may ask it of you. Does anyone else know this story?'

'No. Athelstan asked me one day, but I told him only as much as the world knows. This was my secret, to be revealed only if you asked.'

'I understand. It might be embarrassing for my father if there were too many questions. I think for the time being it would be best to leave things as they are.'

'Very well; it is your choice.' The Abbess smiled at her. 'Now, I am sure you are tired and hungry. The nuns will show you where you may sleep. I fear we have only plain fare here, but you shall not go hungry.'

'Thank you! You are very kind to me.'

'Mathilda was my sister. You gave her many hours of happiness, dear girl.'

'She told me you would receive me for her sake, but I did not know she was your sister.'

'I fear Mathilda never completely forgave me for leaving the world to devote my life to God. I was considered pretty as a girl, and she had great hopes for me.' The Abbess sighed. 'She visited me here only once – when I gave you into her care.'

'I do not believe that was because she could not forgive you. Her husband would not let her visit any of her family. He was increasingly unkind to her as the years passed.' Perdita stopped short of telling her what must hurt her.

'Poor Mathilda.' The Abbess touched the silver cross at her breast. 'I am glad you have told me this. Is there anything more I can do for you?'

'May I have writing-materials? I need to send a letter to someone as quickly as possible.'

'Of course. Whatever we have is yours.'

She rang a little bell, and within a few minutes a nun came to conduct Perdita to a plain, bare cell where she could rest for a while. Lying down on the hard cot, Perdita closed her eyes, thinking about what the Abbess had told her. She remembered the ring Lady Mathilda had given her quite clearly: it was twin to the one she had seen on the hand of the stranger on her first day at the castle. She thought about the hard, angry face of the man who had threatened her, and knew that she had made the right decision. If he was her father, she did not wish to claim the relationship.

Her mind made up, she relaxed and allowed sleep to take her. She would write to Gervase in a little while, when she was rested.

'You took these things from the dead man to pay for his burial?' Balsadare asked. 'Do you know how he died, or whether anyone travelled with him?'

315

'He had a sword in his back, but...' The innkeeper shook his head. 'We found the corpse when the ostlers went to feed the horses. Since no one knew his name or whence he came, we buried him and kept his personal possessions. If you wish to pay the price of the funeral, you can take them.'

Balsadare pointed to the heavy gold medallion with Sir Edmund's crest carved on it. It was a large, impressive piece and would be proof of his identity to show to Athelstan. 'I shall buy that. Name your price for it.'

The bargain was agreed, and he went outside to where Will Turner was waiting with the horses, tucking the medallion inside his thickly-padded jerkin for safety.

'Sir Edmund is dead. The description fits, and I have seen his things. No one knows anything of Perdita, so I think she may have escaped. She may even now be on her way to the castle. It might be best to return there to see if there is news of her.'

'Heaven be praised! Lord Gervase will be pleased to hear this, I'll warrant.'

Something in Turner's voice made Balsadare look at him in sudden suspicion – something in the way he said, 'Lord Gervase'. Then he saw the man's hand move towards the short dagger at his waist, and he knew. He sprang aside, but the blade had already left Will's hand, finding its mark in

Balsadare's breast.

Seeing him stagger and fall, Will laughed harshly. 'My lord will be grateful for your help, sirrah. I hope you like the reward he sent you?' Then he wheeled his horse about and galloped off, leaving Balsadare sprawled in the dust.

'My lady, there is someone who would see you.' Perdita looked up from the bible she was reading as the white-gowned novice entered. 'Will you come to him? I am afraid he may not enter and must wait for you at the gate. It is Lord Gervase of Athelstan.'

Perdita got to her feet with a cry of relief. 'He has come himself? Yes, I shall speak with him at once.'

She followed the young woman eagerly through the Abbey and out into the gardens, running as she saw Gervase at the gate. He came forward to catch her in his arms, hugging her and smiling at her as warmly as he had when they were first friends.

'I have men searching for you everywhere, Perdita. We heard that Sir Edmund Mortimer had abducted you. Was that so?'

'Yes. He was at the tilt, and he prevented me from reaching Athelstan. I was foolish enough to faint. When I came to myself, I was riding in a wagon and bound hand and foot. He tried to rape me when we stopped at an inn, and Fulk killed him.'

'Fulk? It was he that brought your letter. He shall be well rewarded for his deed, Perdita.' Gervase took her hands tightly in his own. 'It is so good to have you back! I was afraid I should never see you again.'

Perdita looked at him uncertainly. 'Have you forgiven me for hurting you, Gervase?'

His smile did not waver as he gazed at her lovely face, hugging his secret knowledge to himself. Soon she would be all his, but he must be patient. Given time, she would turn to him with love in her eyes. She cared for him, and had it not been for Athelstan ... but his brother was gone, and would not dare to return while the threat of excommunication hung over him. A pardon from the Pope would take time, and by then Perdita would be his wife. Yet he must not frighten her, or she might run from him.

'It was a stupid quarrel,' he said. 'We shall forget it and be friends again. Would you like that?'

'Of course! You know I would,' she agreed instantly. 'We must do something to help Athelstan. You will try, Gervase?'

'Naturally. Everything that can be done shall be done. I have already paid the fine imposed on us by Richard and sued for peace. We shall obtain my brother's release, never fear!' Gervase smiled as he lied. Time enough for her to learn what was really in his mind when she was safely within the castle walls. 'I have come to take you home, Perdita. Are you ready to leave?'

'Yes, in a moment. I must first say my farewell to the Abbess.'

'I suppose you must.' He frowned in frustration. 'They will not allow me beyond the gates.'

Perdita laughed. 'You are too handsome, Gervase. They think you might corrupt the novices!'

He smiled, watching as she went back into the Abbey to bid her benefactress goodbye. Little did she know that she was the one woman he desired for himself! So far everything had gone well. If Will Turner had done his work, Perdita need not guess that Athelstan was still alive. Only he and Balsadare knew the truth. Everyone else believed that the Earl had died in the murky waters of the Thames. When he told Perdita eventually that his brother was dead, she would turn to him for comfort...

He was kept waiting for several minutes while Perdita took her leave of all the nuns, but his frustration faded as he saw her returning and relief rose in him. If she had decided to remain, he would have been powerless. No man could invade the sanctuary of a nunnery and escape the fury of the Church. To have taken her by force would have brought down the wrath of all decent folk on his head.

She came to him smiling and he helped her mount her own palfrey. 'You brought Dioscuri! I am so glad he was found safely.' She rubbed the horse's nose affectionately, remembering the happy day Athelstan had given him to her.

'I told you that I have had men searching for you,' said Gervase, frowning as he saw the shadows in her eyes and understood the reason for them.

Perdita nodded, her thoughts elsewhere as she wondered what had become of Balsadare. She had long since realised her foolishness in tricking him, and was sorry that by doing so she had caused so much trouble. She would apologise when they next met, and ask him to forgive her.

A light dusting of snow had begun to cover the trees and fields, and the wind was bitter. It would be good to be back at the castle, she thought, in her own room and with Griselda to scold her. Her only sorrow was that Athelstan would not be there. Tears pricked behind her eyes, but she fought them back. In the hours since they had parted, she had faced the pain of losing him and she knew that she must be brave. There was no use in tormenting herself with imagining his suffering. While Athelstan lived, she would wait and hope.

'Here, put this on,' said Griselda, holding

the pale blue tunic to slip it over Perdita's head. 'Lord Gervase had it brought from London with your other things, and he himself chose it for you to wear tonight.'

The silk tunic was in one of Gervase's favourite shades, edged with silver and girdled with a wide silver belt. As she allowed Griselda to fasten it, Perdita frowned at something that was bothering her. When they had arrived at the castle, she had noticed that the men greeted Gervase with a new respect; and this was the first time she had heard the old nurse speak of him as 'Lord Gervase', though he had always been entitled to the courtesy. What had suddenly changed?

Griselda brought her a matching head-dress of blue and silver, and she sat patiently while it was set in place. Intricately worked silver bangles and the brooch Gervase had given her completed the ensemble. It crossed Perdita's mind that she was wearing nothing that Athelstan had personally chosen for her. It was almost as though, by dressing her in his colours, Gervase had somehow put his mark on her.

In another moment she dismissed the idea as nonsense. Gervase had already said that he was doing all he could to secure his brother's release. She knew that Athelstan would never have agreed to pay the fine the King had imposed on them, but she supposed that it was essential in the circumstances. The charges of witchcraft were, of course false, but only the intervention of His Majesty could secure a swift pardon. Representation from Athelstan's family and friends might be listened to in time, but by then it could be too late. No, Gervase was right to go straight to the King. By paying the fine, he might just manage to soften Richard's heart. So why did she have this uneasy feeling?

'I shall go down now,' she said to Griselda. 'Gervase will be waiting for me.'

There was a gleam of speculation in the woman's eyes that puzzled her, but she knew her moods by now. The familiarity of the castle made her feel warm inside as she walked slowly through the shadowy passages towards the great hall. It was almost as it had been before – except that Athelstan would not be waiting for her. A picture of his face came to her mind, and she was forced to stop for a moment as the pain struck at her heart. She covered her face with her hands, fighting the desire to give way to her tears, then she lifted her head proudly and went on. She would behave in the dignified manner her lord would expect of her.

At the head of the stair, she looked down at the men gathered at table. Something was different – of course! They were all wearing blue and silver. A little shiver ran down her back as Gervase came to greet her with a smile. Why were the men not wearing Athelstan's colours, and why was his brother looking at her in that way? His smile was one of self-satisfaction, as though he was mightily pleased about something.

He held out his hand, and Perdita took it reluctantly, sensing that the atmosphere was all wrong. She felt the men's eyes on her as she walked with Gervase to the high table, aware of the tension in them. What were they waiting for – what did they expect of her? She felt as if they looked to her for a lead, but she did not know how to react to this strange situation. As they neared the high table, she saw that Father Jonathan was looking very solemn. She smiled at him, but he merely nodded his head, saying nothing.

Then, as Gervase took his place at the head of the table, she suddenly knew what was wrong. Gervase was usurping his brother's authority. When he motioned to her to take her seat beside him, she hung back, slowly shaking her head.

'No, I shall not sit beside you while you take my lord's place,' she said clearly. 'I shall not betray him.'

There was an odd silence in the hall. Perdita bit her lip as she saw Gervase's eyes darken with anger, but she did not care. He was trying to make her put the seal of approval on what he had done, and she would not be a party to the conspiracy to rob Athelstan of his rightful position.

'Please sit down, Perdita,' said Gervase, his face white. 'We shall talk about this later.'

'No. I shall not sit at this table and eat with you; neither shall I wear your colours! I am to be Athelstan's wife, and I shall never betray him.'

'Mistress Perdita,' Father Jonathan murmured, 'do you not know...'

A terrible coldness clutched at her breast as she looked into his pitying eyes. 'What–What should I know?'

'Athelstan is dead,' Gervase said bitterly. 'He died while trying to escape.'

'No...' Perdita looked at him, her face draining of colour. 'I don't believe it – I won't believe it! You're lying to me – both of you.' She pressed trembling fingers to her lips, trying to prevent the cry escaping, but it came anyway, sounding like the death agony of a wild creature. 'Noooo...'

As Father Jonathan got to his feet as though to comfort her, she turned and fled through the hall, past the rows of astonished men, on up the stairs and along the passage to her own chamber. Once there, she began to tear at the fine silk of her tunic, stripping it away from her body in a frenzy of disgust. Gervase had tried to trick her tonight, and she hated him for it. He had given her his colours to wear, knowing that Athelstan was dead. No wonder the men had looked at her like that! They had thought her a heartless wanton who would take one husband as willingly as she took another. If Gervase thought she would turn to him to fill the terrible chasm in her heart, he was much mistaken! She could never love anyone again as she had loved Athelstan, and rather than wed another, she would return to the Abbey and give her life to the service of God.

At once she knew that that was what she must do. Athelstan had told her to seek sanctuary at the Abbey if anything should happen to him, and she should have remembered his advice. She had forgotten how bitter Gervase's heart was against his brother. Yet it was not too late! She would leave tonight – this very moment. She reached for the tunic she had worn earlier in the day, relieved that for once Griselda had not taken it away. Perhaps that had been deliberate: the old woman had many strange ways, but she understood more than most gave her credit for. In her heart she must have known that Perdita would not tamely accept all that Gervase planned for her. The girl slipped the tunic over her head just as the door was flung open.

Seeing Gervase standing on the threshold, she stiffened. 'What are you doing here?' she

325

demanded haughtily. 'Please have the decency to knock before you enter my room.'

He came in and slammed the door behind him, his eyes glittering with anger. 'So you will not wear my colours! Why, then, should I let you wear anything?' He took a step towards her, and she retreated as she guessed what he meant to do.

'Touch me, and you will regret it, Gervase. I shall hate you – I'm warning you!'

'You already hate me! I can see it in your eyes. I saw it just now in the hall when you shamed me before them all. But you shall not shame me again, my sweet Perdita...'

'Gervase?' A shiver went through her as he limped purposefully towards her. 'Gervase, you do not mean to...'

'Why should I not have all that was my brother's? You were hot enough for him, so don't look at me with those accusing eyes! You are a whore – like Jania. She went to him because she couldn't control her lust for him, and she died as she deserved. The slut!'

'I am not like Jania,' Perdita defended herself. 'I have never made you any promises. I am leaving here tonight, Gervase, and you need never see me again.'

She tried to brush past him, but he caught her arm, swinging her back to face him. She saw the glazed expression in his eyes as he reached out, pulling her hard against him. His lips closed over hers as his hands went round her throat. She felt them begin to squeeze, and at the same time his body started to shake violently. She was just about to scream when the door was flung wide and Griselda came hobbling in. She moved faster than Perdita had ever seen her, throwing herself at Gervase and clinging on to his arm as she tried to wrench him away from the girl.

His grip was strong and he seemed almost riveted to her as his fit deepened, as if he could not let go even if he wanted to. Perdita pushed at his hands desperately, feeling the pressure tighten until it was almost unbearable and she was fighting for breath. Then she heard a rushing sound from the direction of the doorway and suddenly Balsadare was there. He clutched Gervase round the waist, then brought his arms up hard under the youth's armpits, breaking his hold. Gervase fell to the floor, twitching violently.

'Leave him to me,' Griselda said fiercely. 'Get out of here, both of you! Leave the castle now while you can, or it will happen again. It is as I always feared...'

'Come, do as she says,' Balsadare urged. 'Gervase has already tried to have me murdered, but fortunately a heavy gold medallion and the thickness of my jerkin saved me from the assassin's blade! We must go now before he comes to himself and orders his men to take us prisoner.'

CHAPTER NINE

Perdita could only give a swift glance at Gervase before Balsadare grabbed her arm, hurrying her from the room. He turned away from the passage to the great hall, towards the room she had found by mischance on her first day at the castle. As she hung back, he opened the door and gave her a little push inside.

'There is a secret passage from here,' he explained. 'I do not think anyone will try to stop us leaving, but it is as well to take care. Most of the men are loyal to Athelstan, and once they learn he is alive they will rally to...' He broke off to stare at her white face. 'Are you ill, Mistress Perdita?'

She held on to his arm, the joy leaping wildly in her eyes. 'Athelstan is alive? You are quite sure?'

'I saw him on his way to France myself. I thought Gervase must have told you?'

Perdita shook her head, relating all that had happened earlier in the evening. 'It was such a shock. I ran from the hall, and Gervase came after me. If you had not come when you did, I think he might have killed me.'

'Then we had best leave at once,' said Balsadare. 'Thank God, when I arrived, Fulk warned me that you might be in trouble. He should be waiting outside the walls with the horses and what provisions he could manage to collect.'

He had pulled aside a tapestry while he talked, operating a hidden device so that a section of the wall slid back. They stepped inside, Balsadare pausing momentarily to light a taper and close the entrance. There was a steep spiral staircase leading eventually to a narrow passage. As Perdita had suspected long ago, a network of these secret ways ran beneath the castle, and she had no doubt that they had often been put to good use.

Conversation was almost impossible as they walked in single file, the blackness lit only by the tiny flickering flame. The passage seemed to wind on endlessly until at last there was a glimmer of moonlight through a kind of iron grille. Balsadare released a bolt and the grating swung back into the bush that hid it from prying eyes outside the castle.

'Can you squeeze through?' he asked, holding the branches to one side and then closing the grille after him. 'This entrance can be operated only from inside, but we prefer to keep it as secret as possible.'

'You need not fear that I shall reveal it. But

where is Fulk?'

'I told him to meet us a little further on. I think we can trust him, but only a few know of this entrance.'

'I understand.' She nodded, laying her hand on his arm as he turned to lead the way. 'Where are we going? When I thought Athelstan was dead, I meant to seek refuge at the Abbey, but now everything has changed. If my lord is in exile, I...'

'You want to be with him.' Balsadare smiled. 'I knew that you would. Besides, we must warn him of Gervase's treachery.'

Her eyes twinkled with mischief. 'So you will take me with you?'

'If I refused, I believe you would attempt the journey alone.' He chuckled as he saw the confirmation in her face. 'I have learned my lesson, lady. I shall not try to deny you, though my lord will not be pleased with me. He may have me whipped yet when he learns that you were in danger because of my carelessness!'

'It was my fault, not yours,' she said quickly. 'And since I escaped unharmed, there is no need for Athelstan to know.'

'I shall have to tell him, and risk his wrath. There can be no lies between us.'

'You are very loyal, Balsadare.'

'I love him,' he replied quietly. 'As you do, my lady. When I knew you were in danger it was hard to choose between you – but I remembered your words to me before we left for London, and I knew what you would expect of me.'

'He must always be your first choice,' she said with a smile. 'But I am glad to have you as my friend.'

'Then it is understood between us.' He gave her his hand to help her negotiate the steep path. 'Come, lady, we must be on our way. Before we set sail for France, we must reach the coast, and as soon as Gervase recovers, he will send men out to search for us.'

There was a huge fair in progress in the streets of Nottingham. Crowds of people thronged the market stalls as the three travellers tried to force a passage through the mass of livestock, pedlars and brown-cheeked peasants. The smell of a huge roasting ox seemed to float tantalisingly on the air, mingling with the various scents of humanity and domestic beasts. It was so noisy that Balsadare had to shout to make himself heard.

'We must find a quiet spot to leave the horses. Then I'll come back to buy food.'

'Could we not leave them at those stables,' Perdita asked, pointing just ahead. 'It would be pleasant to stretch our legs for a while and perhaps sample a slice of that roast ox.'

He grinned at her as his stomach juices

rumbled with hunger. 'Indeed it would! We have made good progress so far, and I do not think that an hour's delay could hurt our plans.'

Accordingly the three of them dismounted, and Fulk took the horses to be cared for by an ostler until they were ready to continue their journey. As he rejoined them, they mingled with the cheerful crowds, stopping every now and then to bargain for mugs of cool, sweet ale, cheeses, fruit and bread – and a slice or two of the succulent beef, which tasted every bit as good as the delicious aroma had promised.

Perdita looked about her with interest, enjoying the festive atmosphere of the fair. The people were all dressed in their best clothes, and some had obviously travelled from far afield to stock up on food and spices, horses, household implements and all manner of wonderful things. Stopping for a moment to admire the beautiful velvets and laces of a merchant from London, she shook her head as he spread the cloth for her to admire in an effort to persuade her to buy.

Turning from the merchant's disappointed face, her eye was caught by the antics of the street tumblers and a fool. She laughed as the jester capered and danced, hitting anyone unwise enough to venture within range with his pig's-bladder on a stick. Her attention on the amusing antics of the fool, she did not notice that both Fulk and Balsadare had walked ahead a few steps.

The disturbance happened so swiftly that no one could have forecast the danger. Three noblemen emerged from an inn, their faces flushed from the quantities of wine they had taken. Suddenly the fool cannoned into one of them, pushing him slightly off balance.

'Ho, ho, master,' he cried. 'Can you not see where you're going? If you're that drunk already, I wouldn't care to be your wife when you get home! She'll likely take the broom to you.'

His words set the crowd laughing, but the nobleman was in no mood to accept the buffoon's jests as many an unwilling victim had done before him. As the fool hit him with the bladder, he seized him and knocked him to the ground, kicking him viciously in the head and stomach. The senseless incident incensed the crowd, and without warning, they surged forward to attack the drunken bully and his friends.

All at once, the happy, carefree atmosphere had changed. Fighting was breaking out on all sides as the crowd went mad. Market stalls were overturned in the mêlée, spilling apples and vegetables on the ground. Looting had begun as people saw the chance to turn the fracas into an opportunity for profit.

Caught in the midst of it, Perdita looked for Balsadare and Fulk. She saw them a short distance ahead, but as she tried to push her way through to them, she was roughly shoved back by a fat peasant woman.

'Who do you think you're pushing, wench?' she asked belligerently.

'I must reach my friends,' said Perdita, but even as she spoke, a fresh surge from the crowd thrust her backwards, separating her from the fat woman and carrying her further away from the men. She saw Balsadare raise his arm to indicate that he was aware of her problem, and then he was lost among the mass of hostile faces.

Powerless to act against the tide of surging humanity, Perdita was swept through streets that were strange to her, trapped in the middle of the angry crowd. She was pushed this way and that, bruised and sometimes knocked to the ground as she struggled to work her way through the rampaging mob. Managing to detach herself at last, she limped to a quiet spot at the side of a road just off the market square, knowing that there was no sense in trying to find her friends for the moment. She leaned against a wall, shaking after the frightening experience. She had somehow lost her cloak, her tunic was torn, and she could taste blood at the corner of her mouth. She closed her eyes for a second, trying to calm her nerves, opening them again to find herself staring at an attractive, mature woman in a rich gown of crimson velvet. The woman smiled sympathetically, and touched her arm.

'What a terrible thing to happen! Are you badly hurt? I saw you from my window and came out at once.'

'That was kind.' Perdita smiled at her. 'I am a little bruised and shaken, but I shall be better in a moment.'

'You have been hurt. There is blood on your mouth. You poor child! Will you not step inside my house for a moment and let me give you some refreshment? Come, it is only a few steps away.'

Perdita hesitated, looking about her uncertainly. 'My friends will be looking for me. I should stay here.'

'They will not find you while this fighting is going on. As soon as the trouble is over, we shall go to look for them.' She paused, a slightly mocking smile on her lips. 'I am Mistress Frinton. I assure you that you will be quite safe at my house.'

'Oh, I did not mean to imply...' Perdita blushed. 'It is very kind of you. I would like to sit down for a while, thank you. My legs feel shaky.'

'Of course! And I am not offended. One cannot be too careful these days.' She took Perdita's arm, leading her to a door only a short distance away. 'You will be comfortable now, my dear, and my servants will search for your friends. Now tell me all about yourself and where you come from. Did you journey to the fair?'

'Yes, we came to visit the fair,' Perdita said, feeling it was best not to reveal too much. Mistress Frinton seemed kind, but she had learned not to be too trusting. She would merely rest for a while and then go to look for Balsadare. If she made her way back to where they had left the horses, she would be sure to find them.

Mistress Frinton unlocked the door, smiling as she invited the girl to enter. For a second Perdita hesitated, then glancing over her shoulder, she stiffened. A horseman was leading his mount down the street towards them and he was wearing a tabard of blue and silver – Gervase's colours! It might only be coincidence, but it could be one of the men Gervase had sent out to look for them. She followed Mistress Frinton inside quickly, praying that he had not seen her.

The house seemed warm and peaceful after the noise of the streets, the windows closed and shuttered against a chill in the air. Her hostess ushered Perdita to a settle by the fire, after first giving instructions that wine and cakes should be brought.

'Please do not trouble yourself on my account,' Perdita said hastily. 'I fear I cannot pay you for your hospitality. My friend has charge of what money we have.'

'I would not think of taking your money, my dear. Now let me bathe that little cut on your mouth.' She went to a dresser at the side of the room and poured a pale pink liquid into a bowl. Dipping a silk kerchief in it, she dabbed at the graze. 'This is only rose-water – a recipe I prepare myself each year. It will make you feel fresher if we bathe your face.'

Perdita merely smiled, sitting obediently as the woman fussed over her. It was almost like being with Griselda again. Looking round the room, she saw that it was tastefully furnished and contained several items of value. Obviously it was the house of a gentlewoman. Relaxing, Perdita thanked her benefactress when she had finished. She had been foolish to suspect Mistress Frinton's motives, even for a moment. She was simply a kind, good-natured woman.

The servant arrived with a dish of comfits and the wine. Setting down her tray, she poured wine into a cup and brought it to Perdita with the dish of cakes. Accepting the wine and an almond comfit, Perdita thanked her warmly, then turned to her hostess.

'This is indeed good of you, Mistress Frinton.'

'It is nothing. I am ashamed that you should have been treated so roughly in my city. I cannot understand what came over

338

the crowd. Now drink your wine, my dear. It will steady you and make you feel much better. In a little while we shall go to look for your friends.'

'Are you not having any?'

'Why, of course! Aline, you forgot to serve me, you silly girl!'

Perdita raised the wine cup to her lips, then something made her hesitate. She was not sure whether it was the odd look on the servant's face or the gleam in Mistress Frinton's eyes. But an inner instinct warned her not to drink, and she suddenly knew that the wine was drugged. This was some kind of trap! She set the cup down and got to her feet, trying not to show her alarm.

'I think I shall go now.'

Mistress Frinton looked at her, her eyes narrowing as she realised that the girl was going to prove stubborn after all. 'I am sorry, but I cannot allow you to go yet. The streets are not safe for a young woman alone.'

'They are safe enough,' said Perdita. 'Please stand aside; I wish to leave.'

'But I do not want you to go.' The woman smiled persuasively. 'Would you not like to stay with us? My girls have the best of everything, and I treat them as if they were my own daughters.'

'What is this place?' A look of horror dawned in Perdita's eyes as she realised she had been lured into a brothel. 'I must leave here at once!'

She tried to push past the other woman, struggling as she was held back. They wrestled fiercely until she heard a sound behind her and half turned to investigate; but as she did so, something hard hit the back of her head and she fell forward unconscious into the arms of Mistress Frinton.

'I hope you have not hit her too hard, Gaston! Unless I am much mistaken, I think we have something special here – something my customers will pay well to sample.'

'It was merely a tap on the head. She will be well enough in an hour or so, Mistress Frinton.'

'Very well. Take her upstairs and lock her in the spare room – the room that was Jeanette's. It will take a few days to tame her, and then I think the Count should find this little delicacy to his liking…'

'She cannot have disappeared into thin air,' said Balsadare, his face grey with anxiety. 'She is not a fool. She would have waited until the trouble was over and then made her way back here.'

'If she were able,' Fulk said with a shake of his head. 'Perhaps she has been hurt?'

'We've searched the streets. If she was lying by the side of the road, we must have seen her.'

'Then – do you think someone could have snatched her?'

'I thought I caught a glimpse of Will Turner in one of the side streets, though I may have been wrong.'

'She was not with him?' Fulk looked puzzled. 'You don't think he has her hidden away somewhere?'

Balsadare shook his head. 'He wouldn't dare to try and abduct her on her own. If she saw him, though, she might have taken refuge somewhere.'

'In someone's house, you mean?' Fulk's eyes narrowed. 'That could be dangerous. There are those who would not hesitate to take advantage of a young and beautiful girl.'

'Ay, I've thought of that, too. My lady would not put her trust lightly in a stranger, but that stranger could be a seemingly respectable woman.'

'You think she might have been enticed by a woman into a house of ill-repute?'

'If she was hurt or dizzy after being caught up in that mob, she might have been off her guard. A woman of that kind knows how to handle innocent girls. We shall make enquiries, Fulk. Someone must know if there is a house of that kind in the town. I know Mistress Perdita. If she was captured by force, she would not have gone quietly, and someone will have seen something. You stay here in case she returns, and I'll see what I can find out. But be alert in case there are any more of Gervase's spies about.'

Fulk agreed, realising that Balsadare had the best chance of finding her. He had a way of getting folk to talk, and that was their only hope if Perdita had been lured into danger. It was frustrating to be able to do nothing, but someone had to remain at the stables in case she returned.

'I shall wait and watch,' he promised. 'It may be that she is merely resting and will make her own way back to us.'

'I pray that you are right,' said Balsadare, but he was uneasy as he left Fulk. Instinctively, he knew that Perdita would try to rejoin them as quickly as possible. It was more than an hour since they had been parted, and he felt that something had happened to her. Alone in a strange city and penniless, she was in grave danger from any unscrupulous folk who might seek to take advantage of her – and there was always the chance that Will Turner might find her first. Somehow he had to prevent that. She could not be far away. Someone must have seen her!

She was so cold, and the hounds were chasing her. Perdita woke as the old nightmare gripped her. Shivering in the darkness, wondering what had happened to her, she remembered being struck on the back of the head and was gripped by a terrible anger. Anger against the woman who had trapped her, but also against herself for being so foolish. She should have refused to go with Mistress Frinton and waited in the street until it was quiet. Balsadare would be sick with worry.

Realising that she was naked beneath a thin blanket, she got out of bed, pulling the coverlet with her and wrapping it round her body. She was so cold! The room was in semi-darkness, the only light coming from the narrow window, yet it was sufficient for her to find her way to the door. She tugged at the latch, finding it unyielding as she had suspected. Naturally they would lock her in. She was under no illusions concerning the nature of Mistress Frinton's house, and she fully understood the fate in store for her unless she could escape.

She would be left naked to shiver and starve until she agreed to accept the man they chose to be her first customer. The madame would be well paid for allowing a nobleman to deflower a virgin; and after that there would be one man after another until she was so broken in spirit that she no longer cared about escaping. It was a fate suffered by many an unwary girl, and Perdita felt very foolish at having fallen into such a simple trap. Perhaps that was why it

had succeeded. She would have fought anyone who had used force, but the seemingly
honest concern in Mistress Frinton's face
had tricked her.

'I must get out of here,' Perdita whispered,
tugging at the latch again in frustration. 'I
must find Balsadare. How could I have been
so stupid?'

She left the door, walking to the window to
discover that it was securely fastened with a
latticed shutter. Looking into the street
through the slats, she wondered if it would
be possible to climb down to the ground. It
was a long way, but she would risk the fall if
it meant freedom. She pushed at the catch,
but found the wooden surround had been
nailed together. It was impossible to open it.
As she looked longingly through the thin
slats, she saw a man in the street. He appeared to be looking up towards her window
and her heart lifted with hope. It was
Balsadare. He had found her! She banged at
the wooden bars with her fists, shouting at
the top of her voice.

'Balsadare, help me! I'm a prisoner here.
Help me!' He remained staring up at the
window for a moment more, then turned
and walked away. 'Oh, Balsadare,' she whispered chokily, 'don't leave me. You must
help me...'

Hereford set down his wine goblet as the

visitor was shown into his private apartments, a look of surprise and pleasure on his face. Son and heir of the great John of Gaunt, he had found his exile in France an irksome punishment. Any visitor from his own land was welcome, but none more so than this one.

'Athelstan, I am glad to see you.' He embraced the Earl warmly. 'Have you news from home?'

'None that will give you pleasure, sir. You know that Richard has confiscated your inheritance, of course?'

Anger glinted in the proud eyes. 'He has broken his solemn promise to uphold my right. When will this tyrant learn? I am not a man to sit under this, my lord!'

'Perhaps it is time Richard was brought to see sense. You are not alone in your anger, my lord duke.'

'Then you would advise me to return?'

'The decision is yours, sir – but I believe the time will soon be ripe. There are many who will join you.'

'And you are one of these?' The Duke looked at him intently. 'Why do you come so secretly to me, sir? Is there something else you would tell me?'

'I have come to ask for your help in a certain matter.' Athelstan's face was grim. 'As for my support in your claim to the lands that are yours by right, you know it is yours. You may not wish for it, however, when you know all.'

'What nonsense is this!' The Duke frowned as he saw the stiffness in the Earl. 'Were we not closer than this when we hunted together and your arrow slew the boar that would have killed me?'

'Forgive me.' Athelstan's stern features relaxed. 'I have so many enemies and so few true friends.'

'Do you think I do not understand? You are a powerful man, and your wealth breeds envy. Yet you stood by me when others deserted me. Do you think me capable of less? Come, sit and eat with me. I would know what I can do to help you.'

Perdita clutched at her blanket, eyeing the dish of chicken stew hungrily. The smell was tantalising and she was very hungry. It was now four days since she had eaten more than a dry crust of bread, and her stomach rumbled in protest. How long could she go on refusing food? Her tongue moved restlessly over her dry lips as she shook her head.

'No, take it away. I cannot agree to do as you wish. I prefer to starve.'

Mistress Frinton looked at her in concern. Would she really be thoroughly stubborn, she wondered uneasily. Most of the girls she had enticed into her house had been only too pleased to exchange that blanket for fine clothes, and the dry crust for as much tasty food as they could eat; but then, many of them had come from the poorest families and thought a good home a fair exchange for the pleasure they gave to their clients. She had guessed at the start that this girl was different, but it seemed that she was neither as green nor as biddable as she first appeared.

She clucked her tongue in frustration. 'If you don't eat, you will be ill. Surely you don't want that?'

'If I am ill, you can hardly sell me to a rich client! I have gone without food before this, and survived.'

'You foolish wench!' Mistress Frinton frowned at her. 'You will share in the profit. You will have pretty clothes and trinkets – and a comfortable bed. Once you have settled down, you will discover it is a good life – better than working in the fields or scrubbing floors to earn your bread. Why be obstinate? I don't want to make you suffer like this.'

They would not dare to let her starve. They would give her just enough to keep her alive, relying on breaking her spirit. She lifted her head haughtily. 'I am betrothed to the Earl of Athelstan, and I am on my way to join him at the court of the French King. If you let me die, Athelstan will kill you. I warn you, my lord has a terrible temper.'

'Betrothed to the Earl of Athelstan! And who is he, may I ask?' Mistress Frinton laughed in disbelief. 'Where are your servants and your jewels? A fine story, wench, but I am no fool. I've heard a few lies in my day, but never one as stupid as this!'

'I am not lying. If you sent word to my lord, he would pay you handsomely.'

'Enough of this nonsense, wench.' Mistress Frinton looked at her uncertainly. 'You're no good to me dead, so I'll leave you the food, but you won't escape this room until you agree to my terms. The Count is coming this evening, and I shall send my girls to dress you. If you refuse him, you will suffer for it. Gaston knows how to break the stubborn ones.'

'Who is Gaston?'

'My servant. He carried you up here. He is not gentle, girl. You would not like Gaston! The wench who had this room before you was stubborn, too. Poor Jeanette! Gaston was too rough with her, and she died. Please do not make me send him to you.'

Perdita bit her lip as the woman went out. She hesitated for a moment, then picked up the dish of stew, tasting it cautiously at first and swallowing the next few mouthfuls so quickly that she almost choked. She was so hungry! Even when Sir Edmund had tried to break her pride, he had allowed her sufficient food each day. If she were to be alternately starved and beaten, she was not sure how long she could hold out. It was true that she would rather die than become a harlot, but to die by starvation would be a slow, painful death.

When Perdita had finished eating, she tried to think of a way to escape. There was certainly no chance for her as long as that door remained locked, and it would stay that way until she agreed to do as Mistress Frinton wanted – but they could hardly lock the Count in with her!

Her eyes gleamed as she realised it was the only avenue open to her. If she succeeded, she might trick them all. If she failed, it would end in a beating or something much worse – but what choice did she have? She jumped out of bed, running to the door as if to call Mistress Frinton back. Then she realised that to capitulate too suddenly would make everyone suspicious. No, she must wait and let them persuade her when the girls came to dress her.

Her decision made, she spent a restless afternoon pacing the floor of her prison. It was one thing to take the decision, another to wait calmly for the moment of her ordeal. A hundred times she cursed herself for the carelessness that had led to this predicament. If only she had not lagged behind Balsadare! Would he and Fulk still be waiting for her if she managed to reach the stables, or would they have given her up and gone on to join Athelstan? Would her lord come to look for her? If he did, he would be risking his own life!

It seemed so long since she had seen her beloved lord's face. The desire to be with him, to feel his arms round her and melt beneath the searing passion of his kisses was so strong that she almost swooned. Supposing she did not manage to escape? She dared not face that thought. If the worst happened, she would never see Athelstan again, for she could not bear to see the scorn in his face if...

Her thoughts were suspended as the door opened and three girls came in, followed by Mistress Frinton. They looked at her expectantly, and she saw that they had brought clothes, silken slippers and ornaments for her hair; there was also a pitcher of hot water and a tub of sweet-smelling soap.

'Well, girl, will you let them prepare you, or must I send for Gaston?'

'Please, Mistress Frinton, will you not spare me?' Perdita said tearfully. 'Let me go, and you will be well rewarded.'

'Cease this nonsense immediately! Let the girls dress you, or suffer the consequences.'

A deep shudder ran through Perdita. She closed her eyes for a moment, fighting for the strength to carry out her plan. Then she opened them and looked proudly at the other woman.

'It seems I have no choice. Very well, I shall do as you order, but I demand a share of the price you obtain for me tonight. You can sell my maidenhead only once, and I want something for myself.'

Mistress Frinton smiled in relief. It would have been a shame to let Gaston loose with the girl; she was a bright, pretty thing, and the men liked to see some spirit in the wenches they chose to bed with. She could handle a demand for money – a little greed was no bad thing in a whore, it made them more amenable to … special requests from the customers.

'You shall have five silver marks.' Mistress Frinton stated. 'What is your name? What shall we call you?'

'Rosamund.' Perdita stared at her coldly. 'I am worth more. I want ten marks.'

'Perhaps, if you please the Count.' The woman's eyes gleamed with greed. The Count had promised a rich reward if the girl was truly a virgin. 'The girls will help you to dress – and there must be clean sheets on the bed.' A sudden thought stopped her on her way to the door. 'I suppose you are free of disease?'

A haughty flash from Perdita's dark eyes almost made her believe that the wench was indeed the betrothed of an Earl. It crossed her mind that she might be throwing away the chance of a fortune, but she dismissed it almost at once. The Count was a trusted client; he would pay well for the girl – and it was probably only a lying tale to trick her.

As she went out, the three girls gathered round Perdita, touching her hair, and smiling. They were obviously willing to be friendly, introducing themselves at once. The tallest was Margaret; the pretty fair girl with blue eyes was Fanny, and the little redhead was called Julia. They were talkative, and seemed to admire Perdita for the way she had stood up to Mistress Frinton.

'I wish I had made her give me five silver marks when she sold me for the first time,' Julia said with a pout.

'You have no head for business,' Margaret said dismissively, turning to Perdita with a smirk. 'You will like the Count. He is handsome, and a strong, passionate lover. He can be very generous if you please him.'

The other two girls giggled and winked at each other, making gestures that brought a flush to Perdita's cheeks. She was relieved when Margaret rounded on them fiercely.

'They are fools!' she said scornfully. 'I am glad you have come. At last I shall have someone worth talking to.'

'Do– Do you enjoy working here?' Perdita asked, wondering why the girl was content to stay. 'Did Mistress Frinton trick you, too?'

'No, I came here of my own accord.' Margaret frowned as she poured water into a bowl. 'My father sold me to a man before I was ten. He used to beat me when he was drunk. One day I pushed him in the duck-pond and ran away. For a while I stole to eat or lay with any man who would pay me; then I met Mistress Frinton and she offered me a home. No one has ever beaten me since I've been here, and I get paid for my work. I have been happier here than I ever was before I came.'

Perdita was silent. In the light of the other girl's suffering, her own ordeal was less terrible. Yet she did not believe she would have accepted such a fate. Death seemed preferable to a life of shame!

When the girls left her, she tried to sit calmly, but her restless spirit would not be denied. She paced the floor ceaselessly, digging her nails into the palms of her hands as she heard a key turn in the lock. The time had come when she must face her destiny! The door opened to admit Mistress Frinton and a tall, distinguished-looking man with silver hair.

'Rosamund, my dear,' Mistress Frinton said, a false smile on her lips. 'May I intro-duce you to the Count? He wishes to spend some time alone with you.' She turned to him. 'Will you require supper to be sent up later, my lord?'

The Count nodded, his lips curving in a smile of anticipation as he looked at Perdita. She was even more lovely than he had been led to believe. 'We shall ring if we need anything.'

Perdita stared proudly at her visitor as the woman went out, listening carefully to discover whether the door was to be locked once more. Thankfully, she did not hear the turn of a key, and relief swept over her. So far her plan was working, but now she had to find a way of escaping from the Count. He was not the brute she had feared, but the thought of submitting to him or to any man but Athelstan was abhorrent to her.

'Why do you look at me like that, Rosamund?' he asked. 'Do you find me disgusting?'

She bit her lips, wondering if she dared appeal to his sense of honour. Deciding it was worth a try, she shook her head. 'No, sir. If I were truly the whore you have been led to believe, I should consider it an honour to lie with you – but I am not a harlot. I have been held here as a prisoner and forced to agree to receive you.'

He frowned, a hint of anger in his face. 'What trickery is this? I have paid a good price for you, Rosamund. Is this some notion you have of getting more money?'

'No, sir. I know you have paid for me, but if you were to help me to escape, the Earl of Athelstan would repay you gladly.'

'The Earl...' He glared at her. 'I was told you were a maiden. It seems that I have been cheated. Still, if your protector was an Earl, you must be reasonably fresh.'

'Athelstan is my betrothed, not my protector,' Perdita said haughtily. 'How dare you insult me?'

His lips curved in a sneer. 'I am not quite the fool you think me, wench! This tale is a pretext to cheat me of my prize. If I helped you, you would sneak back so that Mistress Frinton could sell you to another fool. Oh no, Rosamund, I have paid for you, and I mean to have you.'

Perdita retreated as he moved purposefully towards her. Her hands reached behind her back to clasp the heavy iron candlestick. She had tried to reason with him, and now there was no alternative left to her. Before he realised what she meant to do, she lifted her weapon and brought it crashing down on the side of his head. A look of surprise came into his eyes; then he gave a little moan and crumpled into a heap at her feet. She looked at him anxiously, afraid that she might have struck him too hard, but his eyelids were fluttering and it was obvious that he was merely stunned. Giving a sigh of relief, she ran towards the door; but as she reached it, it was thrust back with such a vengeance that she narrowly escaped being knocked down. Her heart jerked as someone stood on the threshold and she screamed, thinking it must be Gaston. Then, as the door swung wider, her eyes opened in astonishment.

'Athelstan! How did you get here?'

His face was black with fury, and he clasped a sword menacingly in one hand; but as his gaze went searchingly over her and then moved on to the moaning figure of the Count, a glint of humour lit the grey eyes.

'I came to rescue you, Perdita,' he said lightly, 'but it seems I am too late. Have you killed him, or is he merely stunned?' As the Count was beginning to twitch, the question was facetious, but she did not laugh.

'Oh, my lord,' she whispered chokily, 'how glad I am to see you! I was so frightened when you opened that door. I thought it was Gaston come to punish me for refusing the Count.'

The smile left his eyes. 'That brute will never harm you, or any other unfortunate girl again – but if she let him touch you, she will pay for it with her life!'

Perdita shook her head, going to his embrace as he sheathed his sword. 'No, I was starved, and locked in this room until I pretended to agree to her demands, but I have not otherwise been harmed.'

'That is enough to seal her fate!'

She felt his arms tighten about her and drew back to gaze up into his face. Seeing the anger there, she reached out to touch his cheek. 'Do not punish her too severely, my lord. I believe she has been kind enough to the other girls – but I was stubborn.'

'She will be punished, but I shall spare her life since you ask for it,' said Athelstan. 'Thank God you had the courage to hold out as long as you did! Balsadare knew you were here, but he dared not try to rescue you. He told Fulk to stand guard and set out for France to find me. It was by the merest chance that he encountered me as I set foot on English soil. One of our horses had cast a shoe... Had it not been for that, we must have missed one another. I should have been on my way to the castle, and he would have sailed for France in vain...' He shuddered, clasping her to him. 'By the time I discovered what had happened, it would have been too late.'

'You have forgotten that I was about to escape!' Perdita's laugh was shaky. She laid her head against his shoulder, feeling the weakness wash over her. It was strange, but now that she was safe, all she wanted to do was weep. She knew that her chances of making a successful escape had been slim, and if Athelstan had not already been on his way home, her fate might have been a grim one.

Sensing how close she was to breaking, Athelstan swept her up in his arms, cradling her to his chest as he carried her from the room. 'Do not think about it,' he whispered. 'It was your own courage that saved you, my darling. You are safe now, and I promise that no one shall ever hurt you again.'

Nestling against his shoulder, she relaxed as the warmth of his body comforted her. 'All I want is to be with you, my lord,' she murmured. 'Please don't leave me again.'

'I swear we shall not be parted in this life,' he said fiercely, and she was content, not even bothering to turn her head as he carried her past the frightened Mistress Frinton and the wide-eyed girls, out into the night to join the small band of armed men he had brought with him from France. 'Can you ride?' he asked, as he set her gently on the ground.

Perdita's head went up, her moment of weakness past. 'Of course I can ride! Where are we going?'

'To my small manor house in Yorkshire. It is but a humble dwelling, but it will serve until I can retake the castle.'

'I care not where we go as long as I can be with you,' Perdita declared. She took a step towards her horse, then stopped as faintness washed over her, swaying on her feet. 'Your pardon, my lord. I have scarce eaten in four days…'

'Forgive me,' said Athelstan, moving quickly to support her. 'I am at fault. Come, my brave love, you shall ride with me.' He lifted her gently on to his horse, swinging easily into the saddle behind her. She sighed as his arms went round her, knowing that the time for stubbornness was past...

The manor was in darkness when they finally arrived. It had taken some days to reach the secluded house at the edge of the moors, and they were clearly not expected. Athelstan had judged it wiser not to send messengers to warn of their coming lest his enemies learn too soon of his return to England. He was still under the threat of excommunication, and until a pardon was issued from the Pope, that could not change. Most of his men were French mercenaries, and he was not sure how far their loyalty would stretch.

'I am sorry to bring you to this place,' he said, as he helped Perdita to dismount. 'I have not been here for several years, and it has suffered neglect. The bailiff and his wife have grown careless...'

'It will suffice,' she said, smiling at him. 'We shall at least be safe here for the moment.'

Athelstan's face was grim as he nodded. The news of his brother's betrayal had come as a shock when Balsadare told him the extent of it. He had always been aware of the bitterness in Gervase, but that his brother should be capable of such treachery! It had given him cause to rethink his plans. He had promised Hereford his support in the matter of the lands and title of Lancaster that was his by right, but to do that he must first take back the castle. Yet, before anything else, must come the safety of the woman he loved. He had come so close to losing her! Had he not been delayed by a horse casting a shoe, he might never have met Balsadare on the road. It was beyond bearing! She had suffered enough, and must not be put at risk again...

Balsadare had succeeded in raising the servants. They came straggling into the main hall, sleepy-eyed and bewildered by the arrival in the middle of the night of a master they had heard was dead. All at once there was frantic activity as torches and fires were lit; the servants rushing to and fro as they found food for the Earl's party. It was a simple meal of cheese, bread, meat and wine, but the weary travellers had no fault to find with it. Nor with the beds that had been swiftly aired, though most had to settle for a straw pallet on the floor.

The bailiff's daughter gave up her own bed to Perdita. She was scarcely fourteen; a neat, serious child who showed great respect for her lord and his lady.

'Go with Marie,' Athelstan said as the girl shyly told them her name. 'You may sleep in peace tonight, my love.'

She looked at him uncertainly, feeling a little intimidated by the fierce emotion she sensed he was barely keeping in check. She wanted to reach out and touch him, to reassure him, to tell him that he must not be so intense, but she could not find the right words. And in her heart she understood why there was fear mixed with the burning hunger in his eyes. It was the same fear she had known when she watched him fight. They had found a refuge for the moment, but they were all still in terrible danger.

She knew that somehow she must find a way to banish that worried look from her lover's eyes. It was because of her that he looked so anxious, but he must not fear for her so much. She did not want to chain him to her, or destroy his sense of purpose. Her vulnerability when he rescued her had made him fearful for her sake; but he was a man who needed to fight for his beliefs, and she would not rob him of that. Somehow she would banish the shadows from his eyes – but it would have to wait for another day. She was too tired to do more than follow Marie to her chamber.

CHAPTER TEN

Perdita was smiling as she went down to join her companions at supper. They had been at the manor a week, and she was feeling fully recovered from her ordeal in Mistress Frinton's house. She had made up her mind that it was her duty to banish the permanently anxious look from the eyes of the man she loved. For the past few days he had hardly left her side, his thoughts only for her. It made her happy to know that he cared for her so deeply, but it must not go on. He would never be content until he was the master of his own destiny once more.

Athelstan kissed her hand as she took her place by his side at the high table. It was a much smaller gathering than they had been used to at the castle, but she recognised a few of the faces now beside those of her lord, Balsadare and Fulk. Somehow a few of the most loyal of the Earl's men seemed to have learned of his whereabouts and slipped away to join him – and there were several young men from the village who had seized the chance to enter their lord's service.

Perdita's mood tonight was one of gaiety, and she teased her companions unmercifully, telling the story of how she had locked Balsadare in her chamber and slipped away to the tournament.

'Poor Balsadare was sure you would have him beaten for it,' she said with a twinkle in her eye. 'It is a wonder that he bothered to look for me when I was lost in Nottingham. I fear he must find me a most troublesome wench!'

'A most troublesome wench,' Athelstan agreed with a twist of his lips. 'Yet it is no more than the rogue deserves for disobeying me. He should have left you safe at the Abbey when he came in search of me, though I believe him when he says you would have come alone if he had not brought you.'

'Indeed I should! Why should you have all the excitement, my lord?' Her eyes sparkled with mischief. 'I remember you once asked me if, for the sake of love, I would sleep under the stars with only a crust to eat. Well, I have tried living on a crust of bread, and I must tell you, sir, I prefer this fine capon…' Her breath caught in her throat as she saw the sudden flame in his eyes. 'But I would take the crust if it meant I could be with you.'

'I believe you would,' he said, his eyes bright with desire as he looked at her and saw the woman she had become. She was no longer an innocent child, but a wonderful, exciting woman who made his pulses race.

'I came to find you,' she whispered, 'and would do so again, despite what happened. No matter where you are, there shall I be, my lord.'

In that moment he understood what she was telling him, and the lines of strain melted away, leaving only the hunger in his eyes. 'Have you eaten enough?' he asked, a hint of impatience in his voice. 'I would be alone with you.'

She nodded, standing up and giving him her hand. He led her from the hall, neither of them noticing the smiles on the faces of their friends. They could see nothing and no one as they gazed into each other's eyes, walking slowly but surely towards Perdita's chamber.

Marie melted away as they entered, disappearing so discreetly that neither noticed her. For a long moment Athelstan looked down into the eyes of his woman, then he bent to touch his lips to hers, brushing them softly at first, then gathering her to him in a demanding embrace.

'I was so afraid that I would never hold you again,' he whispered hoarsely. 'You will never know how much that hurt me, Perdita. I wanted to hold you so much – so very much…'

'You were always with me in my heart.'

'My darling…' His mouth ravaged hers as the passion swept through him. 'I need you more than I ever thought it possible to need another person. We must be married soon, Perdita. I cannot wait much longer.'

'Why should you wait?' she asked softly, her lips curving in invitation. 'I am yours. I was always yours, even when I fought you. Do not torture yourself or me, my lord. I want you to stay with me tonight.'

She felt the deep shudder run through him as he gathered her in his arms and laid her gently on the bed. Their lips met in a long, lingering kiss, and then their bodies were straining to touch in a sudden urgency that would not be denied. Clothes were discarded amid teasing laughter that hid a heart-wrenching need to quench a desire too long suppressed. And yet Athelstan did deny himself, holding back his thrusting passion until she opened to him, and the pain of his entry was a slight discomfort that was soon forgotten in the fulfilment of their love.

The first meeting of their fevered flesh was sweet, but it ended all too soon. Afterwards he held her, stroking and touching with his lips and tongue and fingertips, whispering softly against her cheek until desire quickened in them both once more. This time his need was not so urgent, and his caresses set her blood racing in her veins, making her moan and toss beneath him. He drew her gently towards a tumultuous climax that left her exhausted but contented in his arms, her face nestled into his shoulder as she tasted the salt of his sweat.

For a while they slept in each other's arms, but as the night deepened she woke to feel his kisses on her lips and strained to meet him eagerly, as ready as he for the joy of loving that kept them wakeful through the night. He mounted her a fourth time just as the dawn was breaking, and this time she cried out wildly as the sheer ecstasy swept away all restraint, sending her spiralling into eternity.

And then at last they slept.

Winter had turned to an early spring, and Perdita's days were spent walking or riding in the countryside round the manor with Athelstan and his men. At night they supped together, and afterwards she slept in her lover's arms. Her happiness shone from her lovely eyes, and she blossomed during this time, teasing her companions, bringing laughter and smiles wherever she went. The shadows of the past had at last left her, and her mind was free of all the doubts that had once clouded it.

It was a magic interlude in their lives, and one that Perdita would always remember, but she knew that it could not go on for much longer. They had heard that the Duke of Lancaster was preparing to return to claim his inheritance, and that meant that Athelstan could delay no longer. Yet still he hesitated, although she knew that Balsadare was urging him to make his return known and retake the castle.

She was not sure why he waited, though she believed it might be in the hope of receiving the Pope's blessing. The threat of excommunication was a powerful weapon, and he could not be sure how many of the men who had once served him would be brave enough to disregard it.

He had never mentioned his imprisonment or the sentence laid upon him by the Bishop of Nantes, but she knew that his pride would not let him rest until his name was cleared. At last she knew she must speak. One night when they lay together in the aftermath of love, she raised herself on one elbow, her long hair sweeping his face as she looked down at him.

'When do we return to the castle, Athelstan?'

'There will be time enough for that when we are married.' He pulled her down to kiss her lips, but for once she denied him. He frowned as she withdrew. 'What is this? Do you tire of me already?'

'Foolish man,' she teased, placing one finger against his mouth. 'Could I tire of living? You are the very breath I take, the very beat of my heart.'

'Then come to me, and leave the talking for another day.'

'Not yet.' She smiled as she saw the smouldering frustration in his eyes. 'Do you remember that you once asked what you could give me that would please me?'

'You know that anything I have is yours.' He frowned. 'I shall regain what is mine, never fear it. You shall have clothes that befit your station and fine jewels again.'

'I do not need gold or fine jewels, Athelstan, and I know I have your love. But I would have more.'

'What more can I give you?' His attention was caught now, and his hand ceased to stroke the curve of her breast. 'What would you have of me?'

'I ... would share your thoughts, my lord,' she said, her eyes glowing. 'I would know what worries you. You strive to protect me from anything that might distress me. I know you do it from love, but I would be a part of all that you are. I would share your pain and your sorrow. I know I am not clever enough to understand your work, but I would have you tell me when you fail and share the joy of your success– I would be...'

'My soulmate,' Athelstan said with a kind of reverence. 'The kindred spirit I have looked for all my life. This would be a gift to me, Perdita.' He touched her cheek lovingly. 'How much you have enriched my life already! Now you offer this. I see I have been a fool. I was so frightened of losing you that I sought to make you a pretty toy that I could keep locked up for my own pleasure – but you are so much more.'

'Oh, Athelstan,' she whispered. 'Do not fear for me. I shall always need your strength, but my love for you will never die. I would not have you live a lie to keep me safe. I am willing to face at your side whatever comes.'

Athelstan drew her down beside him, his arm about her as he began to talk. He spoke of his youth, when he had heard stories from his father of Wat Tyler and the peasants' revolt, and had determined that, when he was Earl, he would do all he could to help the needy and oppressed. He told of his sorrow when Gervase was born with a twisted body, and of how he had striven to find some way to help him, and of his hurt at his brother's bitterness against him.

'I did not seduce Jania. She came to my bed when I was sleeping. Gervase saw her there, and his fury awoke me. I had been working late into the night and knew nothing until he accused me of seducing her.'

'Did you tell him the truth?'

'I tried, but he would not listen. I was angry, and I said things I should not. Jania was but a foolish child... I should not have called her a whore. It was not true, though it was not for want of trying on her part.' A rueful smile twisted his mouth, and Perdita laughed.

'It is good that you have told me this. Now, when do we go home?'

'Witch!' He nibbled her earlobe, but she held him back. 'Very well, my lady, but you shall pay for your defiance.'

'Willingly! Tell me, Athelstan?'

'I have heard that the Earl of March has been killed in Ireland. He is Richard's heir and cousin. I think it likely that the King will take a force to seek revenge for the murder, and when he does...'

'Lancaster will return to claim his estates and there will be rebellion in England. Since you will want to support him, you must first retake the castle. So when do we leave?'

His soft laughter set a thrill of pleasure running through her. It was a sound she had not heard for a while – the old, malicious triumph was in his face as he gazed down at her. 'I see I have underestimated you, my lady. I had hoped to wed you first, but the Pope has not yet granted my request.'

'He will,' she said confidently. 'We shall be married at the castle, my lord. Until then, I am content to be your *amour.*'

'Indeed?' His eyes were wicked as they looked at her. 'Then cease this resistance, or I may cast you out into the snow.'

'It is not snowing, my lord,' she whispered demurely as he pressed her back against the pillows, but the laughter bubbled up inside her and she arched to meet his impatient kisses.

His kisses ravaged her generous mouth, then moved on to seek out and tantalise every part of her body. Her creamy flesh quivered and trembled in the candle-light as she moaned beneath the determined assault of his caresses. It was clear that he meant to extract full payment for her defiance, making her wait until the fever in her blood was so strong that she begged him to end the sweet torture.

'Enough!' she moaned, biting her lip. 'I cannot bear it.'

'Will you deny me again?' he asked hoarsely.

'No... Perhaps, if I have cause.'

He laughed in delight, catching her to him to end the torment for them both. There was a new meaning to their love now, and his passion seemed to have intensified, carrying them on to fresh dimensions. Now they were meeting as equals, the white-hot glory of their love something that few are privileged to know.

Perdita was swept away on a tide of desire, waves of sensation washing over her in ever greater intensity until she felt that she would die. At last the fusion of their hearts, minds and bodies became the catalyst that made them one being, one entity, that even death could never sunder.

Exhausted, she lay in his arms, but she would not let sleep claim her until he had answered. 'When do we go home, my lord?' she whispered against his ear.

'Witch,' he murmured lazily. 'Be at peace. We shall leave as soon as I can arrange it.'

Satisfied, she nestled meekly into the satin hardness of his shoulder, hearing his laughter as he acknowledged his defeat. It would always be so for them, he realised, and the anticipation of future challenges made his blood quicken. Somehow he sensed that when he lost to this woman, he won more than he would ever fully know.

The sun was sailing steadily in a blue sky as Perdita sat her horse, watching from a distance the activity before the castle. During the hours of darkness, Athelstan had brought up his engines of war and his men in a display of strength. His force was still greatly outnumbered by the trained men within the fortress, but he hoped that the majority of the soldiers who had once worn his colours would surrender rather than fight against him. Believing him dead, it was natural enough that they should accept Gervase, but few would stand by his brother if he persisted in defying the rightful master of the castle. Especially now that a letter had finally come from France. Lancaster had succeeded in obtaining the pardon from the Pope that they had all hoped for. Athelstan was cleared of the false charges laid against him, and the strain of excommunication had been lifted. The Holy Father had remembered a friend, and given his blessing to the Earl's cause.

Gervase had ordered that the drawbridge should be raised, and Perdita could imagine the consternation that must be going through the minds of all those inside the castle. It was possible that some would be prepared to fight, but she hoped it could yet be a bloodless reconciliation and she knew that it was Athelstan's wish, too.

He had wanted her to stay with the Abbess until it was all over; but he had not insisted when she said that she would rather watch from a safe distance, merely detailing Fulk to accompany her. So she was able to hear and see everything, from the ear-splitting challenge of the horns to the lumbering of heavy weapons as they were trained on the castle walls. Among the fearsome machinery were the new cannon, which Athelstan had told her were capable of smashing walls even as thick as those that protected the castle. They were still risky weapons, liable to explode or misfire, and she knew he would be reluctant to use them, but they would serve as notice of his intent.

'What will happen now, do you suppose?'

she asked, glancing across at Fulk. 'Do you think they will surrender?'

'Lord Athelstan's herald has read out his demands. He has given them one hour to capitulate, and no doubt the men are trying to reason with Lord Gervase. We can only wait and see, my lady.'

Perdita nodded, straining to catch every movement or sound. Would Gervase be sensible, she wondered. Knowing how bitter he was, she felt that he would want to fight – but would the men be prepared to stand with him?

She did not have long to wait and wonder. Before the hour was ended, the blue and silver flag was hauled down, and the black and green colours of Athelstan were soon flying proudly in the breeze. The castle had surrendered without bloodshed, and a tremendous cheer went up from both sides of the walls. Men appeared at the battlements calling Athelstan's name and waving as the bridge was lowered.

'Poor Gervase,' Perdita whispered, realising how deep would be his despair and humiliation at being deserted by the men. 'He will hate his brother even more now.'

Balsadare came riding up to them, his ugly face wreathed in smiles. 'The Earl asks you to join him, my lady. He would have you share his triumph as he rides in.'

'Gladly! I can hardly believe it is over.'

'I always believed the men would rally to Athelstan – even if the Pope's pardon had not arrived.'

'Yes, I know. You never lost faith, good Balsadare.' She smiled at him, urging her mount forward to canter at his side. 'Yet the surrender is almost too wonderful to be true.'

Athelstan was waiting for her a short distance from the drawbridge. She could see the triumph in his eyes as he looked at her, and her love flowed out towards him.

'Ride with me,' he said. 'It is right that you should share this moment with me.'

'I am proud to do so, my lord.'

He nodded approvingly. 'Come, Perdita. I want them all to know that I honour you as much as though you were already my wife.'

She brought her mount level with his, and they moved forward together at a slow walk, the horses' hooves clattering over the wooden bridge. In the courtyard, the men had lined up to wave and cheer, most of them having already donned tunics of black and green. They were shouting and laughing, eager to welcome the Earl home.

The sharp twang of the arrow alerted Perdita. She screamed as she saw it fly through the air, and Athelstan lurched towards her, desperately thrusting her to one side. The missile embedded itself in his shoulder and he slumped forward, almost falling from his horse. Terror swept through her. It was as she had feared: Gervase had seized one last chance to be revenged on his brother. Yet even as her heart jerked with pain, the Earl straightened in the saddle. Deliberately he reached up and snapped the arrow-shaft, then he looked at the men nearest to him, his face grave.

'Find Lord Gervase and bring him to me. I want him alive. Do you understand me?'

'Yes, my lord.'

A dozen or more went off at a run, and Perdita knew that Gervase would not be allowed to escape. Already, Balsadare was sending men to form a cordon round the walls. Even if the Earl's brother were to flee through one of the secret ways, he would be caught and brought back to face the punishment for his treachery.

Glancing at the stern lines of her lover's face, Perdita knew that it would grieve him to do what must be done. Yet Gervase must and would be punished.

Willing hands were there to help the Earl from his horse; he accepted them, but insisted on walking unaided, even though the blood was soaking through his tunic sleeve. He turned, holding out his hand to Perdita with a wry smile.

'A sorry beginning to our triumph, lady. Will you come with me while Griselda tends my wound?'

'I shall tend it myself,' said Perdita. 'The arrowhead must be cut out, and I do not trust her. She is too fond of Gervase.'

'I shall make the cut,' said Balsadare, coming up behind them. 'You must wash away the blood and help me to bind him, my lady.' She nodded, and between them they supported Athelstan to his chamber, refusing to listen to his protests.

'I am not dying,' he muttered. 'It is but a flesh wound.'

'A mere scratch,' Perdita agreed with a smile. 'So why are you making so much fuss?'

'Witch!' He scowled at her. 'I have not forgotten that you once promised to be a scold.'

'You may beat me when I have tended your wound!' His soft laughter reassured her.

Once he was put to bed, it was discovered that the arrow had entered the flesh at the side of his shoulder, fortunately missing the bone. He refused the wine Balsadare offered, watching as he twisted the blade of his knife in a candle-flame and growling at him to get on with it. His body jerked with pain as the slashing cut was made, but he did not cry out and it was swiftly over. When they had bound his wound tightly to stop the blood, he insisted on rising and dressing.

Walking unaided to the great hall, he took his place at the high table, looking round at the expectant faces. The men watched as he held up his hand for complete silence.

'You have been told that I was dead,' he said in a loud, clear voice. 'As you see, I live. Even after my brother broke his promise to surrender peacefully, I live. The stain of excommunication has been lifted. I have the blessing of the Holy Father himself, and I have come to take back what is mine...' He broke off as there was a disturbance at the other end of the hall, and Gervase was dragged in, struggling and cursing. 'Bring him to me.'

Gervase was hustled through the rows of silent men and pushed to his knees before the high table. His face was angry and un-repentant as he looked up at his brother.

'So you have won it all, Athelstan,' he said bitterly. 'Yet I shall curse you – and yours! – with my dying breath. You took Jania from me, and I would have taken Perdita from you if I could. That arrow was meant for her, not you.'

'Be silent, Gervase! What you have just said is enough to hang you.'

'No, my lord.' Perdita laid her hand on his arm. 'He is your brother...'

'And he hates me,' Athelstan said, 'for something that was no fault of mine. I did not take Jania from you, brother. She crept into my bed while I was sleeping, hoping that I would be tempted to make love to her

379

when I woke. It was not the first time she had tried to tempt me. She wanted to be a Countess, Gervase. It was not for love of me that she jilted you.'

'Even if that were true, you drove her to her death!' Gervase flung the accusation at him bitterly.

'No. It was not I who killed her.'

'Liar! You drove her to take her own life.'

'No.' Athelstan's eyes were dark with pain. 'I told that lie to save you from shame. To save you from the knowledge of what you yourself had done…'

Gervase stared at him, his face draining of colour. 'You lie…' he whispered. 'I could not…' As he spoke, the horror dawned in his eyes. 'She was laughing at me … then everything went black… I cannot remember. I cannot remember…'

'Meredith saw you. She came to fetch me, but when I got there, it was too late. Jania was dead, and you were unconscious. I carried the girl to her room, and I told you she had taken poison – but it was not so.'

'No!' Gervase's cry of agony was so terrible that the men released their hold on him. He bent his head, covering his face as he wept. 'Oh God, no,' he cried. 'I killed her… But I loved her. Oh God, how much I loved her…'

All of a sudden he got to his feet and began to stumble away. The men moved to stop him, but Athelstan shook his head.

'No, let him go. He is punished enough.'

'He will always be a danger to you,' Balsadare warned.

'What can he do? He is banished from the castle. I cannot have his blood on my hands. He is my brother.'

'Then let me rid you of him.'

'No, Balsadare, I forbid it.' Athelstan frowned at him. 'He may take anything that is his and leave in peace. It is my wish.'

'I have never disobeyed you yet, my lord. I shall not do so now.'

'Thank you, my friend.' Athelstan smiled grimly as his brother disappeared from view. 'Enough of this gloom! Today is to be a celebration, and I would share it with all my friends. Come, eat your fill, and share my happiness. I would have you all raise your goblets and drink a toast to Lady Perdita, the future Countess of Athelstan.'

They stood to a man, lifting their cups to salute her enthusiastically. 'The Lady Perdita!'

She smiled and thanked them, her eyes bright with tears of joy. Father Jonathan had come to sit beside her, occupying the seat that had been Gervase's, while Balsadare took his place at Athelstan's right hand. She glanced anxiously at her lord's face, seeing the signs of strain that betrayed how much it was costing him to keep his place at table, but she knew his pride would not allow him to leave too soon.

It was late in the evening when he finally stood and held his hand out to her. She took it with a smile, glancing swiftly at Balsadare. Understanding, he rose and walked softly behind them, following until they reached the Earl's chambers. At the door, Athelstan stopped to turn and look wryly at his friend.

'Good-night, Balsadare.'

'Good-night, my lord.' There was not a flicker of emotion on the servant's face.

Inside, Athelstan sighed wearily and almost stumbled, leaning heavily on Perdita's arm as she helped him to the bed. He sat obediently as she unfastened his belt and removed his shoes, a glint of mockery in his eyes.

'What an excellent wife you will be! Yet I prefer to undress you.'

'Be still, my lord,' she scolded. 'Is there nothing that would help to ease the pain?'

'Yes, there is a powder in that casket yonder. Bring it here, and I shall show you what to do.' She obeyed, and he took out a small packet. 'Mix half of this in a cup of wine. Only half, or I shall sleep for ever more.'

She mixed it carefully, and he nodded his approval. 'I can see you will make an excellent sorcerer's apprentice! I shall sleep now, my love, and you would rest easier in your own apartments.'

'Yet I shall stay by you,' she said. 'Sleep, Athelstan. I shall not leave you.'

'Stubborn wench,' he muttered, but there was a smile on his lips as he laid his head on the pillow. 'Come here beside me then.'

She did as he asked, nestling her cheek against his uninjured shoulder. His hand clasped hers, their fingers entwining tightly; but soon the wine began to do its work and his hold slackened as he slept.

Perdita lay wakeful beside him, watching for signs of a fever, but they did not come, and in the end she, too, drifted into peaceful slumber.

Outside his master's door, Balsadare kept a vigil until the dawn had broken, and Fulk came to take his place. While Gervase lived, they would share the watch between them...

Within a week, Athelstan's shoulder had healed enough for him to think of keeping his promise to the Duke of Lancaster. As he had expected, King Richard had crossed over into Ireland to avenge his kinsman. Realising this as his chance, Lancaster had slipped away from the French Court under pretext of a visit to the Duke of Brittany, and had landed at Ravenspur in Yorkshire.

'I must join him within a few days,' said Athelstan, when the news was brought. 'But first we shall be wed, my love. I had hoped to make a show of our wedding at Court, but I fear it must be a simple ceremony after all.'

She smiled at him, her eyes alight with happiness. 'It would please me if we were married by our own dear Father Jonathan, with all our friends around us to wish us well. I have no need of pageantry, my lord.'

'Then so be it.' He bent his head to kiss her lips softly.

They were married in their own chapel, with Balsadare to give the bride into the hands of her husband, and all their friends to wish them long life and happiness. The next day, Athelstan set out on his journey to join Lancaster, who was making a triumphant progress to meet his uncle the Duke of York at Berkeley.

Perdita kissed her husband good-bye, smiling bravely as she waved and watched him ride out with Balsadare at his side. Within her was an aching loneliness that tore at her heart. How could she bear it if he never came back to her? She fought her fear, knowing that there must be many another woman who held her tears back when her husband rode away to war. Like them, she would fill her time with sewing and spinning – and she could study with Father Jonathan. She sighed as she remembered the lessons at the harp she had shared with Gervase, knowing that she could never hate him even though he had tried to kill her. It was sad that life should be so cruel.

She turned and went into the castle. The days seemed to stretch emptily before her, and she thought nostalgically of the time they had spent in the manor house, when Athelstan had devoted all his time to her. She almost wished that she had not persuaded him to return to the castle; then she shook her head, scolding herself for her selfish thoughts.

Alone in her chamber, she sat down to write a letter to the Abbess. Life was too short to bear a grudge against anyone, and it was time she learned the truth about her birth...

Perdita pressed a hand to her aching back, sighing wearily. She laid aside the tiny garment she had been sewing, getting up to take a turn about the room. How long was it since her lord had left to join the Duke of Lancaster, she wondered. Long enough for Athelstan's child to take shape within her womb. She felt it kick, and smiled wistfully. Would her lord be home in time for the birth?

'My lady, there is someone who wishes to speak with you,' Marie said. 'She says her name is Mistress Meredith.'

'Meredith here?' Perdita looked at her maid in surprise. 'I wonder why she has come. We were never friends, and she must have heard that I was married to Athelstan before he left.'

'Shall I tell her that you will not receive her?'

'No...' Perdita hesitated. 'She may have news of my lord. Please ask her to join me here.'

Perdita frowned as the young maid went away. Although she no longer felt the sickness she had suffered early in her pregnancy, she was often tired these days. Griselda told her it was natural and that she was carrying the child well, but her body felt heavy and clumsy and knew she would feel ugly beside the beautiful Meredith.

She got to her feet as Meredith entered, smiling and inviting her to be seated. 'I must confess I am surprised to see you, Meredith. What may I do for you?'

Meredith remained standing, her face hostile as she looked at Perdita and saw the new maturity that was hers. She looked contented and confident in her position as the Countess of Athelstan, and it was obvious that she was carrying her husband's child. It was this that made the jealousy flare suddenly in the older girl. She was bearing Athelstan's son! All hope of displacing her was ended. The bitterness mounted in her as she gazed at the serene face of the girl she hated. Perdita had stolen everything that should have been hers. It ought to have been she, Meredith, who was mistress here, not this usurper! Athelstan should have married *her!* To achieve her ambition, she had schemed and lied and ... and it had all come to nothing because of this dark-eyed harlot. How she hated her!

'So you have it all,' she said bitterly. 'Everything that should have been mine.'

'Why did you come, Meredith?' Perdita pressed a hand to her back and sighed. She might have known that the older girl had not travelled all this way simply to heal the breach between them.

'Athelstan was promised to me.' Meredith went on as if she had not spoken. 'You stole him from me! You lured him to your bed as Jania did. She would have taken him from me if she could but I put an end to her schemes!'

'Athelstan married me because...' Perdita looked at her, wondering at the strange expression in her eyes. There was something very odd in the way she was staring at her. 'What do you mean, you put an end to Jania's schemes? Gervase killed your sister...' Her heart pounded wildly as she saw Meredith's eyes narrow, and she felt sick. Her hand went to her throat as a tingle of fear ran down her back. 'Or did he? You were the only witness, Meredith. You went to fetch Athelstan, but when he got there, Jania was dead and Gervase was unconscious. Who really killed her? Was it Gervase – or you?'

They stared at each other in silence, and the tension was like that moment before the wolf springs to kill. A brittle flame gleamed in the eyes of the older girl, and the world seemed to stop turning for an instant. From somewhere far away there was the sound of shouting, laughter and the clatter of hooves; but for Perdita there was only the awful silence of the question that lay between them, and the touch of madness in Meredith's eyes. And then she spoke, her voice unnaturally calm.

'How clever you are! But I always knew that… That was why you were so dangerous. Jania was a little fool! She thought that she could blackmail Athelstan into marrying her. Her! He was mine from the start. I would never have let her have him. Never!' Meredith laughed harshly. 'The day that she deliberately let Gervase find her in his bed, I made up my mind to be rid of her. I never expected it to be so easy. She was screaming because Gervase was in a fit. I pushed her to the ground, and held a pillow over her face until she ceased to struggle, and then I ran weeping to Athelstan. He believed every word I said. Men are such fools! I could always twist him round my finger – until you came. I might have known that you would guess the truth.'

The bitterness in her voice was lost on Perdita as she stared at her in horror. 'You killed Jania?' she whispered, the sickness turning in her stomach. 'You killed your own sister and let Gervase take the blame? Even now he believes he murdered the girl he loved.'

'And he will go on believing it!' Meredith said triumphantly. 'You asked me why I came. It was to bring you a letter from him. He is about to set out on a pilgrimage to the Holy Land, and he wanted to ask your forgiveness. He thought you would not receive him, so he asked me to bring his letter.'

'You must tell me where he is, Meredith. He must be told the truth. He cannot be made to carry this hurt inside him...'

'No!' Meredith cried, moving closer. 'You will never tell him or anyone else our little secret. If I cannot have Athelstan, neither shall you!'

Suddenly she pulled a long thin dagger from beneath her mantle, coming at Perdita so swiftly that she was unprepared. She screamed, catching at Meredith's arm in a desperate attempt to fend her off. They struggled fiercely, knocking into the furniture and almost tumbling, Perdita's awkwardness making it difficult for her to defend herself. Then there was sudden movement in the room and the sound of a man's startled oath. From the corner of her eye Perdita saw a shadow, and then it became substance as Athelstan seized Meredith from behind, twisting her arm behind her back so that she screamed in agony and dropped the knife. He picked it up and held it at her throat, his face black with fury.

'Be quiet, you vixen, or I shall plunge this into your black heart!'

'She killed Jania!' Perdita cried. 'She murdered her own sister and told you it was Gervase!'

'She lies,' Meredith croaked, her voice harsh with fear. 'It was Gervase. You saw for yourself, Athelstan.'

'Be still, viper.' He flung her away from him in disgust. 'I always knew you were capable of evil, but this is beyond belief.'

Meredith threw herself at his feet, clinging to his legs and weeping loudly. 'Do not look at me so, my lord. I did it for love of you. You were mine, and she tried to take you from me. All I have done was for love of you…'

Athelstan thrust her sharply away. 'You do not know the meaning of the word! For what you tried to do to my wife, I should have you whipped and then beheaded as a murderess!'

'No!' Perdita moved towards him then, and he caught her to him. She gazed up into his face, tears squeezing from beneath her thick lashes. 'Send her away, Athelstan. Banish her from the castle, but let her live. She has not harmed me, and her sin will be punished by a higher authority.'

'She tried to kill you … and yet you plead for her life? She will always be a danger to you, Perdita.'

'And yet I would give her her life – as you gave Gervase his, my lord.'

Athelstan hesitated, then sighed deeply as he turned to Meredith. 'Your brother shall be informed of your wickedness. It will be for him to take what measures he thinks fit. Go now, and never let me see your face here again!'

Meredith's face twisted with spite. 'So she has made you her slave. The great Earl of Athelstan made weak by a wanton's smiles! I loved you once – but now I hate you. I hate you both, and I'll make you sorry you spurned me!'

'Leave, or I shall throw you to my hounds!' Athelstan moved threateningly towards her and she gave a little scream, then ran from the room. He smiled wryly at Perdita. 'I doubt not I should have strangled the vixen – but I had not the heart for it.'

'I am glad you spared her.' Perdita smiled at him lovingly. 'Oh, my lord, I have missed you so much.'

'And I you.' He caught her to him, kissing

her with a hungry passion, holding her so tightly that she was obliged to cry out.

'Have a care for your son, my lord.' She laughed at the expression on his face as he instantly released her, his eyes going over her in incredulous delight. 'Griselda tells me that it will be a boy.'

'Then it probably will be, for she is seldom wrong.' He caressed her cheek softly. 'And you? Are you well, my love?'

'Yes, of course.' Her eyes sparkled and she forgot the ache in her back. 'Why did you send no warning of your arrival?'

'I wanted to surprise you.' He laughed. 'Besides, no messenger could have reached you sooner than I in my impatience. Balsa-dare, a few others and I rode on ahead of the main party.' The smile left his eyes. 'Thank God I did! Meredith might have killed you had I not been at hand.'

She saw the sudden fear in his face, and shook her head. 'In another moment, my screams must have brought the servants in on us. I am well protected, my lord – and you were here when I needed you. Now, come and sit down. I have so much to tell you.'

'And I you...' His arm went round her waist and she leaned her head against his shoulder. 'I have thought of you constantly, my love. Lancaster would have had me stay longer in London, but Richard is safely in the Tower and I could not wait to be with you.'

Perdita nodded, gazing up at him. 'We heard that Richard was captured at Flint Castle after his army deserted him.'

'He succeeded in slipping away from us at Lichfield, but was retaken almost at once. We had tried to treat with him earlier, but as always he promised one thing while plotting another.' Athelstan shrugged. 'Well, now he is in the Tower, and Parliament must decide his fate. Lancaster says he does not want the Crown, though the people would have him as their king.'

She saw the troubled look in his eyes and guessed that he was uneasy in his mind. 'You are concerned about this, are you not?'

'Yes – and a little disappointed. I believe that Richard is a tyrant who does not deserve to rule, but I am not sure that what comes after will be much better.'

'I thought Lancaster was your friend?'

'He is...' Athelstan frowned. 'Power is a strange thing, Perdita. I pray that he will not let it corrupt him. He begins to say that he has as much hereditary right to the throne as Richard. If Richard resigns and the people offer the crown to Lancaster, it will be rightfully his. If that should happen, I would see Richard banished. I fear others would have it otherwise.'

'You think he will be murdered – as his

393

uncle was?'

'He is hated and despised by the people, but he is as much entitled to justice as any man. I like not this smell of corruption and treachery!'

'He would have rejoiced at your death, my lord.'

Athelstan smiled wryly. 'If his death heralds a new dawn for England, then I am content. I do not believe that Parliament will ever be the slave of a monarch so absolutely again. It may be many years before there is true freedom for all, but I truly think that by what we have done we have shown the way for future generations.'

'Then you could do no more, my lord. The minds of men cannot be changed in a single night.'

'No. I expect you are right.' He kissed her brow. 'Enough of politics, my lady. You said you had something to tell me?'

'I have much to tell you,' she said, a hint of anxiety in her voice. 'But first I would speak of Gervase. Meredith said he had written to me asking me to forgive him – and that he was about to set out on a pilgrimage to the Holy Land to do penance for his sins. Should we not try to find him and tell him that he was not guilty of Jania's murder?'

'If you can forgive Gervase, then so can I. I shall send messengers to find him if they can, but I believe it will be best if he does not return too soon. He had become almost a prisoner of his illness, and this may prove a blessing in disguise. Who knows, if he makes this pilgrimage, he might be blessed by Our Lord.'

'You hope for a miracle?'

'A miracle?' His brows went up. 'Perhaps. Yet I have always believed that Gervase was his own worst enemy. It might be that his cure could come from within himself.'

'We must hope and pray that it will be so.' A tiny sigh escaped her, and he looked at her sharply.

'Are you ill? Do you wish to rest?'

'I am a little tired – and a little sad today. I wrote to the Abbess some weeks ago, and I have just heard that she died in her sleep before she could read my letter. It was returned to me unopened. She was Lady Mathilda's sister, and the nearest I had to an aunt.'

'I am sorry to hear of her death. She was a good woman. But why did you write to her?'

'She told me she knew my father's name. At the time, you were imprisoned in the Tower and I could not cope with anything more. I have since thought that it would be good to know who he was.'

'There must surely be some hint among her papers?'

Perdita shook her head. 'No, it was a secret she carried with her to her grave. I do have one tiny clue, but I am not sure that I have the right to use it.' Athelstan looked at her enquiringly and she drew a deep breath. 'Lady Mathilda gave me a ring the night she died. Lord Edmund afterwards said I stole it, but it was not so. The ring was mine by right. It had belonged to my mother.'

'Where is this ring?'

'Sir Edmund took it from me, but I saw its twin on the finger of a man who came secretly to the castle at the time you first brought me here.'

'His name was Lord Edwin Winters.' Athelstan's eyes narrowed in thought. 'He came to bring me word of Hereford. Are you sure it was the same ring, Perdita?'

'I think so…' She gazed up at him. 'If I am his child, he might not want to know it. I think we must forget it, my lord. I have a name now. I need no other.'

He touched his lips to hers. 'I shall make discreet enquiries, my love. If the truth can be discovered and no harm done, I know it would please you.'

'It pleases me that you are home again, my lord.'

She laughed, her arms sliding up round his neck as he held her pressed against him. Her lips parted invitingly for his kiss, softening and opening beneath it. She felt the familiar quickening in her blood, and her heart was racing wildly.

'Are you not hungry?' she asked, her eyes full of mischief. 'Would you not like to rest a while?'

'Your husband has been away for many lonely nights. Have you not a warmer welcome for him, wench?'

'But you must be in need of refreshment?'

'Witch! My hunger is for you – and well you know it!'

Perdita took his hand, leading him towards the inner chamber. 'Then you need fast no longer, my lord,' she whispered.

As their eyes met, the world was forgotten. For this one moment there was nothing but their love. No matter what the future might hold or how many dangers they might face, they would always have this ability to lose themselves in one another. Their love was a source of strength to them both, and because of it they would survive whatever storms lay ahead...

The publishers hope that this book has given you enjoyable reading. Large Print Books are especially designed to be as easy to see and hold as possible. If you wish a complete list of our books please ask at your local library or write directly to:

Magna Large Print Books
Magna House, Long Preston,
Skipton, North Yorkshire.
BD23 4ND